Someone l̲ ̲ ̲ ̲ ̲ ̲ ̲ ̲ ̲ ̲ ̲ ̲ hen abruptly a ̲ ̲ ̲ ̲ ̲ ̲ ̲ ̲ the same voice called aloud, peremptorily: "Open to the law!" The formality was followed up immediately by a strong thrust, hurling the door inwards to the wall, and the doorway was filled by the burly figure of the bearded sergeant from Shrewsbury, with two men-at-arms at his back. Brother Cadfael and William Warden confronted each other at a distance of a couple of feet; mutual recognition made the one bristle and the other grin.

"Well met, Brother Cadfael! And sorry I am I have no writ for you, but my business is with the young man behind you. I'm addressed to Edwin Gurney. And you, I think, my lad, are he?"

Edwin came forward a step from the inner doorway, pale as his shirt and huge-eyed. "That is my name," he said.

"Then I arrest you on suspicion of the murder of Gervase Bonel by poison, and I'm here to take you back in custody to answer the charge in Shrewsbury."

ABOUT THE AUTHOR

Ellis Peters is the nom-de-crime of Edith Pargeter, author of many books under her own name. She is also well know as a translator of prose and poetry from the Czech and has been awarded for her services to Czech literature. Miss Pargeter lives in England. The earlier chronicles of Brother Cadfael are *A Morbid Taste for Bones* and *One Corpse Too Many*.

Monk's-Hood

The Third Chronicle
of Brother Cadfael

Ellis Peters

POPULAR LIBRARY • NEW YORK

MONK'S-HOOD

This book contains the complete text of the original hardcover edition.

Published by Popular Library, CBS Educational and Professional Publishing, a division of CBS Inc., by arrangement with William Morrow and Company, Inc.

ISBN: 0-445-04713-5

Printed in the United States of America

First Popular Library printing: May 1982

10 9 8 7 6 5 4 3 2 1

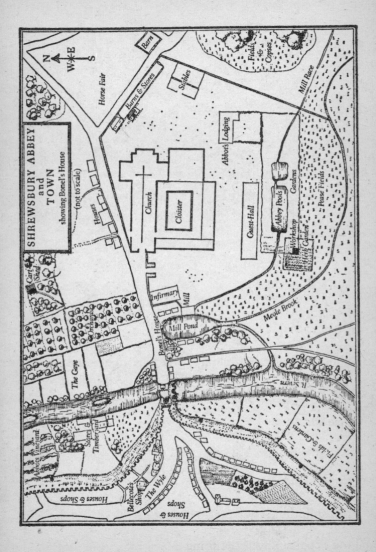

SHREWSBURY ABBEY
and
TOWN
showing Bonel's House
(not to scale)

N
W—E
S

Barn

Horse Fair

Barns & Stores

Stables

Fields &
Copses

Mill Race

Abbot's Lodging

Houses

Church

Cloister

Guest-Hall

Abbey Pools

Gardens

Workshop
Herb Garden

Pease Fields

Cart Shed

Infirmary

Mill

Bonel's House

Mill Pond

Meole Brook

The Gaye

River Severn

Stores of
Timberyards

Fields & Gardens

Abbot's Vineyard

Houses & Shops

Bellecote's Shop

The Wyle

Houses &
Shops

Shops

Monk's-Hood

Chapter 1

On this particular morning at the beginning of December, in the year 1138, Brother Cadfael came to chapter in tranquillity of mind, prepared to be tolerant even towards the dull, pedestrian reading of Brother Francis, and long-winded legal haverings of Brother Benedict the sacristan. Men were variable, fallible, and to be humoured. And the year, so stormy in its earlier months, convulsed with siege and slaughter and disruptions, bade fair to end in calm and comparative plenty. The tide of civil war between King Stephen and the partisans of the Empress Maud had receded into the south-western borders, leaving Shrewsbury to recover cautiously from having backed the weaker side and paid a bloody price for it. And for all the hindrances to good husbandry, after a splendid summer the harvest had been successfully gathered in, the barns were full, the mills were busy, sheep and cattle thrived on pastures still green and lush, and the weather continued surprisingly mild, with only a hint of frost in the early mornings. No one was wilting with cold yet, no one yet was going hungry. It could not last much longer, but every day counted as blessing.

And in his own small kingdom the crop had been rich and varied, the eaves of his workshop in the garden were hung everywhere with linen bags of dried herbs, his jars of wine sat in plump, complacent rows, the shelves were thronging with bottles and pots of specifics for all the ills of winter, from snuffling colds to seized-up joints and sore and wheezing chests. It was a better world than it had looked in the spring, and an ending that improves on its beginning is always good news.

So Brother Cadfael rolled contentedly to his chosen seat in the chapter-house, conveniently retired behind one of the pillars in a dim corner, and watched with half-sleepy benevolence as his brothers of the house filed in and took their places: Abbot Heribert, old and gentle and anxious, sadly worn by the troublous year now near its ending; Prior Robert Pennant, immensely tall and patrician, ivory of face and silver of hair and brows, ever erect and stately, as if he already balanced the mitre for which he yearned. He was neither old nor frail, but an ageless and wiry fifty-one, though he contrived to look every inch a patriarch sanctified by a lifetime of holiness; he had looked much the same ten years ago, and would almost certainly change not at all in the twenty years to come. Faithful at his heels slid Brother Jerome, his clerk, reflecting Robert's pleasure or displeasure like a small, warped mirror. After them came all the other officers, sub-prior, sacristan, hospitaller, almoner, infirmarer, the custodian of the altar of St Mary, the cellarer, the precentor, and the master of the novices. Decorously they composed themselves for what bade fair to be an unremarkable day's business.

Young Brother Francis, who was afflicted with a nasal snuffle and somewhat sparse Latin, made heavy weather of reading out the list of saints and martyrs to be commemorated in prayer during the coming days, and fumbled a pious commentary on the ministry of St Andrew the Apostle, whose day was just past. Brother Benedict the sacristan contrived to make it sound only fair that he, as responsible for the upkeep of church and enclave, should have the major claim on a sum willed jointly for that purpose and to provide lights for the alter of the Lady Chapel, which was Brother Maurice's province. The precentor acknowledged the gift of a new setting for the 'Sanctus', donated by the composer's patron, but by the dubious enthusiasm with which he welcomed so generous a gift, he did not think

10

highly of its merits, and it was unlikely to be heard often. Brother Paul, master of the novices, had a complaint against one of his pupils, suspected of levity beyond what was permitted to youth and inexperience, in that the youngster had been heard singing in the cloisters, while he was employed in copying a prayer of St Augustine, a secular song of scandalous import, purporting to be the lament of a Christian pilgrim imprisoned by the Saracens, and comforting himself by hugging to his breast the chemise given him at parting by his lover.

Brother Cadfael's mind jerked him back from incipient slumber to recognise and remember the song, beautiful and poignant. He had been in that Crusade, he knew the land, the Saracens, the haunting light and darkness of such a prison and such a pain. He saw Brother Jerome devoutly close his eyes and suffer convulsions of distress at the mention of a woman's most intimate garment. Perhaps because he had never been near enough to it to touch, thought Cadfael, still disposed to be charitable. Consternation quivered through several of the old, innocent, lifelong brothers, to whom half the creation was a closed and forbidden book. Cadfael made an effort, unaccustomed at chapter, and asked mildly what defence the youth had made.

'He said,' Brother Paul replied fairly, 'that he learned the song from his grandfather, who fought for the Cross at the taking of Jerusalem, and he found the tune so beautiful that it seemed to him holy. For the pilgrim who sang was not a monastic or a soldier, but a humble person who made the long journey out of love.'

'A proper and sanctified love,' pointed out Brother Cadfael, using words not entirely natural to him, for he thought of love as a self-sanctifying force, needing no apology. 'And is there anything in the words of that song to suggest that the woman he left behind was not his wife? I remember none. And the music is worthy of noting. It is not, surely, the purpose of our order to obliterate or censure the sacrament of marriage, for those who have not a celibate vocation. I think this young man may have done nothing very wrong. Should not Brother Precentor try if he has not a gifted voice? Those who sing at their work commonly have some need to use a God-given talent.'

The precentor, startled and prompted, and none too lavishly provided with singers to be moulded, obligingly opined that he would be interested to hear the novice sing. Prior Robert knotted his austere brows, and frowned down his patrician nose; if it had rested with him, the errant youth would have been awarded a hard penance. But the master of novices was no great enthusiast for the lavish use of the discipline, and seemed content to have a good construction put on his pupil's lapse.

'It is true that he has shown as earnest and willing, Father Abbot, and has been with us but a short time. It is easy to forget oneself at moments of concentration, and his copying is careful and devoted.'

The singer got away with a light penance that would not keep him on his knees long enough to rise from them stiffly. Abbot Heribert was always inclined to be lenient, and this morning he appeared more than usually preoccupied and distracted. They were drawing near the end of the day's affairs. The abbot rose as if to put an end to the chapter.

'There are here a few documents to be sealed,' said Brother Matthew the cellarer, rustling parchments in haste, for it seemed to him that the abbot had turned absent-minded, and lost sight of this duty. 'There is the matter of the fee-farm of Hales, and the grant made by Walter Aylwin, and also the guestship agreement with Gervase Bonel and his wife, to whom we are allotting the first house beyond the mill-pond. Master Bonel wishes to move in as soon as may be, before the Christmas feast...'

'Yes, yes, I have not forgotten.' Abbot Heribert looked small, dignified but resigned, standing before them with a scroll of his own gripped in both hands. 'There is something I have to announce to you all. These necessary documents cannot be sealed today, for sufficient reason. It may well be that they are now beyond my competence, and I no longer have the right to conclude any agreement for this community. I have here an instruction which was delivered to me yesterday, from Westminster, from the king's court. You all know that Pope Innocent has acknowledged King Stephen's claim to the throne of this realm, and in his support has sent over a legate with full powers, Alberic, cardinal-bishop of Ostia. The cardinal proposes to hold a legatine council in London for the reform of the church, and I am summoned to attend, to account for my stewardship as abbot of this convent. The terms make clear,' said Heribert, firmly and sadly, 'that my tenure is at the disposal of the legate. We have lived through a troubled year, and been tossed between two claimants to the throne of our land. It is not a secret, and I acknowledge it, that his Grace, when he was here in the summer, held me in no great favour, since in the confusion of the times I did not see my way clear, and was slow to accept his sovereignty. Therefore I now regard my abbacy as suspended, until or unless the legatine council confirms me in office. I cannot ratify any documents or agreements in the name of our house. Whatever is now uncompleted must remain uncompleted until a firm appointment has been made. I cannot trespass on what may well be another's field.'

He had said what he had to say. He resumed his seat and folded his hands patiently, while their bewildered, dismayed murmurings gradually congealed and mounted into a boiling, bees'-hive hum of consternation. Though not everyone was horrified, as Cadfael plainly saw. Prior Robert, just as startled as the rest, and adept at maintaining a decorous front, none the less glowed brightly behind his ivory face, drawing the obvious conclusion, and Brother Jerome, quick to interpret any message from that quarter, hugged himself with glee inside the sleeves of his habit, while his face exhibited pious sympathy and pain. Not that they had anything against Heribert, except that he continued to hold an office on which impatient subordinates were casting

13

covetous eyes. A nice old man, of course, but out of date, and far too lax. Like a king who lives too long, and positively invites assassination. But the rest of them fluttered and panicked like hens invaded by the fox, clamouring variously:

'But, Father Abbot, surely the king will restore you!'

'Oh, Father, must you go to this council?'

'We shall be left like sheep without a shepherd!'

Prior Robert, who considered himself ideally equipped to deal with the flock of St Peter himself, if need be, gave that complaint a brief, basilisk glare, but refrained from protest, indeed murmured his own commiseration and dismay.

'My duty and my vows are to the Church,' said Abbot Heribert sadly, 'and I am bound to obey the summons, as a loyal son. If it pleases the Church to confirm me in office, I shall return to take up my customary ward here. If another is appointed in my place, I shall still return among you, if I am permitted, and live out my life as a faithful brother of this house, under our new superior.'

Cadfael thought he caught a brief, complacent flicker of a smile that passed over Robert's face at that. It would not greatly disconcert him to have his old superior a humble brother under his rule at last.

'But clearly,' went on Abbot Heribert with humility, 'I can no longer claim rights as abbot until the matter is settled, and these agreements must rest in abeyance until my return, or until another considers and pronounces on them. Is any one of them urgent?'

Brother Matthew shuffled his parchments and pondered, still shaken by the suddenness of the news. 'There is no reason to hurry in the matter of the Aylwin grant, he is an old friend to our order, his offer will certainly remain open as long as need be. And the Hales fee-farm will date only from Lady Day of next year, so there's time enough. But Master Bonel relies on the charter being sealed very soon. He is waiting to move his belongings into the house.'

'Remind me of the terms, if you will,' the abbot requested apologetically. 'My mind has been full of other matters, I have forgotten just what was agreed.'

'Why, he grants to us his manor of Mallilie absolutely, with his several tenants, in return for a messuage here at the abbey—the first house on the town side of the mill-pond is vacant, and the most suitable to his household—together with keep for life for himself and his wife, and for two servants also. The details are as usual in such cases. They shall have daily two monks' loaves and one servants' loaf, two gallons of conventual ale and one of servants' ale, a dish of meat such as the abbey sergeants have, on meat-days, and of fish on fish-days, from the abbot's kitchen, and an intermissum whenever extra dainties are provided. These to be fetched by their manservant. They shall also have a dish of meat or fish daily for their two domestics. Master Bonel is also to have annually a robe such as the senior of the abbey officers receive, and his wife—she so prefers—shall have ten shillings yearly to provide a robe for herself as she chooses. There is also a provision of ten shillings yearly for linen, shoes and firing, and livery for one horse. And at the death of either, the other to retain possession of the house and receive a moiety of all the aforesaid provisions, except that if the wife be the survivor, she need not be provided with stabling for a horse. These are the terms, and I had intended to have witnesses come hither after chapter for the ratification. The justice has a clerk waiting.'

'I fear none the less,' said the abbot heavily, 'that this also must wait. My rights are in abeyance.'

'It will greatly inconvenience Master Bonel,' said the cellarer anxiously. 'They have already prepared to remove here, and expected to do so in the next few days. The Christmas feast is coming, and they cannot well be left in discomfort.'

'Surely,' suggested Prior Robert, 'the move could be countenanced, even if the ratification must wait a while. It's highly unlikely that any abbot appointed would wish to upset this agreement.' Since it was perfectly clear that he himself was in line for the appoint-

15

ment, and knew himself to be in better odour with King Stephen than his superior, he spoke with easy authority. Heribert jumped at the suggestion.

'I think such a move is permissible. Yes, Brother Matthew, you may proceed, pending final sanction, which I feel sure will be forthcoming. Reassure our guest on that point, and allow him to bring his household at once. It is only right that they should feel settled and at peace for the Christmas feast. There is no other case needing attention?'

'None, Father.' And he asked, subdued and thoughtful: 'When must you set forth on this journey?'

'The day after tomorrow I should leave. I ride but slowly these days, and we shall be some days on the road. In my absence, of course, Prior Robert will be in charge of all things here.'

Abbot Heribert lifted a distrait hand in blessing, and led the way out of the chapter-house. Prior Robert, sweeping after, no doubt felt himself already in charge of all things within the pale of the Benedictine abbey of St Peter and St Paul of Shrewsbury, and had every intent and expectation of continuing so to his life's end.

The brothers filed out in mourne silence, only to break out into subdued but agitated conversations as soon as they were dispersed over the great court. Heribert had been their abbot for eleven years, and an easy man to serve under, approachable, kindly, perhaps even a little too easy-going. They did not look forward to changes.

In the half-hour before High Mass at ten, Cadfael betook himself very thoughtfully to his workshop in the herb-gardens, to tend a few specifics he had brewing. The enclosure, thickly hedged and well trimmed, was beginning now to look bleached and dry with the first moderate cold, all the leaves grown elderly and lean and brown, the tenderest plants withdrawing into the warmth of the earth; but the air still bore a lingering, aromatic fragrance compounded of all the ghostly scents of summer, and inside the hut the spicy sweetness made the senses swim. Cadfael regularly

16

took his ponderings there for privacy. He was so used to the drunken, heady air within that he barely noticed it, but at need he could distinguish every ingredient that contributed to it, and trace it to its source.

So King Stephen, after all, had not forgotten his lingering grudges, and Abbot Heribert was to be the scapegoat for Shrewsbury's offence in holding out against his claims. Yet he was not by nature a vindictive man. Perhaps it was rather that he felt a need to flatter and court the legate, since the pope had recognised him as king of England, and given him papal backing, no negligible weapon, in the contention with the Empress Maud, the rival claimant to the throne. That determined lady would certainly not give up so easily, she would be pressing her case strongly in Rome, and even popes may change their allegiance. So Alberic of Ostia would be given every possible latitude in pursuing his plans for the reform of the Church, and Heribert might be but one sacrificial victim offered to his zeal on a platter.

Another curious theme intruded itself persistently into Cadfael's musings. This matter of the occasional guests of the abbey, so-called, the souls who chose to abandon the working world, sometimes in their prime, and hand over their inheritance to the abbey for a soft, shielded, inactive life in a house of retirement, with food, clothing, firing, all provided without the lifting of a finger! Did they dream of it for years while they were sweating over lambing ewes, or toiling in the harvest, or working hard at a trade? A little sub-paradise where meals dropped from the sky and there was nothing to do but bask, in the summer, and toast by the fire with mulled ale in the winter? And when they got to it, how long did the enchantment last? How soon did they sicken of doing nothing, and needing to do nothing? In a man blind, lame, sick, he could understand the act. But in those hale and busy, and used to exerting body and mind? No, that he could not understand. There must be other motives. Not all men could be deceived, or deceive themselves, into mistaking idleness for blessedness. What else could provoke such an act? Want of an heir? An urge, not yet understood, to the monastic life, without the immediate courage to go all the way? Perhaps! In a man with a wife, well advanced in years and growing aware of his end, it might be so. Many a man had taken the habit and the cowl late, after children and grandchildren and the heat of a long day. The grace house and the guest status might be a stage on the way. Or was it possible that men divested themselves of their life's work at last out of pure despite, against the world, against the unsatisfactory son, against the burden of carrying their own souls?

Brother Cadfael shut the door upon the rich horehound reek of a mixture for coughs, and went very soberly to High Mass.

Abbot Heribert departed by the London road, turning his back upon the town of Shrewsbury, in the early morning of a somewhat grey day, the first time there had been the nip of frost in the air as well as the pale sparkle in the grass. He took with him his own clerk, Brother Emmanuel, and two lay grooms who had served here longest; and he rode his own white mule. He put on a cheerful countenance as he took leave, but for all that he cut a sad little figure as the four riders dwindled along the road. No horseman now, if he ever had been much of one, he used a high, cradling saddle, and sagged in it like a small sack not properly filled. Many of the brothers crowded to the gates to watch him as long as he remained in view, and their faces were apprehensive and aggrieved. Some of the boy pupils came out to join them, looking even more dismayed, for the abbot had allowed Brother Paul to conduct his schooling undisturbed, which meant very tolerantly, but with Prior Robert in charge there was no department of this house likely to go its way ungoaded, and discipline might be expected to tighten abruptly.

There was, Cadfael could not but admit, room for a little hard practicality within these walls, if the truth were told. Heribert of late had grown deeply discouraged with the world of men, and withdrawn more and more into his prayers. The siege and fall of Shrewsbury, with all the bloodshed and revenge involved, had been enough to sadden any man, though that was no excuse for abandoning the effort to defend right and oppose wrong. But there comes a time when the old grow very tired, and the load of leadership unjustly heavy to bear. And perhaps—perhaps!—Heribert would not be quite so sad as even he now supposed, if the load should be lifted from him.

Mass and chapter passed that day with unexceptionable decorum and calm, High Mass was celebrated devoutly, the duties of the day proceeded in their smooth and regular course. Robert was too sensible of his own image to rub his hands visibly, or lick his lips before witnesses. All that he did would be done according to just and pious law, with the authority of sainthood. Nevertheless, what he considered his due would be appropriated, to the last privilege.

Cadfael was accustomed to having two assistants allotted to him throughout the active part of the gardening years, for he grew other things in his walled garden besides the enclosure of herbs, though the main kitchen gardens of the abbey were ouside the enclave, across the main highway and along the fields by the river, the lush level called the Gaye. The waters of Severn regularly moistened it in the flood season, and its soil was rich and bore well. Here within the walls he had made, virtually single-handed, this closed garden for the small and precious things, and in the outer levels, running down to the Meole brook that fed the mill, he grew food crops, beans and cabbages and pulse, and fields of pease. But now with the winter closing gently in, and the soil settling to its sleep like the urchins under the hedges, curled drowsily with all their prickles cushioned by straw and dead grass and leaves, he was left with just one novice to help him brew his draughts, and roll his pills, and stir his rubbing oils, and pound his poultices, to medicine not only the brothers, but many who came for help in their troubles, from the town and the Foregate, sometimes even from the scattered villages beyond. He had not been bred to this science, he had learned it by experience, by trial and study, accumulating knowledge over the years, until some preferred his ministrations to those of the acknowledged physicians.

His assistant at this time was a novice of no more than eighteen years, Brother Mark, orphaned, and a trouble to a neglectful uncle, who had sent him into the abbey at sixteen to be rid of him. He had entered tongue-tied, solitary and homesick, a waif who seemed even younger than his years, who did what he was told with apprehensive submission, as though the best to be hoped out of life was to avoid punishment. But some months of working in the garden with Cadfael had gradually loosened his tongue and put his fears to flight. He was still undersized, and slightly wary of authority, but healthy and wiry, and good at making things grow, and he was acquiring a sure and delicate touch with the making of medicines, and an eager interest in them. Mute among his fellows, he made up for it by being voluble enough in the garden workshop, and with none but Cadfael by. It was always Mark, for all his silence and withdrawal about the cloister and court, who brought all the gossip before others knew it.

He came in from an errand to the mill, an hour before Vespers, full of news.

'Do you know what Prior Robert has done? Taken up residence in the abbot's lodging! Truly! Brother Subprior has orders to sleep in the prior's cell in the dormitory from tonight. And Abbot Heribert barely out of the gates! I call it great presumption!'

So did Cadfael, though he felt it hardly incumbent upon him either to say so, or to let Brother Mark utter his thoughts quite so openly. 'Beware how you pass judgment on your superiors,' he said mildly, 'at least until you know how to put yourself in their place and see from their view. For all we know, Abbot Heribert

20

may have required him to move into the lodging, as an instance of his authority while we're without an abbot. It is the place set aside for the spiritual father of this convent.'

'But Prior Robert is not that, not yet! And Abbot Heribert would have said so at chapter if he had wished it so. At least he would have told Brother Sub-prior, and no one did. I saw his face, he is as astonished as anyone, and shocked. *He* would not have taken such a liberty!'

Too true, thought Cadfael, busy pounding roots in a mortar, Brother Richard the sub-prior was the last man to presume; large, good-natured and peace-loving to the point of laziness, he never exerted himself to advance even by legitimate means. It might dawn on some of the younger and more audacious brothers shortly that they had gained an advantage in the exchange. With Richard in the prior's cell that commanded the length of the dortoir, it would be far easier for the occasional sinner to slip out by the night-stairs after the lights were out; even if the crime were detected it would probably never be reported. A blind eye is the easiest thing in the world to turn on whatever is troublesome.

'All the servants at the lodging are simmering,' said Brother Mark. 'You know how devoted they are to Abbot Heribert, and now to be made to serve someone else, before his place is truly vacant, even! Brother Henry says it's almost blasphemy. And Brother Petrus is looking blacker than thunder, and muttering into his cooking-pots something fearful. He said, once Prior Robert gets his foot in the door, it will take a dose of hemlock to get him out again when Abbot Heribert returns.'

Cadfael could well imagine it. Brother Petrus was the abbot's cook, old in his service, and a black-haired, fiery-eyed barbarian from near the Scottish border, at that, given to tempestuous and immoderate declarations, none of them to be taken too seriously; but the puzzle was where exactly to draw the line.

'Brother Petrus says many things he might do well not to say, but he never means harm, as you well know. And he's a prime cook, and will continue to feed the abbot's table nobly, whoever sits at the head of it, because he can do no other.'

'But not happily,' said Brother Mark with conviction.

No question but the even course of the day had been gravely shaken; yet so well regulated was the regime within these walls that every brother, happy or not, would pursue his duties as conscientiously as ever.

'When Abbot Heribert returns, confirmed in office,' said Mark, firmly counting wishes as horses, 'Prior Robert's nose will be out of joint.' And the thought of that august organ bent aside like the misused beak of an old soldier so consoled him that he found heart to laugh again, while Cadfael could not find the heart to scold him, since even for him the picture had its appeal.

Brother Edmund the infirmarer came to Cadfael's hut in the middle of the afternoon, a week after Abbot Heribert's departure, to collect some medicines for his inmates. The frosts, though not yet severe, had come after such mild weather as to take more than one young brother by surprise, spreading a sneezing rheum that had to be checked by isolating the victims, most of them active youngsters who worked outdoors with the sheep. He had four of them in the infirmary, besides the few old men who now spent their days there with none but religious duties, waiting peacefully for their end.

'All the lads need is a few days in the warm, and they'll cure themselves well enough,' said Cadfael, stirring and pouring a large flask into a smaller one, a brown mixture that smelled hot and aromatic and sweet. 'But no need to endure discomfort, even for a few days. Let them drink a dose of this, two or three times in the day and at night, as much as will fill a small spoon, and they'll be the easier for it.'

'What is it?' asked Brother Edmund curiously. Many of Brother Cadfael's preparations he already knew, but there were constantly new developments. Sometimes he wondered if Cadfael tried them all out on himself.

'There's rosemary, and horehound, and saxifrage, mashed into a little oil pressed from flax seeds, and the body is a red wine I made from cherries and their stones. You'll find they'll do well on it, any that have the rheum in their eyes or heads, and even for the cough it serves, too.' He stoppered the large bottle carefully, and wiped the neck. 'Is there anything more you'll be wanting? For the old fellows? They must be in a taking at all these changes we're seeing. Past the three score men don't take kindly to change.'

'Not, at all events, to this change,' owned Brother Edmund ruefully. 'Heribert never knew how he was liked, until they began to feel his loss.'

'You think we have lost him?'

'I fear it's all too likely. Not that Stephen himself bears grudges too long, but what the legate wants, Stephen will let him have, to keep the pope sweet. And do you think a brisk, reforming spirit, let loose here in our realm with powers to fashion the church he wants, will find our abbot very impressive? Stephen cast the doubt, while he was still angry, but it's Alberic of Ostia who will weigh up our good little abbot, and discard him for too soft in grain,' said Brother Edmund regretfully. 'I could do with another pot of that salve of yours for bed-sores. Brother Adrian can't be much longer for this penance, poor soul.'

'It must be pain now, just shifting him for the anointing,' said Cadfael with sympathy.

'Skin and bone, mere skin and bone. Getting food down him at all is labour enough. He withers like a leaf.'

'If ever you want an extra hand to lift him, send for me, I'm here to be used. Here's what you want. I think I have it better than before, with more of Our Lady's mantle in it.'

Brother Edmund laid bottle and pot in his scrip, and considered on other needs, scouring his pointed chin between thumb and forefinger. The sudden chill that blew in through the doorway made them both turn their heads, so sharply that the young man who had opened the door a wary inch or two hung his head in instant apology and dismay.

'Close the door, lad,' said Cadfael, hunching his shoulders.

A hasty, submissive voice called: 'Pardon, brother! I'll wait your leisure.' And the door began to close upon a thin, dark, apprehensively sullen face.

'No, no,' said Cadfael with cheerful impatience, 'I never meant it so. Come into the warm, and close the door on that wicked wind. It makes the brazier smoke. Come in, I'll be with you very shortly, when Brother Infirmarer has all his needs.'

The door opened just wide enough to allow a lean young man to slide in through the aperture, which he thereupon very hastily closed, and flattened his thin person against the door in mute withdrawal, willing to be invisible and inaudible, though his eyes were wide in wonder and curiosity at the storehouse of rustling, dangling, odorous herbs that hung about the place, and the benches and shelves of pots and bottles that hoarded the summer's secret harvest.

'Ah, yes,' said Brother Edmund, recollecting, 'there was one more thing. Brother Rhys is groaning with creaks and pains in his shoulders and back. He gets about very little now, and it does pain him, I've seen it make him jerk and start. You have an oil that gave him ease before.'

'I have. Wait, now, let me find a flask to fill for you.' Cadfael hoisted from its place on a low bench a large stone bottle, and rummaged along the shelves for a smaller one of cloudy glass. Carefully he unstoppered and poured, a viscous dark oil that gave off a strong, sharp odour. He replaced the wooden stopper firmly, bedding it in with a wisp of linen, and with another torn shred scrupulously wiped the lips of both containers, and dropped the rag into the small brazier beside which he had a stoneware pot simmering gently. 'This will answer, all the more if you get someone with good strong fingers to work it well into his joints. But keep it carefully, Edmund, never let it near your lips. Wash your hands well after using it, and make sure any other who handles it does the same. It's good for a man's outside, but bad indeed for his inside. And don't use it where there's any scratch or wound, any break in the skin, either. It's powerful stuff.'

'So perilous? What is it made from?' asked Edmund curiously, turning the bottle in his hand to see the sluggish way the oils moved against the glass.

'The ground root of monk's-hood, chiefly, in mustard oil and oil from flax seeds. It's powerfully poisonous if swallowed, a very small draught of this could kill, so keep it safe and remember to cleanse your hands well. But it works wonders for creaking old joints. He'll notice a tingling warmth when it's rubbed well in, and then the pain is dulled, and he'll be quite easy. There, is that all you need? I'll come over myself presently, and do the anointing, if you wish? I know where to find the aches, and it needs to be worked in deep.'

'I know you have iron fingers,' said Brother Edmund, mustering his load. 'You used them on me once, I thought you would break me apart, but I own I could move the better, the next day. Yes, come if you have time, he'll be glad to see you. He wanders, nowadays, there's hardly one among the young brothers he recognises, but he'll not have forgotten you.'

'He'll remember any who have the Welsh tongue,' said Cadfael simply. 'He goes back to his childhood, as old men do.'

Brother Edmund took up his bag and turned to the door. The thin young man, all eyes, slipped aside and opened it for him civilly, and again closed it upon his smiling thanks. Not such a meagre young man, after all, inches above Cadfael's square, solid bulk, and erect and supple of movement, but lean and wary, with a suggestion of wild alertness in his every motion. He had a shock of light-brown hair, unkempt from the rising wind outside, and the trimmed lines of a fair beard about lips and chin, pointing the hungry austerity of a thin, hawk-featured face. The large, bright-blue eyes, glittering with intelligence and defensive as levelled spears, turned their attention upon Cadfael, and sustained the glance unwavering, lances in rest.

'Well, friend,' said Cadfael comfortably, shifting his pot a shade further from the direct heat, 'what is it I can do for you?' And he turned and viewed the stranger candidly, from head to foot. 'I don't know you, lad,' he said placidly, 'but you're welcome. What's your need?'

'I'm sent by Mistress Bonel,' said the young man, in a voice low-pitched and pleasant to hear, if it had not been so tight and wary, 'to ask you for some kitchen-herbs she needs. Brother Hospitaller told her you would be willing to supply her when her own stocks fail. My master has today moved into a house in the Foregate, as guest of the abbey.'

'Ah, yes,' said Cadfael, remembering the manor of Mallilie, gifted to the abbey in return for the means of life to the giver. 'So they are safely in, are they? God give them joy of it! And you are the manservant who will carry their meals back and forth—yes, you'll need to find your way about the place. You've been to the abbot's kitchen?'

'Yes, master.'

'No man's master,' said Cadfael mildly, 'every man's brother, if you will. And what's your name, friend? For we shall be seeing something of each other in the days to come, we may as well be acquainted.'

'My name is Aelfric,' said the young man. He had come forward from the doorway, and stood looking round him with open interest. His eyes lingered with awe on the large bottle that held the oil of monk's-hood. 'Is that truly so deadly? Even a little of it can kill a man?'

'So can many things,' said Cadfael, 'used wrongly, or used in excess. Even wine, if you take enough of it. Even wholesome food, if you devour it beyond reason. And are your household content with their dwelling?'

'It's early yet to say,' said the young man guardedly. What age would he be? Twenty-five years or so?

Hardly more. He bristled like an urchin at a touch, alert against all the world. Unfree, thought Cadfael, sympathetic; and of quick and vulnerable mind. Servant to someone less feeling than himself? It might well be.

'How many are you in the house?'

'My master and mistress, and I. And a maid.' A maid! No more, and his long, mobile mouth shut fast even on that.

'Well, Aelfric, you're welcome to make your way here when you will, and what I can supply for your lady, that I will. What is it I can send her this time?'

'She asks for some sage, and some basil, if you have such. She brought a dish with her to warm for the evening,' said Aelfric, thawing a little, 'and has it on a hob there, but it wants for sage. She was out. It's a curious time, moving house here, she'll have left a mort of things behind.'

'What's in my way she may send here for, and welcome. Here you are, Aelfric, lad, here's a bunch of either. Is she a good mistress, your lady?'

'She's that!' said the youth, and closed upon it, as he had upon mention of the maid. He brooded, frowning into mixed and confused thoughts. 'She was a widow when she wed him.' He took the bunches of herbs, fingers gripping hard on the stems. On a throat? Whose, then, since he melted at mention of his mistress? 'I thank you kindly, brother.'

He drew back, lissome and silent. The door opening and closing took but a moment. Cadfael was left gazing after him very thoughtfully. There was still an hour before Vespers. He might well go over to the infirmary, and pour the sweet sound of Welsh into Brother Rhys's old, dulled ears, and dig the monk's-hood oil deep into his aching joints. It would be a decent deed.

But that wild young thing, caged with his grievances, hurts and hatreds, what was to be done for him? A villein, if Cadfael knew one when he saw one, with abilities above his station, and some private anguish,

27

maybe more than one. He remembered that mention of the maid, bitten off jealousy between set teeth.

Well, they were but newly come, all four of them. Let the time work for good. Cadfael washed his hands, with all the thoroughness he recommended to his patrons, reviewed his sleeping kingdom, and went to visit the infirmary.

Old Brother Rhys was sitting up beside his neatly made bed, not far from the fire, nodding his ancient, grey-tonsured head. He looked proudly complacent, as one who has got his due against all the odds, stubbly chin jutting, thick old eyebrows bristling in all directions, and the small, sharp eyes beneath almost colourless in their grey pallor, but triumphantly bright. For he had a young, vigorous, dark-haired fellow sitting on a stool beside him, waiting on him good-humouredly and pouring voluble Welsh into his ears like a mountain spring. The old man's gown was stripped down from his bony shoulders, and his attendant was busily massaging oil into the joints with probing fingers, drawing grunts of pleasure from his patient.

'I see I'm forestalled,' said Cadfael into Brother Edmund's ear, in the doorway.

'A kinsmen,' said Brother Edmund as softly. 'Some young Welshman from up in the north of the shire, where Rhys comes from. It seems he came here today to help the new tenants move in at the house by the mill-pond. He's connected somehow—journeyman to the woman's son, I believe. And while he was here he thought to ask after the old man, which was a kind act. Rhys was complaining of his pains, and the young fellow offered, so I set him to work. Still, now you're here, have a word. They'll neither of them need to speak English for you.'

'You'll have warned him to wash his hands well, afterwards?'

'And shown him where, and where to stow the bottle away safely when he's done. He understands. I'd hardly

28

let a man take risks with such a brew, after your lecture. I've told him what the stuff could do, misused.'

The young man ceased his ministrations momentarily when Brother Cadfael approached, and made to stand up respectfully, but Cadfael waved him down again. 'No, sit, lad, I won't disturb you. I'm here for a word with an old friend, but I see you've taken on my work for me, and doing it well, too.'

The young man, with cheerful practicality, took him at his word, and went on kneading the pungent oils into Brother Rhys's aged shoulders. He was perhaps twenty-four or twenty-five years old, sturdily built and strong; his square, good-natured face was brown and weathered, and plentifully supplied with bone, a Welsh face, smooth-shaven and decisive, his hair and brows thick, wiry and black. His manner towards Brother Rhys was smiling, merry, almost teasing, as it probably would have been towards a child; and that was engaging in him, and won Brother Cadfael's thoughtful approval, for Brother Rhys was indeed a child again. Livelier than usual today, however, the visitor had done him a deal of good.

'Well, now, Cadfael!' he piped, twitching a shoulder pleasurably at the young man's probing. 'You see my kinsmen remember me yet. Here's my niece Angharad's boy come to see me, my great-nephew Meurig. I mind the time he was born... Eh, I mind the time she was born, for that matter, my sister's little lass. It's many years since I've seen her—or you, boy, come to think of it, you could have come to see me earlier. But there's no family feeling in the young, these days.' But he was very complacent about it, enjoying handing out praise one moment and illogical reproof the next, a patriarch's privilege. 'And why didn't the girl come herself? Why didn't you bring your mother with you?'

'It's a long journey from the north of the shire,' said the young man Meurig, easily, 'and always more than enough to be done at home. But I'm nearer now, I work for a carpenter and carver in the town here, you'll be seeing more of me. I'll come and do this for you again—

have you out on a hillside with the sheep yet, come spring.'

'My niece Angharad,' murmured the old man, benignly smiling, 'was the prettiest little thing in half the shire, and she grew up a beauty. What age would she be now? Five and forty, it may be, but I warrant she's still as beautiful as ever she was—don't you tell me different, I never yet saw the one to touch her....'

'Her son's not likely to tell you any different,' agreed Meurig comfortably. Are not all one's lost nieces beautiful? And the weather of the summers when they were children always radiant, and the wild fruit they gathered then sweeter than any that grows now? For some years Brother Rhys had been considered mildly senile, his wanderings timeless and disorganised; memory failed, fantasy burgeoned, he drew pictures that never had existed on sea or land. But somewhere else, perhaps? Now, with the stimulus of this youthful and vigorous presence and the knowledge of their shared blood, he quickened into sharp remembrance again. It might not last, but it was a princely gift while it lasted.

'Turn a little more to the fire—there, is that the spot?' Rhys wriggled and purred like a stroked cat, and the young man laughed, and plied deep into the flesh, smoothing out knots with a firmness that both hurt and gratified.

'This is no new skill with you,' said Brother Cadfael, observing with approval.

'I've worked mostly with horses, and they get their troubles with swellings and injuries, like men. You learn to see with your fingers, where to find what's bound, and loose it again.'

'But he's a carpenter now,' Brother Rhys said proudly, 'and working here in Shrewsbury.'

'And we're making a lectern for your Lady Chapel,' said Meurig, 'and when it's done—and it soon will be— I'll be bringing it down to the abbey myself. And I'll come and see you again while I'm here.'

'And rub my shoulder again? It gets winterly now, towards Christmas, the cold gets in my bones.'

'I will so. But that's enough for now, I'll be making you too sore. Have up your gown again, uncle—there, and keep the warmth in. Does it burn?'

'For a while it prickled like nettles, now there's a fine, easy glow. I don't feel any pain there now. But I'm tired...'

He would be, tired and drowsy after the manipulation of his flesh and the reviving of his ancient mind. 'That's right, that's well. Now you should lie down and have a sleep.' Meurig looked to Cadfael to support him. 'Isn't that best, brother?'

'The very best thing. That's hard exercise you've been taking, you should rest after it.'

Rhys was well content to be settled on his bed and left to the sleep that was already overtaking him. His drowsy farewells followed them towards the door, to fade into silence before they reached it. 'Take my greetings to your mother, Meurig. And ask her to come and see me... when they bring the wool to Shrewsbury market... I'm fain to see her again...'

'He set great store by your mother, it seems,' said Cadfael, watching as Meurig washed his hands where Brother Edmund had shown him, and making sure that he was thorough about it. 'Is there a hope that he may see her again?'

Meurig's face, seen in profile as he wrung and scrubbed at his hands, had a gravity and brooding thoughtfulness that belied the indulgent gaiety he had put on for this old man. After a moment he said: 'Not in this world.' He turned to reach for the coarse towel, and looked Cadfael in the eyes fully and steadily. 'My mother has been dead for eleven years this Michaelmas past. He knows it—or he knew it—as well as I. But if she's alive to him again in his dotage, why should I remind him? Let him keep that thought and any other that can pleasure him.'

They went out together in silence, into the chilly air of the great court, and there separated, Meurig striking across briskly towards the gatehouse, Cadfael making for the church, where the Vesper bell could be only a few minutes delayed.

'God speed!' said Cadfael in parting. 'You gave the old man back a piece of his youth today. The elders of your kinship, I think, are fortunate in their sons.'

'My kinship,' said Meurig, halting in mid-stride to stare back with great black eyes, 'is my mother's kinship, I go with my own. My father was not a Welshman.'

He went, lengthening a lusty stride, the square shape of his shoulders cleaving the dusk. And Cadfael wondered about him, as he had wondered about the villein Aelfric, as far as the porch of the church, and then abandoned him for a more immediate duty. These people are, after all, responsible for themselves, and none of his business.

Not yet!

Chapter 2

It was nearing mid-December before the dour manservant Aelfric came again to the herb-gardens for kitchen herbs for his mistress. By that time he was a figure familiar enough to fade into the daily pattern of comings and goings about the great court, and among the multifarious noise and traffic his solitary silence remained generally unremarked. Cadfael had seen him in the mornings, passing through to the bakery and buttery for the day's loaves and measures of ale, always mute, always purposeful, quick of step and withdrawn of countenance, as though any delay on his part might bring penance, as perhaps, indeed, it might. Brother Mark, attracted to a soul seemingly as lonely and anxious as his own had once been, had made some attempt to engage the stranger in talk, and had little success.

'Though he does unfold a little,' said Mark thoughtfully, kicking his heels on the bench in Cadfael's workshop as he stirred a salve. 'I don't think he's an unfriendly soul at all, if he had not something on his mind. When I greet him he sometimes comes near to smiling, but he'll never linger and talk.'

'He has his work to do, and perhaps a master who's hard to please,' said Cadfael mildly.

'I heard he's out of sorts since they moved in,' said Mark. 'The master, I mean. Not really ill, but low and out of appetite.'

'So might I be,' opined Cadfael, 'if I had nothing to do but sit there and mope, and wonder if I'd done well to part with my lands, even in old age. What seems an

33

easy life in contemplation can be hard enough when it comes to reality.'

'The girl,' said Mark judiciously, 'is pretty. Have you seen her?'

'I have not. And you, my lad, should be averting your eyes from contemplation of women. Pretty, is she?'

'Very pretty. Not very tall, round and fair, with a lot of yellow hair, and black eyes. It makes a great effect, yellow hair and black eyes. I saw her come to the stable with some message for Aelfric yesterday. He looked after her, when she went, in such a curious way. Perhaps *she* is his trouble.'

And that might well be, thought Cadfael, if he was a villein, and she a free woman, and unlikely to look so low as a serf, and they were rubbing shoulders about the household day after day, in closer quarters here than about the manor of Mallilie.

'She could as well be trouble for you, boy, if Brother Jerome or Prior Robert sees you conning her,' he said briskly. 'If you must admire a fine girl, let it be out of the corner of your eyes. Don't forget we have a reforming rule here now.'

'Oh, I'm careful!' Mark was by no means in awe of Brother Cadfael now, and had adopted from him somewhat unorthodox notions of what was and was not permissible. In any case, this boy's vocation was no longer in doubt or danger. If the times had been less troublesome he might well have sought leave to go and study in Oxford, but even without that opportunity, Cadfael was reasonably certain he would end by taking orders, and become a priest, and a good priest, too, one aware that women existed in the world, and respectful towards their presence and their worth. Mark had come unwillingly and resisting into the cloister, but he had found his rightful place. Not everyone was so fortunate.

Aelfric came to the hut in the afternoon of a cloudy day, to ask for some dried mint. 'My mistress wants to brew a mint cordial for my master.'

'I hear he's somewhat out of humour and health,' said Cadfael, rustling the linen bags that gave forth such rich, heady scents upon the air. The young man's nostrils quivered and widened with pleasure, inhaling close sweetness. In the soft light within, his wary face eased a little.

'There's not much ails him, more of the mind than the body. He'll be well enough when he plucks up heart. He's out of sorts with his kin most of all,' said Aelfric, growing unexpectedly confiding.

'That's trying for you all, even the lady,' said Cadfael.

'And she does everything woman could do for him, there's nothing he can reproach her with. But this upheaval has him out with everybody, even himself. He's been expecting his son to come running and eat humble pie before this, to try and get his inheritance back, and he's been disappointed, and that sours him.'

Cadfael turned a surprised face at this. 'You mean he's cut off a son, to give his inheritance to the abbey? To spite the young man? That he couldn't, in law. No house would think of accepting such a bargain, without the consent of the heir.'

'It's not his own son.' Aelfric shrugged, shaking his head. 'It's his wife's son by a former marriage, so the lad has no legal claims on him. It's true he'd made a will naming him as his heir, but the abbey charter wipes that out—or will when it's sealed and witnessed. He has no remedy in law. They fell out, and he's lost his promised manor, and that's all there is to it.'

'For what fault could he deserve such treatment?' Cadfael wondered.

Aelfric hoisted deprecating shoulders, lean shoulders but broad and straight, as Cadfael observed. 'He's young and wayward, and my lord is old and irritable, not used to being crossed. Neither was the boy used to it, and he fought hard when he found his liberty curbed.'

'And what's become of him now? For I recall you said you were but four in the house.'

'He has a neck as stiff as my lord's, he's taken himself off to live with his married sister and her family, and learn a trade. He was expected back with his tail between his legs before now, my lord was counting on it, but never a sign, and I doubt if there will be.'

It sounded, Cadfael reflected ruefully, a troublous situation for the disinherited boy's mother, who must be torn two ways in this dissension. Certainly it accounted for an act of spleen which the old man was probably already regretting. He handed over the bunch of mint stems, their oval leaves still well formed and whole, for they had dried in honest summer heat, and had even a good shade of green left. 'She'll need to rub it herself, but it keeps its flavour better so. If she wants more, and you let me know, I'll crumble it fine for her, but this time we'll not keep her waiting. I hope it may go some way towards sweetening him, for his own sake and hers. And yours, too,' said Cadfael, and clapped him lightly on the shoulder.

Aelfric's gaunt features were convulsed for a moment by what might almost have been a smile, but of a bitter, resigned sort. 'Villeins are there to be scapegoats,' he said with soft, sudden violence, and left the hut hurriedly, with only a hasty, belated murmur of thanks.

With the approach of Christmas it was quite usual for many of the merchants of Shrewsbury, and the lords of many small manors close by, to give a guilty thought to the welfare of their souls, and their standing as devout and ostentatious Christians, and to see small ways of acquiring merit, preferably as economically as possible. The conventual fare of pulse, beans, fish, and occasional and meagre meat, benefited by sudden gifts of flesh and fowl to provide treats for the monks of St Peter's. Honey-baked cakes appeared, and dried fruits, and chickens, and even, sometimes, a haunch of venison, all devoted to the pittances that turned a devotional sacrament into a rare indulgence, a holy day into a holiday.

Some, of course, were selective in their giving, and made sure that their alms reached abbot or prior, on the assumption that his prayers might avail them more than those of the humbler brothers. There was a knight of south Shropshire who was quite unaware that Abbot Heribert had been summoned to London to be disciplined, and sent for his delectation a plump partridge, in splendid condition after a fat season. Naturally it arrived at the abbot's lodging to be greeted with pleasure by Prior Robert, who sent it down to the kitchen, to Brother Petrus, to be prepared for the midday meal in fitting style.

Brother Petrus, who seethed with resentment against him for Abbot Heribert's sake, glowered at the beautiful bird, and seriously considered spoiling it in some way, by burning it, or drying it with over-roasting, or serving it with a sauce that would ruin its perfection. But he was a cook of pride and honour, and he could not do it. The worst he could do was prepare it in an elaborate way which he himself greatly loved, with red wine and a highly spiced, aromatic sauce, cooked long and slow, and hope that Prior Robert would not be able to stomach it.

The prior was in high content with himself, with his present eminence, with the assured prospect of elevation to the abbacy in the near future, and with the manor of Mallilie, which he had been studying from the steward's reports, and found a surprisingly lavish gift. Gervase Bonel had surely let his spite run away with his reason, to barter such a property for the simple necessities of life, when he was already turned sixty years, and could hardly expect to enjoy his retirement very long. A few extra attentions could be accorded him at little cost. Brother Jerome, always primed with the news within and without the pale, had reported that Master Bonel was slightly under the weather, with a jaded appetite. He might appreciate the small personal compliment of a dish from the abbot's table. And there was enough, a partridge being a bird of ample flesh.

Brother Petrus was basting the plump little carcase lovingly with his rich wine sauce, tasting delicately, adding a pinch of rosemary and a mere hint of rue, when Prior Robert swept into the kitchen, imperially tall and papally austere, and stood over the pot, his alabaster nostrils twitching to the tantalising scent, and his cool eyes studying the appearance of the dish, which was as alluring as its savour. Brother Petrus stooped to hide his face, which was sour as gall, and basted industriously, hoping his best efforts might meet with an uninformed palate, and disgust where they should delight. Small hope, Robert had such pleasure in the aroma that he almost considered abandoning his generous plan to share the satisfaction. Almost, but not quite. Mallilie was indeed a desirable property.

'I have heard,' said the prior, 'that our guest at the house by the mill-pond is in poor health, and lacks appetite. Set aside a single portion of this dish, Brother Petrus, and send it to the invalid with my compliments, as an intermissum after the main dish for the day. Bone it, and serve it in one of my own bowls. It should tempt him, if he is out of taste with other foods, and he will appreciate the attention.' He condescended, all too genuinely, to add: 'It smells excellent.'

'I do my best,' grated Brother Petrus, almost wishing his best undone.

'So do we all,' acknowledged Robert austerely, 'and so we ought.' And he swept out as he had swept in, highly content with himself, his circumstances, and the state of his soul. And Brother Petrus gazed after him from under lowering brows, and snarled at his two lay scullions, who knew better than to meddle too close while he was cooking, but kept the corners of the kitchen, and jumped to obey orders.

Even for Brother Petrus orders were orders. He did as he had been instructed, but after his own fashion, seeing to it that the portion he set aside for the unoffending guest was the choicest part of the flesh, and laced with the richest helping of the sauce.

'Lost his appetite, has he?' he said, after a final tasting, and unable to suppress his satisfaction in his own skills. 'That should tempt a man on his death-bed to finish it to the last drop.'

* * *

Brother Cadfael on his way to the refectory saw Aelfric crossing the great court from the abbot's kitchen, heading quickly for the gatehouse, bearing before him a high-rimmed wooden tray laden with covered dishes. Guests enjoyed a more relaxed diet than the brothers, though it did not differ greatly except in the amount of meat, and at this time of year that would already be salt beef. To judge by the aroma that wafted from the tray as it passed, beef boiled with onions, and served with a dish of beans. The small covered bowl balanced on top had a much more appetising smell. Evidently the newcomer was to enjoy an intermissum today, before coming to the apples from the orchard. Aelfric carried his burden, which must be quite heavy, with a careful concentration, bent on getting it safely and quickly to the house by the pond. It was not a long journey, out at the gatehouse, a short step to the left, to the limits of the monastery wall, then past the mill-pond on the left, and the first house beyond was Aelfric's destination. Beyond, again, came the bridge over the Severn, and the wall and gate of Shrewsbury. Not far, but far enough in December for food to get cold. No doubt the household, though relieved of the need to do much cooking, had its own fire and hob, and pans and dishes enough, and the fuel was a part of the price of Bonel's manor.

Cadfael went on to the refectory, and his own dinner, which turned out to be boiled beef and beans, as he had foreseen. No savoury intermissum here. Brother Richard, the sub-prior, presided; Prior Robert ate privately in the lodging he already thought of as his own. The partridge was excellent.

They had reached the grace after meat, and were rising from table, when the door flew open almost in Brother Richard's face, and a lay brother from the porter's lodge burst in, babbling incoherently for Brother Edmund, but too short of breath from running to explain the need.

'Master Bonel—his serving-maid has come running

for help...' He gulped breath deep, and suppressed his panting long enough to get out clearly: 'He's taken terribly ill, she said he looks at death's door...the mistress begs someone to come to him quickly!'

Brother Edmund gripped him by the arm. 'What ails him? Is it a stroke? A convulsion?'

'No, from what the girl said, not that. He ate his dinner, and seemed well and well content, and not a quarter of an hour after he was taken with tingling of the mouth and throat, and then willed to vomit, but could not, and lips and neck are grown stiff and hard....So she said!'

By the sound of it, she was a good witness, too, thought Cadfael, already making for the door and his workshop at a purposeful trot. 'Go before, Edmund, I'll join you as fast as I may. I'll bring what may be needed.'

He ran, and Edmund ran, and behind Brother Edmund the messenger scuttled breathlessly towards the gatehouse, and the agitated girl waiting there. Prickling of the lips, mouth and throat, Cadfael was reckoning as he ran, tingling and then rigidity, and urgent need, but little ability, to rid himself of whatever it was he had consumed. And a quarter of an hour since he got it down, more by now, if it was in the dinner he had eaten. It might be late to give him the mustard that would make him sick, but it must be tried. Though surely this was merely an attack of illness from some normal disagreement between an indisposed man and his perfectly wholesome food, nothing else was possible. But then, that prickling of the flesh of mouth and throat, and the stiffness following...that sounded all too like at least one violent illness he had witnessed, which had almost proved fatal; and the cause of that he knew. Hurriedly he snatched from the shelves the preparations he wanted, and ran for the gatehouse.

For all the chill of the December day, the door of the first house beyond the mill-pond stood wide, and for all the awed quietness that hung about it, a quivering of agitation and confusion seemed to well out at the doorway to meet him, an almost silent panic of fluttering movements and hushed voices. A good house, with three rooms and the kitchen, and a small garden behind, running down to the pond; he knew it well enough, having visited a previous inmate upon less desperate business. The kitchen door faced away from the pond, towards the prospect of Shrewsbury beyond the river, and the north light at this time of day and year made the interior dim, although the window that looked out southwards stood unshuttered to let in light and air upon the brazier that did duty as all the cooking facilities such pensioners needed. He caught the grey gleam of a reflection from the water; as the wind ruffled it; the strip of garden was narrow here, though the house stood well above the water level.

By the open inner door through which the murmur of frightened voices emerged, stood a woman, obviously watching for him, her hands gripped tightly together under her breast, and quivering with tension. She started eagerly towards him as he came in, and then he saw her more clearly; a woman of his own years and his own height, very neat and quiet in her dress, her dark hair laced with silver and braided high on her head, her oval face almost unlined except for the agreeable grooves of good-nature and humour that wrinkled the corners of her dark-brown eyes, and made her full mouth merry and attractive. The merriment was quenched now, she wrung her hands and fawned on him; but attractive she was, even beautiful. She had held her own against the years, all forty-two of them that had come between.

He knew her at once. He had not seen her since they were both seventeen, and affianced, though nobody knew it but themselves, and probably her family would have made short work of the agreement if they had known of it. But he had taken the Cross and sailed for the Holy Land, and for all his vows to return to claim her, with his honours thick upon him, he had forgotten everything in the fever and glamour and peril of a life divided impartially between soldier and sailor, and delayed his coming far too long; and she, for all her pledges to wait for him, had tired at last and succumbed to her parents' urgings, and married a more stable character, and small blame to her. And he hoped she had been happy. But never, never had he expected to see her here. It was no Bonel, no lord of a northern manor, she had married, but an honest craftsman of Shrewsbury. There was no accounting for her, and no time to wonder.

Yet he knew her at once. Forty-two years between, and he knew her! He had not, it seemed, forgotten very much. The eager way she leaned to him now, the turn of her head, the very way she coiled her hair; and the eyes, above all, large, direct, clear as light for all their darkness.

At this moment she did not, thank God, know him. Why should she? He must be far more changed than she; half a world, alien to her, had marked, manipulated, adapted him, changed his very shape of body and mind. All she saw was the monk who knew his herbs and remedies, and had run to fetch aids for her stricken man.

'Through here, brother...he is in here. The infirmarer has got him to bed. Oh, please help him!'

'If I may, and God willing,' said Cadfael, and went by her into the next room. She pressed after him, urging and ushering. The main room was furnished with table and benches, and chaotically spread with the remains of a meal surely interrupted by something more than one man's sudden illness. In any case, he was said to have eaten his meal and seemed well; yet there were broken dishes lying, shards on both table and floor. But she drew him anxiously on, into the bedchamber.

Brother Edmund rose from beside the bed, wide and dismayed of eye. He had got the invalid as near rest as he could, wrapped up here on top of the covers, but there was little more he could do. Cadfael drew near, and looked down at Gervase Bonel. A big, fleshy man, thickly capped in greying brown hair, with a short beard now beaded with saliva that ran from both corners of a rigid, half-open mouth. His face was leaden blue, the pupils of his eyes dilated and staring. Fine, strong features were congealed now into a livid mask. The pulse for which Cadfael reached was faint, slow and uneven, the man's breathing shallow, long and laboured. The lines of jaw and throat stood fixed as stone.

'Bring a bowl,' said Cadfael, kneeling, 'and beat a couple of egg-whites into some milk. We'll try to get it out of him, but I doubt it's late, it may do as much damage coming up as going down.' He did not turn his head to see who ran to do his bidding, though certainly someone did; he was hardly aware, as yet, that there were three other people present in the house, in addition to Brother Edmund and Mistress Bonel and the sick man. Aelfric and the maid, no doubt, but he recognised the third only when someone stopped to slide a wooden bowl close to the patient's face, and tilt the livid head to lean over it. Cadfael glanced up briefly, the silent and swift movement pleasing him, and looked into the intent and horrified face of the young Welshman, Meurig, Brother Rhys's great-nephew.

'Good! Lift his head on your hand, Edmund, and hold his brow steady.' It was easy enough to trickle the emetic mixture of mustard into the half-open mouth, but the stiff throat laboured frightfully at swallowing, and much of the liquid ran out again into his beard and the bowl. Brother Edmund's hands quivered, supporting the tormented head. Meurig held the bowl, himself shivering. The following sickness convulsed the big body, weakened the feeble pulse yet further, and produced only a painfully inadequate result. It was indeed late for Gervase Bonel. Cadfael gave up, and let the paroxysms subside, for fear of killing him out of hand.

'Give me the milk and eggs.' This he fed very slowly into the open mouth, letting it slide of itself down the stiff throat, in such small quantities that it could not threaten the patient with choking. Too late to prevent whatever the poison had done to the flesh of Bonel's gullet, it might still be possible to lay a soothing film

43

over the damaged parts, and ease their condition. He spooned patient drop after drop, and dead silence hung all round him, the watchers hardly breathing.

The big body seemed to have shrunk and subsided into the bed, the pulse fluttered ever more feebly, the stare of the eyes filmed over. He lay collapsed. The muscles of his throat no longer made any effort at swallowing, but stood corded and rigid. The end came abruptly, with no more turmoil than the cessation of breathing and pulse.

Brother Cadfael laid the spoon in the little bowl of milk, and sat back on his heels. He looked up at the circle of shocked, bewildered faces, and for the first time saw them all clearly: Meurig, the bowl with its horrid contents shaking in his hands, Aelfric grim-eyed and pale, hovering at Brother Edmund's shoulder and staring at the bed, the girl—Brother Mark had not exaggerated, she was very pretty, with her yellow hair and black eyes—standing frozen, too shocked for tears, both small fists pressed hard against her mouth; and the widow, Mistress Bonel, who had once been Richildis Vaughan, gazing with marble face and slowly gathering tears at what remained of her husband.

'We can do no more for him,' said Brother Cadfael. 'He's gone.'

They all stirred briefly, as though a sudden wind had shaken them. The widow's tears spilled over and ran down her motionless face, as though she were still too bemused to understand what caused them. Brother Edmund touched her arm, and said gently: 'You will need helpers. I am very sorry, so are we all. You shall be relieved of such duties as we can lift from you. He shall lie in our chapel until all can be arranged. I will order it...'

'No,' said Cadfael, clambering stiffly to his feet, 'that can't be done yet, Edmund. This is no ordinary death. He is dead of poison, taken with the food he has recently eaten. It's a matter for the sheriff, and we must disturb nothing here and remove nothing until his officers have examined all.'

After a blank silence Aelfric spoke up hoarsely: 'But how can that be? It can't be so! We have all eaten the same, every one of us here. If there was anything amiss with the food, it would have struck at us all.'

'That is truth!' said the widow shakily, and sobbed aloud.

'All but the little dish,' the maid pointed out, in a small, frightened but determined voice, and flushed at having drawn attention to herself, but went on firmly: 'The one the prior sent to him.'

'But that was part of the prior's own dinner,' said Aelfric, aghast. 'Brother Petrus told me he had orders to take a portion from it and send it to my master with his compliments, to tempt his appetite.'

Brother Edmund shot a terrified look at Brother Cadfael, and saw his own appalling thought reflected back to him. Hastily he said: 'I'll go to the prior. Pray heaven no harm has come to him! I'll send also to the sheriff, or, please God! Prior Robert shall do as much on his own account. Brother, do you stay here until I return, and see that nothing is touched.'

'That,' said Cadfael grimly, 'I will certainly do.'

As soon as the agitated slapping of Brother Edmund's sandals had dwindled along the road, Cadfael shooed his stunned companions into the outer room, away from the horrid air of the bedchamber, tainted wih the foul odours of sickness, sweat and death. Yes, and of something else, faint but persistent even against that powerful combination of odours; something he felt he could place, if he could give it a moment's undisturbed thought.

'No help for this,' he said sympathetically. 'We may do nothing now without authority, there's a death to account for. But no need to stand here and add to the distress. Come away and sit down quietly. If there's wine or ale in that pitcher, child, get your mistress a drink, and do as much for yourself, and sit down and take what comfort you can. The abbey has taken you in, and will stand by you now, to the best it may.'

In dazed silence they did as he bade. Only Aelfric looked helplessly round at the debris of broken dishes and the littered table, and mindful of his usual menial role, perhaps, asked quaveringly: 'Should I not clear this disorder away?'

'No, touch nothing yet. Sit down and be as easy as you can, lad. The sheriff's officer must see what's to be seen, before we remedy any part of it.'

He left them for a moment, and went back into the bedchamber, closing the door between. The curious, aromatic smell was almost imperceptible now, overborne by the enclosed stench of vomit, but he leaned down to the dead man's drawn-back lips, and caught the hint of it again, and more strongly. Cadfael's nose might be blunt, battered and brown to view, but it was sharp and accurate in performance as a hart's.

There was nothing more in this death-chamber to tell him anything. He went back to his forlorn company in the next room. The widow was sitting with hands wrung tightly together in her lap, shaking her head still in disbelief, and murmuring to herself over and over. 'But how could it happen? How could it happen?' The girl, tearless throughout, and now jealously protective, sat with an arm about her mistress's shoulders; clearly there was more than a servant's affection there. The two young men shifted glumly and uneasily from place to place, unable to keep still. Cadfael stood back from them in the shadows, and ran a shrewd eye over the laden table. Three places laid, three beakers, one of them, in the master's place where a chair replaced the backless benches, overturned in a pool of ale, probably when Bonel suffered the first throes and blundered up from his seat. The large dish that had held the main meal was there in the centre, the congealing remains still in it. The food on one trencher was hardly touched, on the others it had been finished decently. Five people—no, apparently six—had eaten of that dish, and all but one were whole and unharmed. There was also the small bowl which he recognised as one of Abbot Heribert's, the same he had seen on Aelfric's tray as he passed through the court. Only the smallest traces of sauce remained in it; Prior Robert's gift to the invalid had clearly been much appreciated.

'None of you but Master Bonel took any of this dish?' asked Cadfael, bending to sniff at the rim carefully and long.

'No,' said the widow tremulously. 'It was sent as a special favour to my husband—a kind attention.'

And he had eaten it all. With dire results.

'And you three—Meurig, Aelfric—and you, child, I don't yet know your name...'

'It's Aldith,' said the girl.

'Aldith! And you three ate in the kitchen?'

'Yes. I had to keep the extra dish hot there until the other was eaten, and to see to the serving. And Aelfric always eats there. And Meurig, when he visits...' She paused for only a second, a faint flush mantling in her cheeks: '...he keeps me company.'

So that was the way the wind blew. Well, no wonder, she was indeed a very pretty creature.

Cadfael went into the kitchen. She had her pots and pans in neat order and well polished, she was handy and able as well as pretty. The brazier had an iron frame built high on two sides, to support an iron hob above the heat, and there, no doubt, the little bowl had rested until Bonel was ready for it. Two benches were ranged against the wall, out of the way, but close to the warmth. Three wooden platters, all used, lay on the shelf under the open window.

In the room at his back the silence was oppressive and fearful, heavy with foreboding. Cadfael went out at the open kitchen door, and looked along the road.

Thank God there was to be no second and even more dismaying death to cope with: Prior Robert, far too dignified to run, but furnished with such long legs that Brother Edmund had to trot to keep up with his rapid strides, was advancing along the highroad in august consternation and displeasure, his habit billowing behind him.

* * *

'I have sent a lay brother into Shrewsbury,' said the prior, addressing the assembled household, 'to inform the sheriff of what has happened, as I am told this death—madam, I grieve for your loss!—is from no natural cause, but brought about by poison. This terrible thing, though clearly reflecting upon our house, has taken place outside the walls, and outside the jurisdiction of our abbey court.' He was grateful for that, at least, and well he might be! 'Only the secular authorities can deal with this. But we must give them whatever help we can, it is our duty.'

His manner throughout, however gracefully he inclined towards the window, and however well chosen his words of commiseration and promises of help and support in the sad obligations of burial, had been one of outrage. How dared such a thing happen in his cure, in his newly acquired abbacy, and through the instrument of his gift? His hope was to soothe the bereaved with a sufficiently ceremonious funeral, perhaps a very obscure place in the actual church precincts if one could be found, bundle the legal responsibility into the sheriff's arms, where it belonged, and hush the whole affair into forgetfulness as quickly as possible. He had baulked in revulsion and disgust in the doorway of the bedchamber, giving the dead man only a brief and appalled reverence and a hasty murmur of prayer, and quickly shut the door upon him again. In a sense he blamed every person there for imposing this ordeal and inconvenience upon him; but most of all he resented Cadfael's blunt assertion that this was a case of poison. That committed the abbey to examine the circumstances, at least. Moreover, there was the problem of the as yet unsealed agreement, and the alarming vision of Mallilie possibly slipping out of his hands. With Bonel dead before the charter was fully legal, to whom did that fat property now belong? And could it still be secured by a rapid approach to the hypothetical heir, before he had time to consider fully what he was signing away?

'Brother,' said Robert, looking down his long, fastidious nose at Cadfael, who was a head shorter, 'you have asserted that poison has been used here. Before so horrid a suggestion is put to the sheriff's officers, rather than the possibility of accidental use, or indeed, a sudden fatal illness—for such can happen even to men apparently in good health!—I should like to hear your reasons for making so positive a statement. How do you know? By what signs?'

'By the nature of his illness,' said Cadfael. 'He suffered with prickling and tingling of lips, mouth and throat, and afterwards with rigidity in those parts, so that he could not swallow, or breathe freely, followed by stiffness of his whole body, and great weakness of his heart-beat. His eyes were greatly dilated. All this I have seen once before, and then I knew what the man had swallowed, for he had the bottle in his hand. You may remember it, some years ago. A drunken carter during the fair, who broke into my store and thought he had found strong liquor. In that case I was able to recover him, since he had but newly drunk the poison. But I recognise all the signs, and I know the poison that was used. I can detect it by smell on his lips, and on the remains of the dish he ate, the dish you sent him.'

If Prior Robert's face paled at the thought of what that might all too easily have meant, the change was not detectable, for his complexion was always of unflawed ivory. To do him justice, he was not a timorous man. He demanded squarely: 'What is this poison, if you are so sure of your judgment?'

'It is an oil that I make for rubbing aching joints, and it must have come either from the store I keep in my workshop, or from some smaller quantity taken from it, and I know of but one place where that could be found, and that is our own infirmary. The poison is monk's-hood—they call it so from the shape of the flowers, though it is also known as wolfsbane. Its roots make an excellent rub to remove pain, but it is very potent poison if swallowed.'

'If you can make medicines from this plant,' said

49

Prior Robert, with chill dislike, 'so, surely, may others, and this may have come from some very different source, and not from any store of ours.'

'That I doubt,' said Cadfael sturdily, 'since I know the odour of my own specific so well, and can detect here mustard and houseleek as well as monk's-hood. I have seen its effects, once taken, I know them again. I am in no doubt, and so I shall tell the sheriff.'

'It is well,' said Robert, no less frigidly, 'that a man should know his own work. You may, then, remain here, and do what you can to provide my lord Prestcote or his deputies with whatever truth you can furnish. I will speak with them first, I am responsible now for the peace and good order of our house. Then I will send them here. When they are satisfied that they have gathered all the facts that can be gathered, send word to Brother Infirmarer, and he will have the body made seemly and brought to the chapel. Madam,' he said in quite different tones, turning to the widow, 'you need have no fear that your tenure here will be disturbed. We will not add to your distresses, we deplore them heartily. If you are in any need, send your man to me.' And to Brother Edmund, who hovered unhappily: 'Come with me! I wish to see where these medicaments are kept, and how accessible they may be to unauthorised people. Brother Cadfael will remain here.'

He departed as superbly as he had come, and at the same speed, the infirmarer scurrying at his heels. Cadfael looked after him with tolerant comprehension; this was certainly a disastrous thing to happen when Robert was new in his eminence, and the prior would do everything he could to smooth it away as a most unfortunate but perfectly natural death, the result of some sudden seizure. In view of the unconcluded charter, it would present him with problems enough, even so, but he would exert himself to the utmost to remove the scandalous suspicion of murder, or, if it must come to that, to see it ebb away into an unsolved mystery, attributed comfortably to some unidentified rogue outside the abbey enclave. Cadfael could not blame him for that; but the work of his own hands, meant to alleviate pain, had been used to destroy a man, and that was something he could not let pass.

He turned back with a sigh to the doleful household within, and was brought up short to find the widow's dark eyes, tearless and bright, fixed upon him with so significant and starry a glance that she seemed in an instant to have shed twenty years from her age and a great load from her shoulders. He had already come to the conclusion that, though undoubtedly shocked, she was not heartbroken by her loss; but this was something different. Now she was unmistakably the Richildis he had left behind at seventeen. Faint colour rose in her cheeks, the hesitant shadow of a smile caused her lips to quiver, she gazed at him as if they shared a knowledge closed to everyone else, and only the presence of others in the room with them kept her from utterance.

The truth dawned on him only after a moment's blank incomprehension, and struck him as the most inconvenient and entangling thing that could possibly have happened at this moment. Prior Robert in departing had called him by his name, no usual name in these parts, and reminder enough to one who had, perhaps, already been pondering half-remembered tricks of voice and movement, and trying to run them to earth.

His impartiality and detachment in this affair would be under siege from this moment. Richildis not only knew him, she was sending him urgent, silent signals of her gratitude and dependence, and her supreme assurance that she could rely on his championship, to what end he hardly dared speculate.

Chapter 3

Gilbert Prestcote, sheriff of Shropshire since the town fell into King Stephen's hands during the past summer, had his residence in Shrewsbury castle, which he held fortified for the king, and managed his now pacified shire from that headquarters. Had his deputy been in Shrewsbury when Prior Robert's message reached the castle, Prestcote would probably have sent him to answer the call, which would have been a relief to Brother Cadfael, who had considerable faith in Hugh Beringar's shrewd sense; but that young man was away on his own manor, and it was a sergeant, with a couple of men-at-arms as escort, who finally arrived at the house by the mill-pond.

The sergeant was a big man, bearded and deep-voiced, in the sheriff's full confidence, and able and willing to act with authority in his name. He looked first to Cadfael, as belonging to the abbey, whence the summons had come, and it was Cadfael who recounted the course of events from the time he had been sent for. The sergeant had already spoken with Prior Robert, who would certainly have told him that the suspected dish had come from his own kitchen and at his own orders.

'And you swear to the poison? It was in this and no other food that he swallowed it?'

'Yes,' said Cadfael, 'I can swear to it. The traces left are small, but even so minute a smear of the sauce, if you put it to your lips, would bring out a hot prickling some minutes later. I have confirmed it for myself. There is no doubt.'

'And Prior Robert, who ate the remainder of the bird, is live and well, God be praised. Therefore somewhere between the abbot's kitchen and yonder table, poison was added to the dish. It is not a great distance, or a great time. You, fellow, you fetch the meals from the kitchen to this house? And did so today? Did you halt anywhere by the way? Speak to any? Set down your tray anywhere?'

'I did not,' said Aelfric defensively. 'If I delay, or the food is cold, I have to answer for it. I do to the letter what I am supposed to do, and so I did today.'

'And here? What did you do with the dishes when you came in?'

'He delivered them to me,' said Aldith, so quickly and firmly that Cadfael looked at her with new interest. 'He put down the tray on the bench by the brazier, and I myself set the small dish on the hob to keep warm, while we two served the main dish to our lord and lady. He told me the prior had kindly sent it for the master. When I had served them within, we sat down in the kitchen to eat our own meal.'

'And none of you noticed anything wrong with the partridge? In odour or appearance?'

'It was a very rich, spiced sauce, it had a fine smell. No, there was nothing to notice. The master ate it and found nothing wrong until his mouth began to prick and burn, and that was afterwards.'

'Both scent and savour,' confirmed Cadfael, consulted with a rapid glance, 'could well be covered by such a sauce. And the amount needed would not be so great.'

'And you...' The sergeant turned to Meurig. 'You were also here? You belong to the household?'

'Not now,' said Meurig readily. 'I come from Master Bonel's manor, but I'm working now for the master-carpenter Martin Bellecote, in the town. I came here today to visit an old great-uncle of mine in the infirmary, as Brother Infirmarer will tell you, and being about the abbey I came to visit here also. I came into the kitchen just when Aldith and Aelfric were about

53

to share out their own meal, and they bade me join them, and I did.'

'There was enough,' said Aldith. 'The abbot's cook is generous-handed.'

'So you were the three eating here together. And giving the little dish a stir now and then? And within...' He passed through the doorway and looked a second time about the debris of the table. 'Master Bonel and the lady, naturally.' No, he was not a stupid man, he could count, and he had noted the absence of one person both from the house and from their talk, as if they were all united to smooth the sixth trencherman out of sight. 'Here are three places laid. Who was the third?'

There was no help for it, someone had to answer. Richildis made the best of it. With apparently ingenuous readiness, rather as though surprised at the introduction of an irrelevancy, she said: 'My son. But he left well before my husband was taken ill.'

'Without finishing his dinner! If this was his place?'

'It was,' she said with dignity, and volunteered nothing more.

'I think, madam,' said the sergeant, with a darkly patient smile, 'you had better sit down and tell me more about this son of yours. As I have heard from Prior Robert, your husband was by way of granting his lands to the abbey in return for this house and guest status for the rest of his life and yours. After what has happened here, that agreement would seem to be forcibly in abeyance, since it is not yet sealed. Now, it would be greatly to the advantage of an heir to those lands, supposing such to be living, to have your husband removed from this world before the charter was ratified. Yet if there was a son of your marriage, his consent would have been required before any such agreement could have been drawn up. Read me this riddle. How did he succeed in disinheriting his son?'

Plainly she did not want to volunteer anything more than she must, but she was wise enough to know that too stubborn reticence would only arouse suspicion.

54

Resignedly she replied: 'Edwin is my son by my first marriage. Gervase had no paternal obligation to him. He could dispose of his lands as he wished.' There was more, and if she left it to be ferreted out through others it would sound far worse. 'Though he had previously made a will making Edwin his heir, there was nothing to prevent him from changing his mind.'

'Ah! So there was, it seems, an heir who was being dispossessed by this charter, and had much to regain by rendering it void. And limited time for the business—only a few days or weeks, until a new abbot is appointed. Oh, don't mistake me, my mind is open. Every man's death may be convenient to someone, often to more than one. There could be others with something to gain. But you'll grant me, your son is certainly one such.'

She bit her lip, which was unsteady, and took a moment to compose herself before she said gallantly: 'I don't quarrel with your reasoning. I do know that my son, however much he may have wanted his manor, would never have wanted it at this price. He is learning a trade, and resolved to be independent and make his own future.'

'But he was here today. And departed, it appears, in some haste. When did he come?'

Meurig said readily: 'He came with me. He's apprenticed himself to Martin Bellecote, who is his sister's husband and my master. We came here together this morning, and he came with me, as he has once before, to see my old uncle in the infirmary.'

'Then you arrived at this house together? You were together throughout that time? A while ago you said *you* came into the kitchen—"I", you said, no "we".'

'He came before me. He was restive after a while...he's young, he grew tired of standing by the old man's bed while we spoke only Welsh together. And his mother was here waiting to see him. So he went ahead. He was in at the table when I got here.'

'And left the table almost dinnerless,' said the sergeant very thoughtfully. 'Why? Can that have been a very comfortable dinner-table, a young man come to eat with the man who disinherited him? Was this the first time they had so met, since the abbey supplanted him?'

He had his nose well down on a strong trail now, and small blame to him, it reeked enough to lure the rawest pup, and this man was far from being that. What would I have said to such a strong set of circumstances, Cadfael wondered, had I been in his shoes? A young man with the most urgent need to put a stop to this charter, while he had time, and into the bargain, here on the scene just prior to the disaster, and fresh from the infirmary, which he had visited before, and where the means to the end was to be found. And here was Richildis, between holding the sheriff's sergeant fast with huge, challenging eyes, shooting desperate glances in Cadfael's direction, crying out to him silently that he must help her, or her darling was deep in the mire! Silently, in turn, he willed her to spill out at once everything that could count against her son, leave nothing untold, for only so could she counter much of what might otherwise be alleged against him.

'It was the first time,' said Richildis. 'And it was a most uneasy meeting, but it was for my sake Edwin sought it. Not because he hoped to change my husband's mind, only to bring about peace for me. Meurig, here, has been trying to persuade him to visit us, and today he prevailed, and I'm grateful to him for his efforts. But my husband met the boy with illwill, and taunted him with coming courting for his promised manor—for it *was* promised!—when Edwin intended no such matter. Yes, there was a quarrel! They were two hasty people, and they ended with high words. And Edwin flung out, and my husband threw that platter after him—you see the shards there against the wall. That's the whole truth of it, ask my servants. Ask Meurig, he knows. My son ran out of the house and back into Shrewsbury, I am sure, to where he now feels his home to be, with his sister and her family.'

'Let me understand you clearly,' said the sergeant,

a thought too smoothly and reasonably. 'Ran out of the house through the kitchen, you say?—where you three were sitting?' The turn of his head towards Aldith and the young men was sharp and intent, not smooth at all. 'So you saw him leave the house, without pause on the way?'

All three hesitated a brief instant, each casting uncertain glances aside at the others, and that was a mistake. Aldith said for them all, resignedly: 'When they began to shout and throw things, we all three ran in there, to try and calm the master down...or at least to...'

'To be there with me, and some comfort,' said Richildis.

'And there you remained after the boy had gone.' He was content with his guess, their faces confirmed it, however unwilling. 'So I thought. It takes time to placate a very angry man. So none of you saw whether this young fellow paused in the kitchen, none of you can say he did not stop to take his revenge by dosing the dish of partridge. He had been in the infirmary that morning, as he had once before, he may well have known where to find this oil, and what its powers could be. He may have come to this dinner prepared either for peace or war, and failed of getting peace.'

Richildis shook her head vigorously. 'You don't know him! It was *my* peace he wanted to secure. And besides, it was no more than a few minutes before Aelfric ran out after him, to try to bring him back, and though he followed almost to the bridge, he could not overtake him.'

'It's true,' said Aelfric. 'He surely had no time to check at all. I ran like a hare and called after him, but he would not turn back.'

The sergeant was unconvinced. 'How long does it take to empty a small vial into an open dish? One twirl of the spoon, and who was to know? And when your master was calm again, no doubt the prior's gift made a very handy and welcome sop to his pride, and he ate it gladly.'

'But did this boy even know,' asked Cadfael, intervening very gingerly, 'that the dish left in the kitchen was meant solely for Master Bonel? He would hardly risk harm to his mother.'

The sergeant was by that time too certain of his quarry to be impressed by any such argument. He eyed Aldith hard, and for all her resolution she paled a little.

'With such a strange gathering to wait on, was it likely the girl would miss the chance of a pleasant distraction for her master? When you went in to serve him his meat, did you not tell him of the prior's kind attention, and make the most of the compliment to him, and the treat in store?'

She cast down her eyes and pleated the corner of her apron. 'I thought it might sweeten him,' she said despairingly.

The sergeant had all he needed, or so he thought, to lay his hands promptly upon the murderer. He gave a final look round the shattered household, and said: 'Well, I think you may put things in order here, I've seen all there is to be seen. Brother Infirmarer is prepared to help you take care of your dead. Should I need to question you further, I must be sure of finding you here.'

'Where else should we be?' asked Richildis bleakly. 'What is it you mean to do? Will you at least let me know what happens, if you...if you should...' She could not put it into words. She stiffened her still straight and lissome back, and said with dignity: 'My son has no part in this villainy, and so you will find. He is not yet fifteen years old, a mere child!'

'The shop of Martin Bellecote, you said.'

'I know it,' said one of the men-at-arms.

'Good! Show the way, and we'll see what this lad has to say for himself.' And they turned confidently to the door and the highway.

Brother Cadfael saw fit to toss one disturbing ripple, at least, into the pool of their complacency. 'There is the matter of a container for this oil. Whoever purloined it, whether from my store or from the infirmary, must

58

have brought a vial to put it in. Meurig, did you see any sign of such about Edwin this morning? You came from the shop with him. In a pocket, or a pouch of cloth, even a small vial would hang in a noticeable way.'

'Never a sign of anything such,' said Meurig stoutly.

'And further, even well stoppered and tied down, such an oil is very penetrating, and can leave both a stain and an odour where even a drop seeps through or is left on the lip. Pay attention to the clothing of any man you think suspect in this matter.'

'Are you teaching me my business, brother?' enquired the sergeant with a tolerant grin.

'I am mentioning certain peculiarities about *my* business, which may be of help to you and keep you from error,' said Cadfael placidly.

'By your leave,' said the sergeant over his shoulder, from the doorway, 'I think we'll first lay hands on the culprit. I doubt if we shall need your learned advice, once we have him.' And he was off along the short path to the roadway where the horses were tethered, and his two men after him.

The sergeant and his men came to Martin Bellecote's shop on the Wyle late in the afternoon. The carpenter, a big, comely fellow in his late thirties, looked up cheerfully enough from his work, and enquired their business without wonder or alarm. He had done work for Prestcote's garrison once or twice, and the appearance of one of the sheriff's officers in his workshop held no menace for him. A brown-haired, handsome wife looked out curiously from the house-door beyond, and three children erupted one by one from that quarter to examine the customers fearlessly and frankly. A grave girl of about eleven, very housewifely and prim, a small, square boy of eight or so, and an elfin miss no more than four, with a wooden doll under her arm. All of them gazed and listened. The door to the house remained open, and the sergeant had a loud, peremptory voice.

'You have an apprentice here by the name of Edwin. My business is with him.'

'I have,' agreed Martin loudly, rising and dusting the resin of polish from his hands. 'Edwin Gurney, my wife's young brother. He's not yet home. He went down to see his mother in the Foregate. He should have been back before this, but I daresay she's wanted to keep him longer. What's your will with him?' He was still quite serene; he knew of nothing amiss.

'He left his mother's house above two hours since,' said the sergeant flatly. 'We are come from there. No offence, friend, if you say he's not here, but it's my duty to search for him. You'll give us leave to go through your house and yard?'

Martin's placidity had vanished in an instant, his brows drew into a heavy frown. His wife's beech-brown head appeared again in the doorway beyond, her fair, contented face suddenly alert and chill, dark eyes intent. The children stared unwaveringly. The little one, voice of natural justice in opposition to law, stated firmly: 'Bad man!' and nobody hushed her.

'When I say he is not here,' said Martin levelly, 'you may be assured it is true. But you may also assure yourselves. House, workshop and yard have nothing to hide. Now what are *you* hiding? This boy is my brother, through my wife, and my apprentice by his own will, and dear to me either way. Now, why are you seeking him?'

'In the house in the Foregate where he visited this morning,' said the sergeant deliberately, 'Master Gervase Bonel, his step-father, who promised him he should succeed to the manor of Mallilie and then changed his mind, is lying dead at this moment, murdered. It is on suspicion of his murder that I want this young man Edwin. Is that enough for you?'

It was more than enough for the eldest son of this hitherto happy household, whose ears were stretched from the inner room to catch this awful and inexplicable news. The law nose-down on Edwin's trail, and Edwin should have been back long ago if everything had gone even reasonably well! Edwy had been uneasy for some time, and was alert for disaster where his elders took it for granted all must be well. He let himself out in haste by the back window on to the yard, before the officers could make their way into the house, clambered up the stacked timber and over the wall like a squirrel, and was away at a light, silent run towards the slope that dived riverwards, and one of the tight little posterns through the town wall, open now in time of peace, that gave on to the steep bank, not far from the abbot's vineyard. Several of the businesses in town that needed bulky stores had fenced premises here for their stock, and among them was Martin Bellecote's wood-yard where he seasoned his timber. It was an old refuge when either or both of the boys happened to be in trouble, and it was the place Edwin would make for if...oh, no, not if he had killed, because that was ridiculous!...but if he had been rejected, affronted, made miserably unhappy and madly angry. Angry almost to murder, but never, never quite! It was not in him.

Edwy ran, confident of not being followed, and fell breathless through the wicket of his father's enclosure, and headlong over the splayed feet of a sullen, furious, tear-stained and utterly vulnerable Edwin.

Edwin, perhaps because of the tear-stains, immediately clouted Edwy as soon as he had regained his feet, and was clouted in his turn just as indignantly. The first thing they did, at all times of stress, was to fight. It meant nothing, except that both were armed and on guard, and whoever meddled with them in the matter afterwards had better be very careful, for their practice on each other would be perfected on him. Within minutes Edwy was pounding his message home into bewildered, unreceptive, and finally convinced and dismayed ears. They sat down cheek by jowl to do some frantic planning.

Aelfric appeared in the herb-gardens an hour before Vespers. Cadfael had been back in his solitude no more than half an hour then, after seeing the body cleansed,

61

made seemly, and borne away into the mortuary chapel, the bereaved house restored to order, the distracted members of the household at least set free to wander and wonder and grieve as was best for them. Meurig was gone, back to the shop in the town, to tell the carpenter and his family word for word what had befallen, for what comfort or warning that might give them. By this time, for all Cadfael knew, the sheriff's men had seized young Edwin...Dear God, he had even forgotten the name of the man Richildis had married, and Bellecote was only her son-in-law.

'Mistress Bonel asks,' said Aelfric earnestly, 'that you'll come and speak with her privately. She entreats you for old friendship, to stand her friend now.'

It came as no surprise. Cadfael was aware that he stood on somewhat perilous ground, even after forty years. He would have been happier if the lamentable death of her husband had turned out to be no mystery, her son in no danger, and her future none of his business, but there was no help for it. His youth, a sturdy part of the recollections that made him the man he was, stood in her debt, and now that she was in need he had no choice but to make generous repayment.

'I'll come,' he said. 'You go on before, and I'll be with her within a quarter of an hour.'

When he knocked at the door of the house by the mill-pond, it was opened by Richildis herself. There was no sign either of Aelfric or Aldith, she had taken good care that the two of them should be able to talk in absolute privacy. In the inner room all was bare and neat, the morning's chaos smoothed away, the trestle table folded aside. Richildis sat down in the great chair which had been her husband's, and drew Cadfael down on the bench beside her. It was dim within the room, only one small rush-light burning; the only other brightness came from her eyes, the dark, lustrous brightness he was remembering more clearly with every moment.

'Cadfael...' she said haltingly, and was silent again for some moments. 'To think it should really be you!

I never got word of you, after I heard you were back home. I thought you would have married, and been a grandsire by this. As often as I looked at you, this morning, I was searching my mind, why I should be so sure I ought to know you... And just when I was in despair, to hear your name spoken!'

'And you,' said Cadfael, 'you came as unexpectedly to me. I never knew you'd been widowed from Eward Gurney—I remember now that was his name!—much less that you'd wed again.'

'Three years ago,' she said, and heaved a sigh that might have been of regret or relief at the abrupt ending of this second match. 'I mustn't make you think ill of him, he was not a bad man, Gervase, only elderly and set in his ways, and used to being obeyed. A widower he was, many years wifeless, and without any children, leastways none by the marriage. He courted me a long time, and I was lonely, and then he promised, you see... Not having a legitimate heir, he promised if I'd have him he'd make Edwin his heir. His overlord sanctioned it. I ought to tell you about my family. I had a daughter, Sibil, only a year after I married Eward, and then, I don't know why, time went on and on, and there were no more. You'll remember, maybe, Eward had his business in Shrewsbury as a master-carpenter and carver. A good workman he was, a good master and a good husband.'

'You were happy?' said Cadfael, grateful at hearing it in her voice. Time and distance had done well by the pair of them, and led them to their proper places, after all.

'Very happy! I couldn't have had a better man. But there were no more children then. And when Sibil was seventeen she married Eward's journeyman, Martin Bellecote, and a good lad he is, too, and she's as happy in her match as I was in mine, thank God! Well, then, in two years the girl was with child, and it was like being young again myself—the first grandchild!—it's always so. I was so joyful, looking after her and making plans for the birth, and Eward was as proud as I was,

63

and what with one thing and another, you'd have thought we old folk were young newlyweds again ourselves. And I don't know how it happens, but when Sibil was four months gone, what should I find but I was carrying, too! After all those years! And I in my forty-fourth year—it was like a miracle! And the upshot is, she and I both brought forth boys, and though there's the four months between them, they might as well be twins as uncle and nephew—and the uncle the younger, at that! They even look very much like, both taking after my man. And from the time they were first on their feet they've been as close as any brothers, and closer than most, and both as wild as fox-cubs. So that's my son Edwin and my grandson Edwy. Not yet turned fifteen, either of them. It's for Edwin I'm praying your help, Cadfael. For I swear to you he never did nor even could do such wicked harm, but the sheriff's man has it fixed fast in his head that it was Edwin who put poison in the dish. If you knew him, Cadfael, if only you knew him, you'd know it's madness.'

And so it sounded when her fond, maternal voice spoke of it, yet sons no older than fourteen had been known to remove their fathers to clear their own paths, as Cadfael knew well enough. And this was not Edwin's own father, and little love lost between them.

'Tell me,' he said, 'about this second marriage, and the bargain you struck.'

'Why, Eward died when Edwin was nine years old, and Martin took over his shop, and runs it as Eward did before him, and as Eward taught him. We all lived together until Gervase came ordering some panelling for his house, and took a strong fancy to me. And he was a fine figure of a man, too, and in good health, and very attentive.... He promised if I would have him he'd make Edwin his heir, and leave Mallilie to him. And Martin and Sibil had three more children to provide for by then, so with all those mouths to feed he needed what the business can bring in, and I thought to see Edwin set up for life.'

'But it was not a success,' said Cadfael, 'understandably. A man who had never had children, and getting on in years, and a lusty lad busy growing up—they were bound to cross swords.'

'It was ten of one and half a score of the other,' she owned, sighing. 'Edwin had been indulged, I fear, he was used to his freedom and to having his own way, and he was for ever running off with Edwy, as he'd always been used to do. And Gervase held it against him that he ran with simple folk and craftsmen—he thought that low company, beneath a young man with a manor to inherit, and that was bound to anger Edwin, who loves his kin. Not to claim that he had not some less respectable friends, too! They rubbed each other the wrong way daily. When Gervase beat him, Edwin ran away to Martin's shop and stayed for days. And when Gervase locked him up, he'd either make his way out all the same, or else take his revenge in other ways. In the end Gervase said as the brat's tastes obviously ran to mere trade, and running loose with all the scallywags of the town, he might as well go and apprentice himself in good earnest, it was all he was fit for. And Edwin, though he knew better, pretended to take that, word for word, as well meant, and went and did that very thing, which made Gervase more furious than ever. That was when he vowed he'd hand over his manor by charter to the abbey, and live here retired. "He cares nothing for the lands I meant to leave him," he said, "why should I go on nursing them for such an ingrate?" And he did it, there and then, while he was hot, he had this agreement drawn up, and made ready to move here before Christmas.'

'And what did the boy say to that? For I suppose he never realised what was intended?'

'He did not! He came with a rush, penitent but indignant, too. He swore he does love Mallilie, he never meant to scorn it, and he would take good care of it if it came to him. But my husband would not give way, though we all pleaded with him. And Edwin was bitter, too, for he had been promised, and a promise should be kept. But it was done, and nobody could make my lord undo it. not being his own son, Edwin's consent was never asked nor needed—it would never have been given! He went flying back to Martin and Sibil with his raging grievance, and I haven't seen him again until this day, and I wish he'd never come near us today. But he did, and now see how the sheriff's man is hunting him as a villain who would kill his own mother's husband! Such a thought could never enter that child's head, I swear to you, Cadfael, but if they take him...Oh, I can't bear to think of it!'

'You've had no word since they left here? News travels this highroad fast. I think it would have reached us before now if they had found him at home.'

'Not a word yet. But where else would he go? He knew no reason why he should hide. He ran from here knowing nothing of what was to happen after his going, he was simply sore about his bitter welcome.'

'Then he might not wish to take such a mood home with him, not until he'd come to terms with it. Hurt things hide until the fright and pain wears off. Tell me all that happened at this dinner. It seems Meurig has been a go-between for you, and tried to bring him to make peace. Some mention was made of a former visit...'

'Not to me,' said Richildis sadly. 'The two of them came to bring down the lectern Martin has been making for the Lady Chapel, and Meurig took my boy with him to see the old brother, his kinsman. He tried to persuade Edwin then to come and see me, but he would not. Meurig is a good fellow, he's done his best. Today he did prevail on Edwin to come, but see what came of it! Gervase was in high glee about it, and monstrously unfair—he taunted my boy with coming like a beggar to plead to be restored, and get his inheritance back, which was never Edwin's intent. He'd die sooner! Tamed at last, are you, says Gervase! Well, if you go down on your knees, he says, and beg pardon for your frowardness, who knows, I might relent yet. Crawl, then, he says, and beg for your manor! And so it went, until Edwin blazed out that he was not and never would

66

be tamed by a wicked, tyrannical, vicious old monster—which I grant you,' she sighed hopelessly, 'Gervase was not, only a stubborn and ill-tempered one. Oh, I can't tell you all they yelled at each other! But I do say this, it took a lot of goading today to get Edwin to blaze, and that's credit to him. For my sake he would have borne it, but it was too much for him. So he said what he had to say, very loudly, and Gervase flung the platter at him, and a beaker, too, and then Aldith and Aelfric and Meurig came rushing in to try and help me calm him down. And Edwin stamped out—and that was all.'

Cadfael was silent for a moment, ruminating on these other members of the household. A hot-tempered, proud, affronted boy seemed to him a possible suspect had Bonel been struck down with fist or even dagger, but a very unlikely poisoner. True, the lad had been twice with Meurig in the infirmary, and probably seen where the medicines were kept, he had a reason for action, he had the opportunity; but the temperament for a poisoner, secret, dark and bitter, surely that was an impossibility to such a youngster, by all his breeding and training open, confident, with a fine conceit of himself. There were, after all, these others, equally present.

'The girl, Aldith—you've had her long?'

'She's distant kin to me,' said Richildis, almost startled into a smile. 'I've known her from a child, and took her when she was left orphan, two years ago. She's like my own girl.'

It was what he had supposed, seeing Aldith so protective while they waited for the law. 'And Meurig? I hear he was also of Master Bonel's household once, before he went to work for your son-in-law.'

'Meurig—ah, well, you see, it's this way with Meurig. His mother was a Welsh maidservant at Mallilie, and like so many such, bore her master a by-blow. Yes, he's Gervase's natural son. My lord's first wife must have been barren, for Meurig is the only child he ever fathered, unless there are one or two we don't know of, somewhere about the shire there. He maintained Angharad decently until she died, and he had Meurig taken care of, and gave him employment on the manor. I was not easy about him,' she admitted, 'when we married. Such a good, willing, sensible young man, and with no claims on any part of what was his father's, it seemed hard. Not that he ever complained! But I asked him if he would not be glad to have a trade of his own, that would last him for life, and he said he would. So I persuaded Gervase to let Martin take him, to teach him all he knew. And I did ask him,' said Richildis, with a quaver in her voice, 'to keep a watch on Edwin, after he ran from us, and try to bring him to make terms with Gervase. I never expected my son to give way, for he's able, too, and he could make his own road. I just wanted to have him back. There was a time when he blamed me—as having to choose between them, and choosing my husband. But I'd married him... and I was sorry for him....' Her voice snapped off short, and she was silent a moment. 'I've been glad of Meurig, he has stood friend to us both.'

'He got on well enough with your husband, did he? There was no bad blood between them?'

'Why, no, none in the world!' She was astonished at the question. 'They rubbed along together quietly, and never any sparks. Gervase was generous to him, you know, though he never paid him much attention. And he makes him a decent living allowance—that is, he did.... Oh, how will he fare now, if that ends? I shall have to have advice, law is a tangle to me....'

Nothing there to raise a brow, it seemed, even if Meurig knew as well as anyone how to lay hands on poison. So did Aelfric, who had been in the workshop and seen it dispensed. And whoever gained by Bonel's death, it seemed, Meurig stood only to lose. Manorial bastards were thick on the ground everywhere, the lord who had but one had been modest and abstemious indeed, and the by-blow who was set up with an expanding trade and an allowance to provide for him was fortunate, and had no cause for complaint. Good cause, in fact, to lament his father's passing.

'And Aelfric?'

The darkness outside had made the light of the little lamp seem brighter; her face, oval and grave, shone in the pallid radiance, and her eyes were round as moons. 'Aelfric is a hard case. You must not think my husband was worse than his kind, or ever knowingly took more than was his by law. But the law limps, sometimes. Aelfric's father was born free as you or I, but younger son in a holding that was none too large even for one, and rather than have it split, when *his* father died, he left it whole for his brother, and took a villein yardland that had fallen without heirs, on my husband's manor. He took it on villein tenure, to do the customary duties for it, but never doubting to keep his status as a free man, doing villein service of his own undertaking. And Aelfric in his turn was a younger son, and foolishly accepted service in the manor household when his elder had family enough to run his yardland without him. So when the manor was to be surrendered, and we were ready to come here, Gervase chose him to be his man-servant, for he was the neatest-handed and best we had. And when Aelfric chose rather to go elsewhere and find employment, Gervase brought suit that he was villein, both his brother and his father having done customary service for the land they held. And the court found that it was so, and he was bound, however free-born his father had been. He takes it hard,' said Richildis ruefully. 'He never felt himself villein before, he was a free man doing work for pay. Many and many a one has found himself in the same case, never having dreamed of losing his freedom until it was lost.'

Cadfael's silence pricked her. He was reflecting that here was another who had a burning grudge, knew where to find the means, and of all people had the opportunity; but her mind was on the painful picture she had just drawn, and she mistook his brooding for disapproval of her dead husband, censure he was unwilling to express to her. Valiantly she sought to do justice, at least, if there was no affection left.

'You are wrong if you think the fault was all on one

side. Gervase believed he was doing no more than his right, and the law agreed with him. I've never known him wilfully cheat any man, but he did stand fast on his own dues. And Aelfric makes his own situation worse. Gervase never used to harry or press him, for he worked well by nature, but now he's unfree he sticks stubbornly on every last extreme of servile labour, purposely, drives home his villein condition at every turn... It is not servility, but arrogance, he deliberately rattles his chains. He did give offence by it, and truly I think they grew to hate each other. And then, there's Aldith.... Oh, Aelfric never says word of it to her, but I know! He looks after her as if his heart's being drawn out of him. But what has he to offer a free girl like her? Even if Meurig wasn't casting an eye in that direction, too, and he so much more lively company. Oh, I tell you, Cadfael, I've had such trouble and grief with all this household of mine. And now this! Do help me! Who else will, if not you? Help my boy! I do believe you can, if you will.'

'I can promise you,' said Cadfael after scrupulous thought, 'that I'll do everything I can to find out the murderer of your husband. That I must, whoever he may be. Will that content you?'

She said: 'Yes! I *know* Edwin is guiltless. You don't, yet. But you will!'

'Good girl!' said Cadfael heartily. 'That's how I remember you from when time was. And even now, before your knowledge becomes my knowledge also, I can promise you one thing more. Yes, I will help your son to the utmost I may, guilty or innocent, though not by hiding the truth. Will that do?'

She nodded, for the moment unable to speak. The stresses not only of this disastrous day, but of many days before, showed suddenly in her face.

'I fear,' said Cadfael gently, 'you went too far aside from your own kind, Richildis, in marrying the lord of the manor.'

'I did so!' she said, and incontinently burst into tears at last, and wept, alarmingly, on his shoulder.

Chapter 4

Brother Denis the hospitaller, who always had all the news of the town from the wayfarers who came to the guest-hall, reported on the way to Vespers that the story of Bonel's death and the hunt for his stepson was all over Shrewsbury, and the sheriff's sergeant had drawn a blank at Martin Bellecote's shop. A thorough search of the premises had turned up no trace of the boy, and the sergeant was having him cried through the streets; but if the populace joined in the hunt with no more than their usual zeal for the sheriff's law, it was likely the crier would be wasting his breath. A boy not yet fifteen, and known to a great many of the town, and with nothing against him but a bit of riotous mischief now and then...no, they were not likely to give up their night's sleep to help in his capture.

The first necessity, it seemed to Cadfael no less than to the sergeant, was to find the boy. Mothers are partial, especially towards only sons, late sons conceived after hope of a son has faded. Cadfael felt a strong desire to see and hear and judge for himself before he made any other move in the matter.

Richildis, relieved by her fit of weeping, had told him where to find her son-in-law's shop and house, and it fell blessedly at the near end of the town. A short walk past the mill-pond, over the bridge, in through the town gates, which would be open until after Compline, and it was but a couple of minutes up the steep, curving Wyle to Bellecote's premises. Half an hour to go and return. After supper, and a quick supper at that, he would slip away, cutting out Collations—safe enough, for Prior Robert would absent himself on principle, standing on his privacy as abbot-designate, and leaving the mundane direction of the house to Brother Richard, who certainly would not meddle where it might cost him effort.

Supper was salt fish and pulse, and Cadfael disposed of it with scant attention, and made off across the great court in haste, and out at the gates. The air was chill, but as yet barely on the edge of frost, and there had been no snow at all so far. All the same, he had muffled his sandalled feet in well-wound strips of wool, and drawn his hood close.

The town porters saluted him respectfully and cheerfully, knowing him well. The right-hand curve of the Wyle drew him upward, and he turned off, again to the right, into the open yard under the eaves of Bellecote's house. After his knock at the closed door there was a longish silence, and that he could well understand, and forbore from knocking again. Clamour would only have alarmed them. Patience might reassure.

The door opened cautiously on a demure young person of about eleven years, erect and splendidly on guard for a troubled household at her back; all of whom, surely, were stretching sharp ears somewhere there beyond. She was bright, well primed and vulnerable; she saw the black Benedictine habit, drew deep breath, and smiled.

'I'm come from Mistress Bonel,' said Cadfael, 'with a word to your father, child, if he'll admit me. There's none else here, never fear.'

She opened the door with a matron's dignity, and let him in. The eight-year-old Thomas and the four-year-old Diota, naturally the most fearless creatures in the house, erupted round her skirts to examine him with round, candid eyes, even before Martin Bellecote himself appeared from a half-lit doorway within, and drew the younger children one either side of him, his hands spread protectively round their shoulders. A pleasant, square-built, large-handed man with a wide, wholesome face, and a deep reserve in his eyes, which Cadfael was glad to see. Too much trust is folly, in an imperfect world.

'Step in, brother,' said Martin, 'and, Alys, do you close and bar the door.'

'Forgive me if I'm brisk,' said Cadfael as the door was closed behind him, 'but time's short. They came looking for a lad here today, and I'm told they did not find him.'

'That's truth,' said Martin. 'He never came home.'

'I don't ask you where he is. Tell me nothing. But I do ask you, who know him, is it possible he can have done what they are urging against him?'

Bellecote's wife came through from the inner room, a candle in her hand. A woman like enough to be known for her mother's daughter, but softer and rounder and fairer in colouring, though with the same honest eyes. She said with indignant conviction: 'Rankly impossible! If ever there was a creature in the world who made his feelings known, and did all his deeds in the daylight, that's my brother. From an imp just crawling, if he had a grievance everyone within a mile round knew it, but grudges he never bore. And my lad's just such another.'

Yes, of course, there was the as yet unseen Edwy, to match the elusive Edwin. No sign of either of them here.

'You must be Sibil,' said Cadfael. 'I've been lately with your mother. And for my credentials—did ever you hear her speak of one Cadfael, whom she used to know when she was a girl?'

The light from the candle was reflected pleasingly in eyes suddenly grown round and bright with astonishment and candid curiosity. 'You are Cadfael? Yes, many a time she talked of you, and wondered...' She viewed his black habit and cowl, and her smile faded into a look of delicate sympathy. Of course! She was reflecting, woman-like, that he must have been heartbroken at coming home from the holy wars to find his old love married, or he would never have taken these bleak vows. No use telling her that vocations strike from heaven like random arrows of God, by no means

73

all because of unrequited love. 'Oh, it must be comfort to her,' said Sibil warmly, 'to find you near her again, at this terrible pass. You she would trust!'

'I hope she does,' said Cadfael, gravely enough. 'I know she may. I came only to let you know that I am there to be used, as she already knows. The specific that was used to kill was of my making, and that is something that involves me in this matter. Therefore I am friend to any who may fall suspect unjustly. I will do what I can to uncover the guilty. Should you, or anyone, have reason to speak with me, anything to tell me, anything to ask of me, I am usually to be found between offices in the workshop in the herb-gardens, where I shall be tonight until I go to Matins at midnight. Your journeyman Meurig knows the abbey grounds, if he has not been to my hut. He is here?'

'He is,' said Martin. 'He sleeps in the loft across the yard. He has told us what passed at the abbey. But I give you my word, neither he nor we have set eyes on the boy since he ran from his mother's house. What we know, past doubt, is that he is no murderer, and never could be.'

'Then sleep easy,' said Cadfael, 'for God is awake. And now let me out again softly, Alys, and bar the door after me, for I must hurry back for Compline.'

The young girl, great-eyed, drew back the bolt and held the door. The little ones stood with spread feet, sturdily staring him out of the house, but without fear or hostility. The parents said never a word but their still: 'Good night!' but he knew, as he hastened down the Wyle, that his message had been heard and understood, and that it was welcome, here in this beleaguered household.

'Even if you are desperate to have a fresh brew of cough syrup boiled up before tomorrow,' said Brother Mark reasonably, coming out from Compline at Cadfael's side, 'is there any reason why I should not do it for you? Is there any need for you, after the day you've had, to be stravaiging around the gardens all night, into the

74

bargain? Or do you think I've forgotten where we keep mullein, and sweet cicely, and rue, and rosemary, and hedge mustard?' The recital of ingredients was part of the argument. This young man was developing a somewhat possessive sense of responsibility for his elder.

'You're young,' said Brother Cadfael, 'and need your sleep.'

'I forbear,' said Brother Mark cautiously, 'from making the obvious rejoinder.'

'I think you'd better. Very well, then, you have signs of a cold, and should go to your bed.'

'I have not,' Brother Mark disagreed firmly. 'But if you mean that you have some work on hand that you'd rather I did not know about, very well, I'll go to the warming-room like a sensible fellow, and then to bed.'

'What you know nothing about can't be charged against you,' said Brother Cadfael, conciliatory.

'Well, then, is there anything I can be doing for you in blessed ignorance? I was bidden to be obedient to you, when they sent me to work under you in the garden.'

'Yes,' said Cadfael. 'You can secure me a habit much your own size, and slip it into my cell and out of sight under my bed before you sleep. It may not be needed, but...'

'Enough!' Brother Mark was cheerful and unquestioning, though that did not prove he was not doing some hard and accurate thinking. 'Will you be needing a scissor for the tonsure, too?'

'You are growing remarkably saucy,' observed Cadfael, but with approval rather than disapproval. 'No, I doubt that would be welcomed, we'll rely on the cowl, and a chilly morning. Go away, boy, go and get your half-hour of warmth, and go to bed.'

The concoction of a syrup, boiled up lengthily and steadily with dried herbs and honey, made the use of the brazier necessary; should a guest have to spend the night in the workshop, he would be snug enough until morning. In no haste, Cadfael ground his herbs to a

75

finer powder, and began to stir the honeyed brew on the hob over his brazier. There was no certainty that the bait he had laid would be taken, but beyond doubt young Edwin Gurney was in urgent need of a friend and protector to help him out of the morass into which he had fallen. There was no certainty, even, that the Bellecote household knew where to find him, but Cadfael had a shrewd inkling that the eleven-year-old Alys of the matronly dignity and the maidenly silence, even if she were not in her own brother's confidence, would be very well acquainted with what he probably considered his secrets. Where Edwy was, there would Edwin be, if Richildis had reported them truly. When trouble threatened the one, the other would be by his side. It was a virtue Cadfael strongly approved.

The night was very still, there would be sharp frost by dawn. Only the gentle bubbling of his brew and the occasional rustling of his own sleeve as he stirred punctured the silence. He had begun to think that the fish had refused the bait, when he caught, past ten o'clock, and in the blackest of the darkness, the faint, slow sound of the door-latch being carefully raised. A breath of cold air came in as the door opened a hair's-breadth. He sat still and gave no sign; the frightened wild thing might be easily alarmed. After a moment a very light, young, wary voice outside uttered just above a whisper: 'Brother Cadfael...?'

'I'm here,' said Cadfael quietly. 'Come in and welcome.'

'You're alone?' breathed the voice.

'I am. Come in and close the door.'

The boy stole in fearfully, and pushed the door to at his back, but Cadfael noticed that he did not latch it. 'I got word...' He was not going to say through whom. 'They told me you spoke with my sister and brother this evening, and said you would be here. I do need a friend... You said you knew my gr—my mother, years ago, you are the Cadfael she used to speak about so often, the one who went to the Crusade... I swear I had no part in my stepfather's death! I never knew any

76

harm had come to him, till I was told the sheriff's men were hunting for me as a murderer. You said my mother knows you for a good friend, and can rely on your help, so I've come to you. There's no one else I can turn to. Help me! Please help me!'

'Come to the fire,' said Cadfael mildly, 'and sit down here. Draw breath and answer me one thing truly and solemnly, and then we can talk. On your soul, mind! Did you strike the blow that laid Gervase Bonel dead in his blood!'

The boy had perched himself gingerly on the edge of the bench, almost but not quite within touch. The light from the brazier, cast upwards over his face and form, showed a rangy, agile youngster, lightly built but tall for his years, in the long hose and short cotte of the country lads, with capuchon dangling at his back, and a tangled mop of curling hair uncovered. By this reddish light it looked chestnut-brown, by daylight it might well be the softer mid-brown of seasoned oak. His face was still childishly rounded of cheek and chin, but fine bones were beginning to give it a man's potential. At this moment half the face was two huge, wary eyes staring unwaveringly at Brother Cadfael.

Most earnestly and vehemently the boy said: 'I never raised hand against him. He insulted me in front of my mother, and I hated him then, but I did not strike him. I swear it on my soul!'

Even the young, when bright in the wits and very much afraid, may exercise all manner of guile to protect themselves, but Cadfael was prepared to swear there was no deceit here. The boy really did not know how Bonel had been killed; that could not have been reported to his family or cried in the streets, and murder, most often, means the quick blow with steel in anger. He had accepted that probability without question.

'Very well! Now tell me your own story of what happened there today, and be sure I'm listening.'

The boy licked his lips and began. What he had to tell agreed with the account Richildis had given; he had gone with Meurig, at his well-intentioned urging, to make his peace with Bonel for his mother's sake. Yes, he had felt very bitter and angry about being cheated out of his promised heritage, for he loved Mallilie and had good friends there, and would have done his best to run it well and fairly when it came to him; but also he was doing well enough at learning his craft, and pride would not let him covet what he could not have, or give satisfaction to the man who had taken back what he had pledged. But he did care about his mother. So he went with Meurig.

'And went with him first to the infirmary,' Cadfael mentioned helpfully, 'to see his old kinsman Rhys.'

The boy was brought up short in surprise and uncertainty. It was then that Cadfael got up, very gently and casually, from his seat by the brazier, and began to prowl the workshop. The door, just ajar, did not noticeably draw him, but he was well aware of the sliver of darkness and cold lancing in there.

'Yes...I...'

'And you had been there with him, had you not, once before, when you helped Meurig bring down the lectern for our Lady Chapel.'

He brightened, but his brow remained anxiously knotted. 'Yes, the—yes, we did bring that down together. But what has that...'

Cadfael in his prowling had reached the door, and laid a hand to the latch, hunching his shoulders, as though to close and fasten it, but as sharply plucked it wide open on the night, and reached his free hand through, to fasten on a fistful of thick, springy hair. A muted squeal of indignant outrage rewarded him, and the creature without, abruptly scorning the flight shock had suggested to him, reared upright and followed the fist into the workshop. It was, in its way, a magnificent entrance, erect, with jutted jaw and blazing eyes, superbly ignoring Cadfael's clenched hold on his curls, which must have been painful.

A slender, athletic, affronted young person the image of the first, only, perhaps, somewhat darker and fiercer, because more frightened, and more outraged by his fear.

'Master Edwin Gurney?' enquired Cadfael gently, and released the topknot of rich brown hair with a gesture almost caressing. 'I've been expecting you.' He closed the door, thoroughly this time; there was no one now left outside there to listen, and take warning by what he heard, like a small, hunted animal crouching in the night where the hunters stirred. 'Well, now that you're here, sit down with your twin—is it uncle or nephew? I shall never get used to sorting you!—and put yourself at ease. It's warmer here than outside, and you are two, and I have just been reminded gently that I am not as young as once I was. I don't propose to send for help to deal with you, and you have no need of help to deal with me. Why should we not put together our versions of the truth, and see what we have?'

The second boy was cloakless like the first, and shivering lightly with cold. He came to the bench by the brazier gladly, rubbing numbed hands, and sat down submissively beside his fellow. Thus cheek to cheek they were seen to share a very strong family likeness, in which Cadfael could trace subtle recollections of the young Richildis, but they were not so like as to give rise to any confusion when seen together. To encounter one alone might present a problem of identification, however.

'So, as I thought,' observed Cadfael, 'Edwy has been playing Edwin for my benefit, so that Edwin could stay out of the trap, if trap it turned out to be, and not reveal himself until he was certain I had no intention of making him prisoner and handing him over to the sheriff. And Edwy was well primed, too...'

'And still made a hash of it,' commented Edwin, with candid and tolerant scorn.

'I did not!' retorted Edwy heatedly. 'You never told me more than half a tale. What was I supposed to answer when Brother Cadfael asked me about going to the infirmary this morning? Never a word you said about that.'

'Why should I? I never gave it a thought, what difference could it make? And you *did* make a hash of it. I heard you start to say grandmother instead of mother—yes, and they instead of we. And so did Brother Cadfael, or how did he guess I was listening outside?'

'He heard you, of course! Blowing like a wheezy old man—and shivering,' added Edwy for good measure.

There was no ill-will whatever in these exchanges, they were the normal endearments current between these two, who would certainly have championed each other to the death against any outside threat. There was no malice in it when Edwin punched his nephew neatly and painfully in the muscles of the upper arm, and Edwy as promptly plucked Edwin round by the shoulder while he was less securely balanced, and spilled him on to the floor. Cadfael took them both by the scruff of the neck, a fistful of capuchon in either hand, and plumped them back firmly on to the bench, a yard apart this time, rather in defence of his softly bubbling syrup than in any very serious exasperation. The brief scuffle had warmed them, and shaken fear away to a magical distance; they sat grinning, only slightly abashed.

'Will you sit still a minute, and let me get the measure of you? You, Edwin, are the uncle, and the younger...yes, I could know you apart. You're darker, and sturdier in the build, and I think your eyes must be brown. And Edwy's...'

'Hazel,' said Edwin helpfully.

'And you have a small scar by your ear, close to the cheekbone. A small white crescent.'

'He fell out of a tree, three years ago,' Edwy informed him. 'He never could climb.'

'Now, enough of that! Master Edwin, now that you are here, and I know which one you are, let me ask you the same question I asked your proxy here a while ago. On your soul and honour, did you strike the blow that killed Master Bonel?'

The boy looked back at him with great eyes suddenly

solemn enough, and said firmly: 'I did not. I carry no weapon, and even if I did, why should I try to harm him? I know what they must be saying of me, that I grudged it that he broke his word, for so he did. But I was not born to a manor, but to trade, and I can make my way in trade, I would be ashamed if I could not. No, whoever wounded him to the death—but how could it happen, so suddenly?—it was not I. On my soul!'

Cadfael was in very little doubt of him by then, but he gave no sign yet. 'Tell me what did happen.'

'I left Meurig in the infirmary with the old man, and went on to my mother's house alone. But I don't understand about the infirmary. Is that important?'

'Never mind that now, go on. How were you welcomed?'

'My mother was pleased,' said the boy. 'But my step-father crowed over me like a cock that's won its bout. I answered him as little as I might, and bore it for my mother's sake, and that angered him more, so that he *would* find some way to sting me. We were three sitting at table, and Aldith had served the meat, and she told him the prior had paid him the compliment of sending a dish for him from his own table. My mother tried to talk about that, and flatter him with the distinction of it, but he wanted me to burn and smart at all costs, and he wouldn't be put off. He said I'd come, as he knew I would, my tail between my legs, like a whipped hound, to beg him to change his mind and restore me my inheritance, and he said if I wanted it, I should kneel and beg him, and he might take pity on me. And I lost my temper, for all I could do, and shouted back at him that I'd see him dead before I'd so much as once ask him a favour, let alone crawl on my knees. I don't know now all I said, but he began throwing things, and...and my mother was crying, and I rushed out, and straight back over the bridge and into the town.'

'But not to Master Bellecote's house. And did you hear Aelfric calling after you as far as the bridge, to fetch you back?'

'Yes, but what would have been the use? It would only have made things worse.'

'But you did not go home.'

'I was not fit. And I was ashamed.'

'He went to brood in Father's wood-store by the river,' said Edwy helpfully. 'He always does when he's out of sorts with the world. Or if we're in trouble, we hide there until it's blown over, or at least past the worst. That's where I found him. When the sheriff's sergeant came to the shop, and said they wanted him, and his stepfather was murdered, I knew where to look for him. Not that I ever supposed he'd done any wrong,' stated Edwy firmly, 'though he can make a great fool of himself sometimes. But I knew something bad must have happened to him. So I went to warn him, and of course he knew nothing whatever about the murder, he'd left the man alive and well, only in a rage.'

'And you've both been hiding since then? You've not been home?'

'*He* couldn't, could he? They'll be watching for him. And I had to stay with him. We had to leave the wood-yard, we knew they'd come there. But there are places we know of. And then Alys came and told us about you.'

'And that's the whole truth,' said Edwin. 'And now what are we to do?'

'First,' said Cadfael, 'let me get this brew of mine off the fire, and stand it to cool before I bottle it. There! You got in here, I suppose, by the parish door of the church, and through the cloisters?' The west door of the abbey church was outside the walls, and never closed except during the bad days of the siege of the town, that part of the church being parochial. 'And followed your noses, I daresay, once you were in the gardens. This syrup-boiling gives off a powerful odour.'

'It smells good,' said Edwy, and his respectful stare ranged the workshop, and the bunches and bags of dried herbs stirring and rustling gently in the rising heat from the brazier.

'Not all my medicines smell so appetising. Though myself I would not call even this unpleasant. Powerful,

82

certainly, but a fine, clean smell.' He unstoppered the great jar of anointing oil of monk's-hood, and tilted the neck beneath Edwin's inquisitive nose. The boy blinked at the sharp scent, drew back his head, and sneezed. He looked up at Cadfael with an open face, and laughed at his own pricked tears. Then he leaned cautiously and inhaled again, and frowned thoughtfully.

'It smells like that stuff Meurig was using to rub the old man's shoulder. Not this morning, the last time I came with him. There was a flask of it in the infirmary cupboard. Is it the same?'

'It is,' said Cadfael, and hoisted the jar back to its shelf. The boy's face was quite serene, the odour meant nothing more to him than a memory blessedly removed from any connection with tragedy and guilt. For Edwin, Gervase Bonel had died, inexplicably suddenly, of some armed attack, and the only guilt he felt was because he had lost his temper, infringed his own youthful dignity, and made his mother cry. Cadfael no longer had any doubts at all. The child was honest as the day, and caught in a deadly situation, and above all, badly in need of friends.

He was also very quick and alert of mind. The diversion began to trouble him just as it was over. 'Brother Cadfael...' he began hesitantly, the name new and almost reverent on his lips, not for this elderly and ordinary monk, but for the crusader Cadfael he had once been, fondly remembered even by a happy and fulfilled wife and mother, who had certainly much exaggerated his good looks, gallantry and daring. 'You knew about my going to the infirmary with Meurig...you asked Edwy about it. I couldn't understand why. Is it important? Has it something to do with my stepfather's death? I can't see how.'

'That you can't see how, child,' said Brother Cadfael, 'is your proof of an innocence we may have difficulty in proving to others, though I accept it absolutely. Sit down again by your nephew—dear God, shall I ever get these relationships straight?—and refrain from fighting him for a little while, till I explain to you what isn't yet public knowledge outside these walls. Yes, your two visits to the infirmary are truly of great importance, and so is this oil you have seen used there, though I must say that many others know of it, and are better acquainted than you with its properties, both bad and good. You must forgive me if I gave you to understand that Master Bonel was hacked down in his blood with dagger or sword. And forgive me you should, since in accepting that tale you quite delivered yourselves from any guilt, at least to my satisfaction. It was not so, boys. Master Bonel died of poison, given in the dish the prior sent him, and the poison was this same oil of monk's-hood. Whoever added it to the partridge drew it either from this workshop or from the flask in the infirmary, and all who knew of either source, and knew the peril if it was swallowed, are in suspicion.'

The pair of them, soiled and tired and harried as they were, stared in horrified understanding at last, and drew together on the bench as threatened litters of young in burrow and nest huddle for comfort. Years bordering on manhood dropped from them; they were children indeed, frightened and hunted. Edwy said strenuously: 'He didn't know! All they said was, dead, murdered. But so quickly! He ran out, and there was nobody there but those of the house. He never even saw any dish waiting...'

'I did know,' said Edwin, 'about the dish. She told us, I knew it was there. But what did it matter to me? I only wanted to go home...'

'Hush, now, hush!' said Cadfael chidingly. 'You speak to a man convinced. I've made my own tests, all I need. Now sit quiet, and trouble your minds no more about me, I know you have nothing to repent.' That was much, perhaps, to say of any man, but at least these two had nothing on their souls but the ordinary misdemeanours of the energetic young. And now that he had leisure to look at them without looking for prevarication or deceit, he was able to notice other things. 'You must give me a little while for thought, but the time need not be wasted. Tell me, has either of you eaten, all these hours? The one of you, I know, made a very poor dinner.'

They had been far too preoccupied with worse problems, until then, to notice hunger, but now that they had an ally, however limited in power, and shelter, however temporary, they were suddenly and instantly ravenous.

'I've some oat-cakes here of my own baking, and a morsel of cheese, and some apples. Fill up the hollows, while I think what's best to be done. You, Edwy, had best make your way home as soon as the town gates open in the morning, slip in somehow without being noticed, and make as though you've never been away but on some common errand. Keep a shut mouth except with those you're sure of.' And that would be the whole united family, embattled in defence of their own. 'But for you, my friend—you're a very different matter.'

'You'll not give him up?' blurted Edwy round a mouthful of oat-cake, instantly alarmed.

'That I certainly will not do.' Yet he might well have urged the boy to give himself up, stand fast on his innocence, and trust in justice, if he had had complete trust himself in the law as being infallibly just. But he had not. The law required a culprit, and the sergeant was comfortably convinced that he was in pursuit of the right quarry, and would not easily be persuaded to look further. Cadfael's proofs he had not witnessed, and would shrug off contemptuously as an old fool fondly believing a cunning young liar.

'I can't go home,' said Edwin, the solemnity of his face in no way marred by one cheek distended with apple, and a greenish smudge from some branch soiling the other. 'And I can't go to my mother's. I should only be bringing worse trouble on her.'

'For tonight you can stay here, the pair of you, and keep my little brazier fed. There are clean sacks under the bench, and you'll be warm and safe enough. But in the day there's coming and going here from time to time, we must have you out early, the one of you for home, the other.... Well, we'll hope you need stay hidden only a matter of a few days. As well close here at the abbey as anywhere, they'll hardly look for you here.' He considered, long and thoughtfully. The lofts over the stables were always warmed from the hay, and the bodies of the horses below, but too many people came and went there, and with travellers on the roads before the festival, there might well be servants required to sleep there above their beasts. But outside the enclave, at one corner of the open space used for the horse-fairs and the abbey's summer fair, there was a barn where beasts brought to market could be folded before sale, and the loft held fodder for them. The barn belonged to the abbey, but was open to all travelling merchants. At this time of year its visitors would be few or none, and the loft well filled with good hay and straw, a comfortable enough bed for a few nights. Moreover, should some unforeseen accident threaten danger to the fugitive, escape from outside the walls would be easier than from within. Though God forbid it should come to that!

'Yes, I know a place that will serve, we'll get you to it early in the morning, and see you well stocked with food and ale for the day. You'll need patience, I know, to lie by, but that you must endure.'

'Better,' said Edwin fervently, 'than falling into the sheriff's clutches, and I do thank you. But...how am I bettered by this, in the end? I can't lie hidden for ever.'

"There's but one way,' said Cadfael emphatically, 'that you can be bettered in this affair, lad, and that's by uncovering the man who did the thing you're charged with doing. And since you can hardly undertake that yourself, you must leave the attempt to me. What I can do, I'll do, for my own honour as well as for yours. Now I must leave you and go to Matins. In the morning before Prime I'll come and see you safely out of here.'

Brother Mark had done his part, the habit was there, rolled up beneath Brother Cadfael's bed. He wore it under his own, when he rose an hour before the bell for Prime, and left the dortoir by the night stairs and the church. Winter dawns come very late, and this night had been moonless and overcast; the darkness as he crossed the court from cloister to gardens was profound, and there was no one else stirring. There was perfect cover for Edwy to withdraw unobserved through the church and the parish door, as he had come, and make his chilly way to the bridge, to cross into Shrewsbury as soon as the gate was opened. Doubtless he knew his own town well enough to reach his home by ways devious enough to baffle detection by the authorities, even if they were watching the shop.

As for Edwin, he made a demure young novice, once inside the black habit and the sheltering cowl. Cadfael was reminded of Brother Mark, when he was new, wary and expecting nothing but the worst of his enforced vocation; the springy, defensive gait, the too tightly folded hands in the wide sleeves, the flickering sideglances, wild and alert for trouble. But there was something in this young thing's performance that suggested a perverse enjoyment, too; for all the danger to himself, and his keen appreciation of it, he could not help finding pleasure in this adventure. And whether he would manage to behave himself discreetly in hiding, and bear the inactive hours, or be tempted to wander and take risks, was something Cadfael preferred not to contemplate.

Through cloister and church, and out at the west door, outside the walls, they went side by side, and turned right, away from the gatehouse. It was still fully dark.

'This road leads in the end to London, doesn't it?' whispered Edwin from within his raised cowl.

'It does so. But don't try leaving that way, even if you should have to run, which God forbid, for they'll have a check on the road out at St Giles. You be sensible and lie still, and give me a few days, at least, to find out what I may.'

The wide triangle of the horse-fair ground gleamed

faintly pallid with light frost. The abbey barn loomed at one corner, close to the enclave wall. The main door was closed and fastened, but at the rear there was an outside staircase to the loft, and a small door at the top of it. Early traffic was already abroad, though thin at this dark hour, and no one paid attention to two monks of St Peter's mounting to their own loft. The door was locked, but Cadfael had brought the key, and let them in to a dry, hay-scented darkness.

'The key I can't leave you, I must restore it, but neither will I leave you locked in. The door must stay unfastened for you until you may come forth freely. Here you have a loaf, and beans, and curd, and a few apples, and here's a flask of small ale. Keep the gown, you may need it for warmth in the night, but the hay makes a kindly bed. And when I come to you, as I will, you may know me at the door by this knock.... Though no one else is likely to come. Should anyone appear without my knock, you have hay enough to hide in.'

The boy stood, suddenly grave and a little forlorn. Cadfael reached a hand, and put back the cowl from the shock-head of curls, and there was just filtering dawn-light enough to show him the shape of the solemn oval face, all steady, dilated, confronting eyes.

'You have not slept much. If I were you, I'd burrow deep and warm, and sleep the day out. I won't desert you.'

'I know,' said Edwin firmly. He knew that even together they might avail nothing, but at least he knew he was not alone. He had a loyal family, with Edwy as link, and he had an ally within the enclave. And he had one other thinking of him and agonising about him. He said in a voice that lost its firmness only for one perilous instant, and stubbornly recovered: 'Tell my mother I did not ever do him or wish him harm.'

'Fool child,' said Cadfael comfortably, 'I've been assured of that already, and who do you suppose told me, if not your mother?' The very faint light was magically soft, and the boy stood at that stage between childhood and maturity when his face, forming but not yet
88

formed, might have been that of boy or girl, woman or man. 'You're very like her,' said Cadfael, remembering a girl not much older than this sprig, embraced and kissed by just such a clandestine light, her parents believing her abed and asleep in virginal solitude. At this pass he had momentarily forgotten all the women he had known between, east and west, none of them, he hoped and believed, left feeling wronged. 'I'll be with you before night,' he said, and withdrew to the safety of the winter air outside.

Good God, he thought with reverence, making his way back by the parish door in good time for Prime, that fine piece of young flesh, as raw and wild and faulty as he is, he might have been mine! He and the other, too, a son and a grandson both! It was the first and only time that ever he questioned his vocation, much less regretted it, and the regret was not long. But he did wonder if somewhere in the world, by the grace of Arianna, or Bianca, or Mariam, or—were there one or two others as well loved here and there, now forgotten?—he had left printings of himself as beautiful and formidable as this boy of Richildis's bearing and another's getting.

Chapter 5

It was now imperative to find the murderer, otherwise the boy could not emerge from hiding and take up his disrupted life. And that meant tracing in detail the passage of the ill-fated dish of partridge from the abbot's kitchen to Gervase Bonel's belly. Who had handled it? Who could have tampered with it? Since Prior Robert, in his lofty eminence within the abbot's lodging, had eaten, appreciated and digested the rest of it without harm, clearly it had been delivered to him in goodwill and in good condition. And he, certainly without meddling, had delivered it in the same condition to his cook.

Before High Mass, Cadfael went to the abbot's kitchen. He was one of a dozen or so people within these walls who were not afraid of Brother Petrus. Fanatics are always frightening, and Brother Petrus was a fanatic, not for his religion or his vocation, those he took for granted, but for his art. His dedicated fire tinted black hair and black eyes, scorching both with a fiery red. His northern blood boiled like his own cauldron. His temper, barbarian from the borders, was as hot as his own oven. And as hotly as he loved Abbot Heribert, for the same reasons he detested Prior Robert.

When Cadfael walked in upon him, he was merely surveying the day's battlefield, and mustering his army of pans, pots, spits and dishes, with less satisfaction than the exercise should have provided, because it was Robert, and not Heribert, who would consume the result of his labours. But for all that, he could not relax his hold on perfection.

'That partridge!' said Petrus darkly, questioned on the day's events. 'As fine a bird as ever I saw, not the biggest, but the best-fed and plumpest, and could I have dressed it for my abbot, I would have made him a masterwork. Yes, this prior comes in and bids me set aside a portion—for one only, mark!—to be sent to the guest at the house by the mill-pond, with his compliments. And I did it. I made it the best portion, in one of Abbot Heribert's own dishes. *My* dishes, says Robert! Did anyone else here touch it? I tell you, Cadfael, the two I have here know me, they do what I say, and let all else ride. Robert? He came in to give his orders and sniff at my pan, but it was all in one pan then, it was only after he left my kitchen I set aside the dish for Master Bonel. No, take it as certain, none but myself touched that dish until it left here, and that was close on the dinner hour, when the manservant—Aelfric, is it?— brought his tray.'

'How do you find this man Aelfric?' asked Cadfael. 'You're seeing him daily.'

'A surly fellow, or at least a mute one,' said Petrus without animosity, 'but keeps exact time, and is orderly and careful.'

So Richildis had said, perhaps even to excess, and with intent to aggrieve his master.

'I saw him crossing the court with his load that day. The dishes were covered, he has but two hands, and certainly he did not halt this side the gatehouse, for I saw him go out.' But once through the gate there was a bench set in an alcove in the wall, where a tray could easily be put down for a moment, on pretense of adjusting to a better balance. And Aelfric knew his way to the workshop in the garden, and had seen the oil dispensed. And Aelfric was a soured man on two counts. A man of infinite potential, since he let so little of himself be known to any.

'Ah, well, it's certain nothing was added to the food here.'

'Nothing but wholesome wine and spices. Now if it had been the rest of the bird that was poisoned,' said

Petrus darkly, 'I'd give you leave to look sideways at me, for you'd have reason. But if ever I did go so far as to prepare a monk's-hood stew for that one, be sure I'd make no mistake about which bowl went to which belly.'

No need, thought Cadfael, crossing the court to Mass, to take Brother Petrus's fulminations too seriously. For all his ferocity he was a man of words rather than actions. Or ought it, after all, to be considered as worth pondering? The idea that a mistake had been made, and the dish intended for Robert sent instead to Bonel, had never entered Cadfael's head until now, but clearly Petrus had credited him with just such a notion, and made haste to hammer it into absurdity before it was uttered. A shade too much haste? Murderous hatreds had been known to arise between those who were sworn to brotherhood, before this, and surely would so arise again. Brother Petrus might have started the very suspicion he had set out to scotch. Not, perhaps, a very likely murderer. But bear it in mind!

The few weeks before the main festivals of the year always saw an increase in the parochial attendance at Mass, the season pricking the easy consciences of those who took their spiritual duties lightly all the rest of the year. There were a creditable number of local people in the church that morning, and it was no great surprise to Cadfael to discover among them the white coif and abundant yellow hair of the girl Aldith. When the service ended he noticed that she did not go out by the west door, like the rest, but passed through the south door into the cloister, and so out into the great court. There she drew her cloak around her, and sat down on a stone bench against the refectory wall.

Cadfael followed, and saluted her gravely, asking after her mistress. The girl raised to him a fair, composed face whose soft lines seemed to him to be belied by the level dark force of her eyes. She was, he reflected, as mysterious in her way as Aelfric, and what she did not choose to reveal of herself it would be hard to discover unaided.

'She's well enough in body,' she said thoughtfully, 'but distressed in mind for Edwin, naturally. But there's been no word of his being taken, and I'm sure we should have heard if he had been. That's some comfort. Poor lady, she's in need of comfort.'

He could have sent her some reassurance by this messenger, but he did not. Richildis had taken care to speak with him alone, he should respect that preference. In so tight and closed a situation, where only the handful of people involved in one household seemed to be at risk, how could Richildis be absolutely sure even of her young kinswoman, even of her stepson or her manservant? And could he, in the end, even be sure of Richildis? Mothers may be driven to do terrible things in defence of the rights of their children. Gervase Bonel had made a bargain with her, and broken it.

'If you'll permit, I'll sit with you a little while. You're not in haste to return?'

'Aelfric will be coming for the dinner soon,' she said. 'I thought I would wait for him, and help him carry everything. He'll have the ale and the bread as well.' And she added, as Cadfael sat down beside her: 'It's ill for him, having to do that same office daily, after what fell on us yesterday. To think that people may be eyeing him and wondering. Even you, brother. Isn't it true?'

'No help for that,' said Cadfael simply, 'until we know the truth. The sheriff's sergeant believes he knows it already. Do you agree with him?'

'No!' She was mildly scornful, it even raised the ghost of a smile. 'It isn't the wild, noisy, boisterous boys, the ones who let the world all round know their grievances and their tantrums and their pleasures, who use poison. But what avails my telling you this, saying I believe or I don't believe, when I'm deep in the same coil myself? As you know I am! When Aelfric came into my kitchen with the tray, and told me about the prior's gift, it was I who set the dish to keep hot on the hob, while Aelfric carried the large dish into the room, and

I followed with the platters and the jug of ale. The three of them were in there at table, they knew nothing about the partridge until I told them...thinking to please the master, for in there the air was so chill you could hardly breathe. I think I was back in the kitchen first of the two of us, and I sat by the hob to eat my meal, and I stirred the bowl when it simmered. More than once, and moved it aside from the heat, too. What use my saying I added nothing? Of course that is what I, or any other in my shoes would say, it carries no weight until there's proof, one way or the other.'

'You are very sensible and very just,' said Cadfael. 'And Meurig, you say, was just coming in at the door when you returned to the kitchen. So he was not alone with the dish...even supposing he had known what it was, and for whom it was intended.'

Her dark brows rose, wonderfully arched and vivid and striking under the pale brow and light-gold hair. 'The door was wide open, that I recall, and Meurig was just scraping the dirt from his shoes before coming in. But what reason could Meurig have, in any case, to wish his father dead? He was not lavish with him, but he was of more value to him alive than dead. He had no hope of inheriting anything, and knew it, but he had a modest competence to lose.'

That was simple truth. Not even the church would argue a bastard's right to inherit, while the state would deny it even where marriage of the parents, every way legal, followed the birth. And this had been a commonplace affair with one of his own maidservants. No, Meurig had no possible stake in this death. Whereas Edwin had a manor to regain, and Richildis, her adored son's future. And Aelfric?

She had reared her head, gazing towards the gatehouse, where Aelfric had just appeared, the high-rimmed wooden tray under his arm, a bag for the loaves slung on his shoulder. She gathered her cloak and rose.

'Tell me,' said Cadfael, mild-voiced beside her, 'now that Master Bonel is dead, to whom does Aelfric belong? Does he go with the manor, to the abbey or some other lord? Or was he excluded from the agreement, conceded to Master Bonel as manservant in villeinage for life?'

She looked back sharply in the act of going to meet Aelfric. 'He was excluded. Granted to be my lord's villein personally.'

'Then whatever happens to the manor now, he will go to whoever inherits the personal effects ... to widow or son, granted the son escapes a criminal charge. And Aldith, you know Mistress Bonel's mind, would you not say that she would at once give Aelfric his freedom, with a glad heart? And would the boy do any other?'

All she gave him by way of answer was a brief, blinding flash of the black, intelligent eyes, and the sudden, veiling swoop of large lids and long dark lashes. Then she went to cross Aelfric's path, and fall in beside him on his way to the abbot's lodging. Her step was light and easy, her greeting indifferent, her manner dutiful. Aelfric trudged by her side stiff and mute, and would not let her take the bag from his shoulder. Cadfael sat looking after them for a long moment, observing and wondering, though after a while the wonder subsided into mild surprise, and by the time he set off to wash his hands before dinner in the refectory, even surprise had settled into conviction and reassessment.

It was mid-afternoon, and Cadfael was picking over the stored trays of apples and pears in the loft of the abbot's barn, discarding the few decayed specimens before they could infect their neighbours, when Brother Mark came hallooing for him from below.

'The sheriff's man is back,' he reported, when Cadfael peered down the ladder at him and demanded what the noise was about, 'and asking for you. And they've not captured their man—if it's any news I'm telling you.'

'It's no good news that I should be wanted,' admitted Cadfael, descending the ladder backwards, as nimbly as a boy. 'What's his will? Or his humour, at least?'

'No menace to you, I think,' said Mark, considering. 'Vexed at not laying his hands on the boy, naturally, but I think his mind's on small things like the level of that rubbing oil in your store. He asked me if I could tell if any had been removed from there, but I'm a slipshod hand who notices nothing, as you'll bear witness. He thinks you'll know to the last drop.'

'Then he's the fool. It takes a mere mouthful or two of that to kill, and in a container too wide to get the fingers of both hands around, and tall as a stool, who's to know if ten times that amount has been purloined? But let's at least pick his brains of what he's about now, and how far he thinks he has his case proven.'

In the workshop the sheriff's sergeant was poking his bushy beard and hawk's beak into all Cadfael's sacks and jars and pots in somewhat wary curiosity. If he had brought an escort with him this time, he must have left them in the great court or at the gatehouse.

'You may yet be able to help us, brother,' he said as Cadfael entered. 'It would be a gain to know from which supply of this oil of yours the poison was taken, but the young brother here can't say if any is missing from this store. Can you be more forthcoming?'

'On that point,' said Cadfael bluntly, 'no. The amount needed would be very small, and my stock, as you see, is large. No one could pretend to say with certainty whether any had been taken out unlawfully. This I can tell you, I examined the neck and stopper of this bottle yesterday, and there is no trace of oil at the lip. I doubt if a thief in haste would stop to wipe the lip clean before stoppering it, as I do.'

The sergeant nodded, partially satisfied that this accorded with what he believed. 'It's more likely it was taken from the infirmary, then. And that's a smaller flask by much than this, but I've been there, and they can none of them hazard an opinion. Among the old the oil is in favoured use now, who can guess if it was used one more time without lawful reason?'

'You've made little progress, I fear,' said Brother Cadfael.

'We have not caught our man, yet. No knowing where Edwin Gurney is hiding, but there's been no trace of him round Bellecote's shop, and the carpenter's horse is in its stable. I'd wager the boy is still somewhere within the town. We're watching the shop and the gates, and keeping an eye on his mother's house. It is but a matter of time before we take him.'

Cadfael sat back on his bench and spread his hands on his knees. 'You're very sure of him. Yet there are at least four others who were there in the house, and any number more who, for one reason or another, know the use and abuse of this preparation. Oh, I know the weight of the case you can make against this boy. I could make as good a case against one or two more, but that I won't do. I'd rather by far consider those factors that might provide, not suspicion, but proof, and not against one chosen quarry, but against the person, whoever he may be, towards whom the facts point. The time concerned is tight, half an hour at most. I myself saw the manservant fetch the dishes from the abbot's kitchen, and carry them out at the gate. Unless we are to look seriously at those who serve the abbot's kitchen, the dish was still harmless when it left our enclave. I don't say,' he added blandly, 'that you should, because we wear the cowl, write off any man of us as exempt from suspicion, myself included.'

The sergeant was intelligent, though not impressed. 'Then what limiting factors, what firm facts, do you refer to, brother?'

'I mentioned to you yesterday, and if you care to sniff at that bottle, and try a drop of it on your sleeve, you'll note for yourself, that it makes itself apparent both to the nose and eye. You would not easily wash out the greasy mark from cloth, nor get rid of the smell. It is not the wolfsbane that smells so sharp and acrid, there's also mustard and other herbs. Whoever you seize upon, you must examine his clothing for these signs. I don't say it's proof of innocence if no such signs are found, but it does weaken the evidence of guilt.'

'You are interesting, brother,' said the sergeant, 'but not convincing.'

'Then consider this. Whoever had used that poison

would be in haste to get rid of the bottle as soon as possible, and as cleanly. If he lingered, he would have to hide it about him, and risk marking himself, or even having it discovered on him. You will conduct your business as you see fit. But I, were I in your shoes, would be looking very carefully for a small vial, anywhere within a modest distance of that house, for when you find it, the place where it was discarded will tell a great deal about the person who could have cast it there.' And with certainty he added: 'You'll be in no doubt of it being the right vial.'

He did not at all like the expression of indulgent complacency that was creeping over the sergeant's weathered countenance, as though he enjoyed a joke that presently, when he chose to divulge it, would quite take the wind out of Cadfael's sails. He himself admitted he had not captured his man, but there was certainly some other secret satisfaction he was hugging to his leather bosom.

'You have not found it already?' said Cadfael cautiously.

'Not found it, no. Nor looked for it very hard. But for all that, I know where it is. Small use looking now, and in any case, no need.' And now he was openly grinning.

'I take exception to that,' said Cadfael firmly. 'If you have not found it, you cannot *know* where it is, you can only surmise, which is not the same thing.'

'It's as near the same thing as we're likely to get,' said the sergeant, pleased with his advantage. 'For your little vial has gone floating down the Severn, and may never be seen again, but we know it was tossed in there, and we know who tossed it. We've not been idle since we left here yesterday, I can tell you, and we've done more than simply pursue a young fox and lose his trail a while. We've taken witness from any we could find who were moving about the bridge and the Foregate around the dinner hour, and saw Bonel's manservant running after the boy. We found a carter who was crossing the bridge just at that time. Such a chase, he pulled

98

up his cart, thinking there was a hue and cry after a thief, but when the boy had run past him he saw the pursuer give up the chase, short of the bridge, for he had no chance of overtaking his quarry. The one shrugged and turned back, and when the carter turned to look after the other he saw him slow in his running for a moment, and hurl some small thing over the downstream parapet into the water. It was young Gurney, and no other, who had something to dispose of, as soon as possible after he'd tipped its contents into the dish for his stepfather, given the spoon a whirl or two, and rushed away with the bottle in his hand. And what do you say to that, my friend?'

What, indeed? The shock was severe, for not one word had Edwin said about this incident, and for a moment Cadfael did seriously consider that he might have been hoodwinked for once by a cunning little dissembler. Yet cunning was the last thing he would ever have found in that bold, pugnacious face. He rallied rapidly, and without betraying his disquiet.

'I say that "some small thing" is not necessarily a vial. Did you put it to your carter that it might have been that?'

'I did, and he would not say yes or no, only that whatever it was was small enough to hold in the closed hand, and flashed in the light as it flew. He would not give it a shape or a character more than that.'

'You had an honest witness. Now can you tell me two things more from his testimony. At exactly what point on the bridge was the boy when he threw it? And did the manservant also see it thrown?'

'My man says the fellow running after had halted and turned back, and only then did he look round and catch the other one in the act. The servant could not have seen. And as for where the lad was at that moment, he said barely halfway across the drawbridge.'

That meant that Edwin had hurled away whatever it was as soon as he felt sure he was above the water, clear of the bank and the shore, for it was the outer section of the bridge that could be raised. And at that, he might have miscalculated and been in too big a hurry. The bushes and shelving slope under the abutments ran well out below the first arch. There was still a chance that whatever had been discarded could be recovered, if it had fallen short of the current. It seemed, also, that Aelfric had not concealed this detail, for he had not witnessed it.

'Well,' said Cadfael, 'by your own tale the boy had just gone running past a halted cart, with a driver already staring at him, and no doubt, at that hour, several other people within view, and made no secret of getting rid of whatever it was he threw. Nothing furtive about that. Hardly the way a murderer would go about disposing of the means, to my way of thinking. What do you say?'

The sergeant hitched at his belt and laughed aloud. 'I say you make as good a devil's advocate as ever I've heard. But lads in a panic after a desperate deed don't stop to think. And if it was not the vial he heaved into the Severn, you tell me, brother, what was it?' And he strode out into the chill of the early evening air, and left Cadfael to brood on the same question.

Brother Mark, who had made himself inconspicuous in a corner all this time, but with eyes and ears wide and sharp for every word and look, kept a respectful silence until Cadfael stirred at length, and moodily thumped his knees with clenched fists. Then he said, carefully avoiding questions: 'There's still an hour or so of daylight left before Vespers. If you think it's worth having a look below the bridge there?'

Brother Cadfael had almost forgotten the young man was present, and turned a surprised and appreciative eye on him. 'So there is! And your eyes are younger than mine. The two of us might at least cover the available ground. Yes, come, for better or worse we'll venture.'

Brother Mark followed eagerly across the court, out at the gatehouse, and along the highroad towards the bridge and the town. A flat, leaden gleam lay over the mill-pond on their left, and the house beyond it showed only a closed and shuttered face. Brother Mark stared at it curiously as they passed. He had never seen Mistress Bonel, and knew nothing of the old ties that linked her with Cadfael, but he knew when his mentor and friend was particularly exercised on someone else's behalf, and his own loyalty and partisan fervour, after his church, belonged all to Cadfael. He was busy thinking out everything he had heard in the workshop, and making practical sense of it. As they turned aside to the right, down the sheltered path that led to the riverside and the main gardens of the abbey, ranged along the rich Severn meadows, he said thoughtfully:

'I take it, brother, that what we are looking for must be small, and able to take the light, but had better *not* be a bottle?'

'You may take it,' said Cadfael, sighing, 'that whether it is or not, we must try our best to find it. But I would very much rather find something else, something as innocent as the day.'

Just beneath the abutments of the bridge, where it was not worth while clearing the ground for cultivation, bushes grew thickly, and coarse grass sloped down gradually to the lip of the water. They combed the tufted turf along the edge, where a filming of ice prolonged the ground by a few inches, until the light failed them and it was time to hurry back for Vespers; but they found nothing small, relatively heavy, and capable of reflecting a flash of light as it was thrown, nothing that could have been the mysterious something tossed away by Edwin in his flight.

Cadfael slipped away after supper, absenting himself from the readings in the chapter-house, helped himself to the end of a loaf and a hunk of cheese, and a flask of small ale for his fugitive, and made his way discreetly to the loft over the abbey barn in the horse-fair. The night was clear overhead but dark, for there was no moon as yet. By morning the ground would be silvered over, and the shore of Severn extended by a new fringe of ice.

101

His signal knock at the door at the head of the stairs produced only a profound silence, which he approved. He opened the door and went in, closing it silently behind him. In the darkness within nothing existed visibly, but the warm, fresh scent of the clean hay stirred in a faint wave, and an equally quiet rustling showed him where the boy had emerged from his nest to meet him. He moved a step towards the sound. 'Be easy, it's Cadfael.'

'I knew,' said Edwin's voice very softly. 'I knew you'd come.'

'Was it a long day?'

'I slept most of it.'

'That's my stout heart! Where are you...? Ah!' They moved together, uniting two faint warmths that made a better warmth between them; Cadfael touched a sleeve, found a welcoming hand. 'Now let's sit down and be blunt and brief, for time's short. But we may as well be comfortable with what we have. And here's food and drink for you.' Young hands, invisible, clasped his offerings gladly. They felt their way to a snug place in the hay, side by side.

'Is there any better news for me?' asked Edwin anxiously.

'Not yet. What I have for you, young man, is a question. Why did you leave out half the tale?'

Edwin sat up sharply beside him, in the act of biting heartily into a crust of bread. 'But I didn't! I told you the truth. Why should I keep anything from you, when I came asking for your help?'

'Why, indeed! Yet the sheriff's men have had speech with a certain carter who was crossing the bridge from Shrewsbury when you went haring away from your mother's house, and he testifies that he saw you heave something over the parapet into the river. Is that true?'

Without hesitation the boy said: 'Yes!' his voice a curious blend of bewilderment, embarrassment and anxiety. Cadfael had the impression that he was even blushing in the darkness, and yet obviously with no sense of guilt at having left the incident unmentioned, rather as though a purely private folly of his own had been accidentally uncovered.

'Why did you not tell me that yesterday? I might have had a better chance of helping you if I'd known.'

'I don't see why.' He was a little sullen and on his dignity now, but wavering and wondering. 'It didn't seem to have anything to do with what happened...and I wanted to forget it. But I'll tell you now, if it does matter. It isn't anything bad.'

'It matters very much, though you couldn't have known that when you threw it away.' Better tell him the reason now, and show that by this examiner, at least, he was not doubted. 'For what you sent over the parapet, my lad, is being interpreted by the sheriff's man as the bottle that held the poison, newly emptied by you before you ran out of the house, and disposed of in the river. So now, I think, you had better tell me what it really was, and I'll try to convince the law they are on the wrong scent, over that and everything else.'

The boy sat very still, not stunned by this blow, which was only one more in a beating which had already done its worst and left him still resilient. He was very quick in mind, he saw the implications, for himself and for Brother Cadfael. Slowly he said: 'And you don't need first to *be* convinced?'

'No. For a moment I may have been shaken, but not longer. Now tell me!'

'I didn't know! How could I know what was going to happen?' He drew breath deeply, and some of the tension left the arm and shoulder that leaned confidingly into Cadfael's side, 'No one else knew about it, I hadn't said a word to Meurig, and I never got so far as to show it even to my mother—I never had the chance. You know I'm learning to work in wood, and in fine metals, too, a little, and I had to show that I meant to be good at what I did. I made a present for my stepfather. Not because I liked him,' he made haste to add, with haughty honesty, 'I didn't! But my mother was unhappy about our quarrel, and it had made him hard and ill-tempered even to her—he never used to be, he *was* fond of her, I know. So I made a present as a peace offering...and to show I should make a craftsman, too, and be able to earn my living without him. He had a relic he valued greatly, he bought it in Walsingham when he was on pilgrimage, a long time ago. It's supposed to be a piece of Our Lady's mantle, from the hem, but I don't believe it's true. But *he* believed it. It's a slip of blue cloth as long as my little finger, with a gold thread in the edge, and it's wrapped in a bit of gold. He paid a lot of money for it, I know. So I thought I would make him a little reliquary just the right size for it, a little box with a hinge. I made it from pear-wood, and jointed and polished it well, and inlaid the lid with a little picture of Our Lady in nacre and silver, and blue stone for the mantle. I think it was not bad.'

The light ache in his voice touched Brother Cadfael's relieved heart; he had loved his work and destroyed it, he was entitled to grieve.

'And you took it with you to give to him yesterday?' he asked gently.

'Yes.' He bit that off short. Cadfael remembered how he had been received, according to Richildis, when he made his difficult, courageous appearance at their table, his gift secreted somewhere upon him.

'And you had it in your hand when he drove you out of the house with his malice. I see how it could happen.'

The boy burst out bitterly, shivering with resentment still: 'He said I'd come to crawl to him for my manor...he taunted me, and if I kneeled to him...How could I offer him a gift, after that? He would have taken it as proof positive...I couldn't bear that! It was meant to be a gift, without any asking.'

'I should have done what you did, boy, kept it clutched in my hand, and run from there without a word more.'

'But not thrown it in the river, perhaps,' sighed Edwin ruefully. 'Why? I don't know...Only it had been meant for him, and I had it in my hand, and Aelfric was running after me and calling, and I couldn't go back...It wasn't his, and it wasn't any more mine, and I threw it over to be rid of it...'

So that was why neither Richildis nor anyone else had mentioned Edwin's peace offering. Peace or war, for that matter? It had been meant to assert both his forgiveness and his independence, neither very pleasing to an elderly autocrat. But well-meant, for all that, an achievement, considering the lad was not yet fifteen years old. But no one had known of it. No one but the maker had ever had the chance to admire—as Richildis would have done most dotingly!—the nice dove-tailing of the joints of his little box, or the fine setting of the slips of silver and pearl and lapis which had flashed just once in the light as they hurtled into the river.

'Tell me, this was a well-fitted lid, and closed when you threw it over?'

'Yes.' He was very fairly visible now, and all startled eyes. He did not understand the question, but he was sure of his work. 'Is that important, too, I wish now I hadn't done it, I see I've made everything worse. But how was I to know? There wasn't any hue and cry for me then, there wasn't any murder, I knew I hadn't done anything wrong.'

'A small wooden box, tightly closed, will float gallantly where the river carries it, and there are men who live by the river traffic and fishing, yes, and poaching, too, and they'll know every bend and beach from here to Atcham where things fetch up on the current. Keep your heart up, lad, you may yet see your work again if I can get the sheriff to listen to me, and put out the word to the watermen to keep a watch. If I give them a description of what was thrown away—oh, be easy, I'll not reveal how I got it!—and somewhere downstream that very thing is discovered, that's a strong point in your favour, and I may even be able to get them to look elsewhere for the bottle, somewhere where Edwin Gurney was not, and therefore could not have left it. You bide yet a day or two here in quiet, if you can bear it, and if need be, I'll get you away to some

105

more distant place, where you can wait the time out in better comfort.'

'I can bear it,' said Edwin sturdily. And added ruefully: 'But I wish it may not be long!'

The brothers were filing out at the end of Compline when it dawned upon Cadfael that there was one important question which he and everyone else had neglected to ask, and the only person he could think of who might conceivably be able to answer it was Richildis. There was still time to ask it before night, if he gave up his final half-hour in the warming-room. Not, perhaps, a tactful time to visit, but everything connected with this business was urgent, and Richildis could at least sleep a little more easily for the knowledge that Edwin was, thus far at least, safe and provided for. Cadfael drew up his cowl, and made purposefully for the gates.

It was bad luck that Brother Jerome should be coming across the court towards the porter's lodge at the same time, probably with some officious orders for the morrow, or some sanctimonious complaint of irregularities today. Brother Jerome already felt himself to be in the exalted position of clerk to the abbot-elect, and was exerting himself to represent adequately his master Robert, now that that worthy man had availed himself of the abbot's privilege and privacy. Authority delegated to Brother Richard, and sedulously avoided by him wherever possible, would be greedily taken up by Brother Jerome. Some of the novices and boy pupils had already had cause to lament his zeal.

'You have an errand of mercy at so late an hour, brother?' smiled Jerome odiously. 'Can it not wait until morning?'

'At the risk of further harm,' snapped Cadfael, 'it might.' And he made no further halt, but proceeded on his way, well aware of the narrowed eyes following his departure. He had, within reason, authority to come and go as he thought fit, even to absent himself from services if his aid was required elsewhere, and he was certainly not going to explain himself, either truthfully or mendaciously, to Brother Jerome, however others less bold might conform for the sake of staying out of Robert's displeasure. It was unfortunate, but he had nothing ill to conceal, and to turn back would have suggested the contrary.

There was still a small light burning in the kitchen of the house beyond the mill-pond, he could see it through a tiny chink in the shutter as he approached. Yes, now, *there* was something he had failed to take into account: the kitchen window overlooked the pond, and close, at that, closer than from the road, and yesterday it had been open because of the brazier standing under it, an outlet for the smoke. An outlet, too, for a small vial hurled out there as soon as emptied, to be lost for ever in the mud at the bottom of the pond? What could be more convenient? No odour on clothing, no stains, no dread of being discovered with the proof.

Tomorrow, thought Cadfael, elated, I'll search from that window down to the water. Who knows but this time the thing thrown may really have fallen short, and be lying somewhere in the grass by the water's edge for me to find? That would be something gained! Even if it cannot prove who threw it there, it may still tell me something.

He knocked softly at the door, expecting Aldith to answer, or Aelfric, but it was the voice of Richildis herself that called out quietly from within: 'Who's there?'

'Cadfael! Open to me for a few minutes.'

His name had been enough, she opened eagerly, and reached a hand to draw him into the kitchen. 'Hush, softly! Aldith is asleep in my bed, and Aelfric within, in the room. I could not sleep yet, I was sitting late, thinking about my boy. Oh, Cadfael, can you give me no comfort? You will stand his friend if you can?'

'He is well, and still free,' said Cadfael, sitting down beside her on the bench against the wall. 'But mark me, you know nothing, should any ask. You may truly
107

say he has not been here, and you don't know where he is. Better so!'

'But you do know!' The tiny, steady light of the rush-candle showed him her face smoothed of its ageing lines and softly bright, very comely. He did not answer; she might read that for herself, and could still say truly that she knew nothing.

'And that's all you can give me?' she breathed.

'No, I can give you my solemn word that he never harmed his stepfather. That I know. And truth must come out. That you must believe.'

'Oh, I will, I do, if you'll help to uncover it. Oh, Cadfael, if you were not here I should despair. And such constant vexations, pin-pricks, when I can think of nothing but Edwin. And Gervase not in his grave until tomorrow! Now that he's gone, I no longer have a claim to livery for his horse, and with so many travellers coming now before the feast, they want his stable-room, and I must move him elsewhere, or else sell him...But Edwin will want him, if...' She shook her head distractedly, and would not complete that doubt. 'They told me they'll find him a stall and feed somewhere until I can arrange for him to be stabled elsewhere. Perhaps Martin could house him...'

They might, Cadfael thought indignantly, have spared her such small annoyances, at least for a few days. She had moved a little closer to him, her shoulder against his. Their whispering voices in the dimly lit room, and the lingering warmth from a brazier now mostly ash, took him back many years, to a stolen meeting in her father's outhouse. Better not linger, to be drawn deeper still!

'Richildis, there's something I came to ask you. Did your husband ever actually draw up and seal the deed that made Edwin his heir?'

'Yes, he did.' She was surprised by the question, 'It was quite legal and binding, but naturally this agreement with the abbey has a later date, and makes the will void now. Or it did...' She was brought back sharply to the realisation that the second agreement,

108

too, had been superseded, more roughly even than the first. 'Of course, that's of no validity now. So the grant to Edwin stands. It must, our man of law drew it properly, and I have it in writing.'

'So all that stands between Edwin and his manor, now, is the threat of arrest for murder, which we know he did not do. But tell me this, Richildis, if you know it: supposing the worst happened—which it must not and will not—and he was convicted of killing your husband—then what becomes of Mallilie? The abbey cannot claim it, Edwin could not then inherit it. Who becomes the heir?'

She managed to gaze resolutely beyond the possibility of the worst, and considered what sense law would make of what was left.

'I suppose I should get my dower, as the widow. But the manor could only revert to the overlord, and that's the earl of Chester, for there's no other legitimate heir. He could bestow it where he pleased, to his best advantage. It might go to any man he favoured in these parts. Sheriff Prestcote, as like as not, or one of his officers.'

It was true, and it robbed all others here, except Edwin, of any prospect of gaining by Bonel's death; or at least, of any material gain. An enemy sufficiently consumed by hate might find the death in itself gain enough, yet that seemed an excessive reaction to a man no way extreme, however difficult Edwin had found him.

'You're sure? There's no nephew, or cousin of his somewhere about the shire?'

'No, no one, or he would never have promised me Mallilie for Edwin. He set great store by his own blood.'

What had been going through Cadfael's mind was the possibility that someone with his own fortune in view might have planned to remove at one stroke both Bonel and Edwin, by ensuring the boy's arrest for the man's murder. But evidently that was far from the mark. No one could have calculated with any certainty on securing for himself what the house of Bonel forfeited.

By way of comfort and encouragement, Cadfael laid his broad, gnarled hand on her slender one, and marked in the slanting light, with roused tenderness, its enlarged knuckles and tracery of violet veins, more touching than any girlish smoothness could ever have been. Her face was beautiful, too, even in its ageing, lined, now that he saw it almost at peace, with good-humour and the long experience of happiness, which this brief ordeal of exasperation, disruption and pain could do little now to deflower. It was his youth he was lamenting, not any waste of Richildis. She had married the right man and been blessed, and a late mistake with the wrong man was over without irreparable damage, provided her darling could be extricated from his present danger. That, and only that, Cadfael thought gratefully, is my task.

The warm hand under his turned and closed, holding him fast. The still beguiling face turned to gaze at him closely and earnestly, with limpid, sympathetic eyes and a mouth with delicate, self-congratulatory guilt. 'Oh, Cadfael, did you take it so hard? Did it have to be the cloister? I wondered about you so often, and so long, but I never knew I had done you such an injury. And you have forgiven me that broken promise?'

'The whole fault was mine,' said Cadfael, with somewhat over-hearty fervour. 'I've wished you well always, as I do now.' And he made to rise from the bench, but she kept her hold on his hand and rose with him. A sweet woman, but dangerous, like all her innocent kind.

'Do you remember,' she was saying, in the hushed whisper the hour demanded, but with something even more secret in its intimacy, 'the night we pledged our troth? That was December, too. I've been thinking of it ever since I knew you were here—a Benedictine monk! Who would ever have dreamed it would end so! But you stayed away so long!'

It was certainly time to go. Cadfael retrieved his

hand gently, made her a soothing good night, and discreetly withdrew, before worse could befall him. Let her by all means attribute his vocation to the loss of her own delightful person, for the conviction would stand by her well until her world was restored in safety. But as for him, he had no regrets whatever. The cowl both fitted and became him.

He let himself out and returned enlarged through the chill and sparkle of the frosty night, to the place he had chosen, and still and for ever now preferred.

Behind him, as he neared the gatehouse, a meagre shadow detached itself from the shelter of the eaves of Richildis's house, and slid contentedly along the road after him, keeping well to the side in case he looked back. But Brother Cadfael did not look back. He had just had a lesson in the perils of that equivocal exercise; and in any case, it was not his way.

Chapter 6

Chapter next morning promised to be as dull as usual, once Brother Andrew's readings were done, and the business of the house reached; but Cadfael, dozing gently behind his pillar, remained alert enough to prick his ears, when Brother Matthew the cellarer announced that the guest-hall was full to capacity, and more stabling space was needed for still more expected gentlefolk, so that it would be necessary to transfer some of the horses and mules belonging to the abbey to some other housing, to accommodate the travellers' beasts within the walls. Late merchants, taking advantage of the clement autumn after the summer of siege and disorder, were now on the roads making for home for the feast, and nobles with manors in the county were seeking their own retired firesides, to celebrate Christmas away from the burden of arms and the stress of faction in the south. It was manifestly true that the stables were overcrowded, and the great court daily brighter and busier with arrivals and departures.

'There is also the matter of the horse that belonged to Master Gervase Bonel,' said Brother Matthew, 'who is to be buried today. Our responsibility to provide stabling and feed is now at an end, though I know the case is in suspense until the matter of the man's death and the disposal of his property is cleared up. But the widow as survivor is certainly not entitled to livery for a horse. She has a daughter married in the town, and doubtless will be able to make provision for the beast, and of course we must house it until she so disposes, but it need not occupy a stall in our main stables. Have I your

112

approval to move it out with our own working beasts to the stabling under our barn in the horse-fair ground?'

Most certainly he had not Cadfael's approval! He sat stiff with alarm and exasperation, fuming at his own unfortunate choice of hiding-place rather than Matthew's practical dispositions. Yet how could he have foreseen this? Very seldom had it been necessary to make use of the stalls at the barn, apart from its actual purpose as temporary accommodation at the horse-fairs and St Peter's fair. And now how was he to get to Edwin in time to remove him from the peril of discovery? In broad daylight, and with the inescapable spiritual duties of the day confining his movements?

'That should certainly provide adequate stabling,' agreed Prior Robert. 'It would be well to make the transfer at once.'

'I will give instructions to the grooms. And you agree also, Father, to the Widow Bonel's horse being removed with them?'

'By all means!' Robert no longer had quite the same interest in the Bonel family, now that it seemed doubtful he would ever lay his hands on the manor of Mallilie, though he did not intend to give up without a struggle. The unnatural death and its consequences irked him like a thorn in his flesh, and he would gladly have removed not merely the horse but the whole household, could he have done so with propriety. He did not want murder associated with his convent, he did not want the sheriff's officers probing among his guests, or the whiff of notoriety hanging round the monastery buildings like a bad odour. 'It will be necessary to go into the legal complications on the vexed question of the charter, which inevitably lapses now unless a new lord chooses to endorse and complete it. But until after Master Bonel's burial, of course, nothing should be done. The horse, however, can well be moved. I doubt if the widow will now have any use for a mount, but that is not yet our problem.'

He is already regretting, thought Cadfael, that in the first flush of sympathy and concern he authorised a grave for Bonel in the transept. But his dignity will not let him withdraw the concession now. God be thanked, Richildis will have whatever comfort there is in a solemn and dignified funeral, since all that Robert does must be done with grandeur. Gervase has lain in state in the mortuary chapel of the abbey, and will lie in abbey ground by nightfall. She would be soothed and calmed by that. She felt, he was sure, a kind of guilt towards the dead man. Whenever she was solitary she would be playing the ageless, debilitating game of: If only...If only I'd never accepted him...if only I had managed affairs between him and Edwin better...if only—then he might have been alive and hale today!

Cadfael closed his ears to the desultory discussion of a possible purchase of land to enlarge the graveyard, and gave his mind to the consideration of his own more pressing problem. It would not be impossible to find himself an errand along the Foregate when the grooms were stabling the horses in their new quarters, and the lay brothers would not question any movements of his. He could as well bring Edwin out of his retreat in a Benedictine habit as lead him into it, provided he took care to time the exit properly. And once out, then where? Certainly not towards the gatehouse. There were people in one or two houses along the highroad towards St Giles who had had dealings with him when sick, some whose children he had attended in fever. They might give shelter to a young man at his recommendation, though he did not much like the idea of involving them. Or there was, at the end of this stretch of road, the leper hospital of St Giles, where young brothers often served a part of their novitiate in attendance on those less fortunate. Something, surely, might be arranged to hide one haunted boy.

Incredulously, Cadfael heard his own name spoken, and was jerked sharply out of his planning. Across the chapter-house, in his stall as close as possible to Prior Robert, Brother Jerome had risen, and was in full spate, his meagre figure deceptively humble in stance, his sharp eyes half-hooded in holy meekness. And he had just uttered Brother Cadfael's name, with odious concern and affection!

'...I do not say, Father, that there has been any impropriety in our dearly valued brother's conduct. I do but appeal for aid and guidance for his soul's sake, for he stands in peril. Father, it has come to my knowledge that many years since, before his call to this blessed vocation, Brother Cadfael was in a relationship of worldly affection with the lady who is now Mistress Bonel, and a guest of this house. By reason of the death of her husband he was drawn back into contact with her, by no fault of his, oh, no, I do not speak of blame, for he was called to help a dying man. But consider, Father, how severe a test may be imposed upon a brother's sincere devotion, when he is again brought unexpectedly into so close touch with a long-forgotten attachment according to this world!'

To judge by Prior Robert's loftily erected head and stretched neck, which enabled him to look from an even greater height down his nose at the imperilled brother, he was indeed considering it. So was Cadfael, with astonished indignation that congealed rapidly into cool, inimical comprehension. He had underestimated Brother Jerome's audacity, no less than his venom. That large, sinewy ear must have been pressed lovingly to the large keyhole of Richildis's door, to have gathered so much.

'Do you allege,' demanded Robert incredulously, "that Brother Cadfael has been in unlawful conversation with this woman? On what occasion? We ourselves know well that he attended Master Bonel's death-bed, and did his best for the unfortunate, and that the unhappy wife was then present. We have no reproach to make upon that count, it was his duty to go where he was needed.'

Brother Cadfael, as yet unaddressed, sat grimly silent, and let them proceed, for obviously this attack came as unexpectedly to Robert as to him.

'Oh, no man of us can question that,' agreed Jerome obligingly. 'It was his Christian duty to give aid according to his skills, and so he did. But as I have learned, our brother has again visited the widow and spoken with her, only last night. Doubtless for purposes of comfort and blessing to the bereaved. But what dangers may lurk in such a meeting, Father, I need not try to express. God forbid it should ever enter any mind, that a man once betrothed, and having lost his affianced wife to another, should succumb to jealousy in his late years, after abandoning the world, when he once again encounters the former object of his affections. No, that we may not even consider. But would it not be better if our beloved brother should be removed utterly even from the temptations of memory? I speak as one having his wellbeing and spiritual health at heart.'

You speak, thought Cadfael, grinding his teeth, as one at last provided with a weapon against a man you've hated for years with little effect. And, God forgive me, if I could wring your scrawny neck now, I would do it and rejoice.

He rose and stood forth from his retired place to be seen. 'I am here, Father Prior, examine me of my actions as you wish. Brother Jerome is somewhat overtender of my vocation, which is in no danger.' And that, at least, was heartfelt.

Prior Robert continued to look down at him all too thoughtfully for Cadfael's liking. He would certainly fight any suggestion of misconduct among his flock, and defend them to the world for his own sake, but he might also welcome an opportunity of curbing the independent activities of a man who always caused him slight discomfort, as though he found in Cadfael's blunt, practical, tolerant self-sufficiency a hidden vein of desire of satire and amusement. He was no fool, and could hardly have failed to notice that he was being obliquely invited to believe that Cadfael might, when confronted with his old sweetheart married to another, have so far succumbed to jealousy as to remove his rival from the world with his own hands. Who, after all, knew the properties of herbs and plants better, or the proportions in which they could be used for good or ill?

God forbid it should enter any mind, Jerome had said piously, neatly planting the notion as he deplored it. Doubtful if Robert would seriously entertain any such thought, but neither would he censure it in Jerome, who was unfailingly useful and obsequious to him. Nor could it be argued that the thing was altogether impossible. Cadfael had made the monk's-hood oil, and knew what could be done with it. He had not even to procure it secretly, he had it in his own charge; and if he had been sent for in haste to a man already sick to death, who was to say he had not first administered the poison he feigned to combat? And I watched Aelfric cross the court, thought Cadfael, and might easily have stopped him for a word, lifted the lid in curiosity at the savoury smell, been told for whom it was sent, and added another savour of my own making? A moment's distraction, and it could have been done. How easy it is to bring on oneself a suspicion there's no disproving!

'Is it indeed truth, brother,' asked Robert weightily, 'that Mistress Bonel was intimately known to you in your youth, before you took vows?'

'It is,' said Cadfael directly, 'if by intimately you mean only well and closely, on terms of affection. Before I took the Cross we held ourselves to be affianced, though no one else knew of it. That was more than forty years ago, and I had not seen her since. She married in my absence, and I, after my return, took the cowl.' The fewer words here, the better.

'Why did you never say word of this, when they came to our house?'

'I did not know who Mistress Bonel was, until I saw her. The name meant nothing to me, I knew only of her first marriage. I was called to the house, as you know, and went in good faith.'

'That I acknowledge,' conceded Robert. 'I did not observe anything untoward in your conduct there.'

'I do not suggest, Father Prior,' Jerome made haste to assure him, 'that Brother Cadfael has done anything deserving of blame...' The lingering ending added silently: '...as yet!' but he did not go so far as to utter it.

'I am concerned only for his protection from the snares of temptation. The devil can betray even through a Christian affection.'

Prior Robert was continuing his heavy and intent study of Cadfael, and if he was not expressing condemnation, there was no mistaking the disapproval in his elevated eyebrows and distended nostrils. No inmate of his convent should even admit to noticing a woman, unless by way of Christian ministry or hard-headed business. 'In attending a sick man, certainly you did only right, Brother Cadfael. But is it also true that you visited this woman last night? Why should that be? If she was in need of spiritual comfort, there is here also a parish priest. Two days ago you had a right and proper reason for going there, last night you surely had none.'

'I went there,' said Cadfael patiently, since there was no help in impatience, and nothing could mortify Brother Jerome so much as to be treated with detached forbearance, 'to ask certain questions which may bear upon her husband's death—a matter which you, Father Prior, and I, and all here, must devoutly wish to be cleared up as quickly as possible, so that this house may be in peace.'

'That is the business of the sheriff and his sergeants,' said Robert curtly, 'and none of yours. As I understand it, there is no doubt whose is the guilt, and it is only a matter of laying hands upon the youth who did so vile a thing. I do not like your excuse, Brother Cadfael.'

'In due obedience,' said Cadfael, 'I bow to your judgment, but also must not despise my own. I think there *is* doubt, and the truth will not be easily uncovered. And my *reason* was not an excuse; it was for that purpose I went to the house. It was my own preparation, meant to bring comfort and relief from pain, that was used to bring death, and neither this house nor I, as a brother herein, can be at peace until the truth is known.'

'In saying so, you show lack of faith in those who uphold the law, and whose business justice is, as yours it is not. It is an arrogant attitude, and I deplore it.'

What he meant was that he wished to distance the Benedictine house of St Peter and St Paul from the ugly thing that had happened just outside its walls, and he would find a means of preventing the effective working of a conscience so inconvenient to his aims. 'In my judgment, Brother Jerome is right, and it is our duty to ensure that you are not allowed, by your own folly, to stray into spiritual danger. You will have no further contact with Mistress Bonel. Until her future movements are decided, and she leaves her present house, you will confine yourself to the enclave, and your energies to your proper function of work and worship within our walls only.'

There was no help for it. Vows of obedience, voluntarily taken, cannot be discarded whenever they become inconvenient. Cadfael inclined his head—bowed would have been the wrong word, it was more like a small, solid and formidable bull lowering its armed brow for combat!—and said grimly: 'I shall observe the order laid upon me, as in duty bound.'

'But you, young man,' he was saying to Brother Mark in the garden workshop, a quarter of an hour later, with the door shut fast to contain the fumes of frustration and revolt, rather Mark's than his own, 'you have no such order to observe.'

'That,' said Brother Mark, taking heart, 'is what I was thinking. But I was afraid you were not.'

'I would not involve you in my sins, God knows,' sighed Cadfael, 'if this was not urgent. And perhaps I should not...Perhaps he must be left to fend for himself, but with so much against him...'

'He!' said Brother Mark thoughtfully, swinging his thin ankles from the bench. 'The he whose *something*, that was not a vial, we did not find? From all I gather, he's barely out of childhood. The Gospels are insistent we should take care of the children.'

Cadfael cast him a mild, measuring and affectionate look. This child was some four years older than the other, and his childhood, since his mother's death when he was three years old, no one had cared for, beyond throwing food and grudged shelter his way. The other had been loved, indulged and admired all his life, until these past months of conflict, and the present altogether more desperate danger.

'He is a spirited and able child, Mark, but he relies on me. I took charge of him and gave him orders. Had he been left on his own, I think he would have managed.'

'Tell me only where I must go, and what I must do,' said Mark, quite restored to cheerfulness, 'and I will do it.'

Cadfael told him. 'But not until after High Mass. You must not be absent, or any way put your own repute in peril. And should there be trouble, you'll hold aloof and safe — you hear?'

'I hear,' said Brother Mark, and smiled.

By ten o'clock of that morning, when High Mass began, Edwin was heartily sick of obedience and virtue. He had never been so inactive for so long since he had first climbed mutinously out of his cradle and crawled into the yard, to be retrieved from among the wagon wheels by a furious Richildis. Still, he owed it to Brother Cadfael to wait in patience, as he had promised, and only in the darkest middle of the night had he ventured out to stretch his legs and explore the alleys and lanes about the horse-fair, and the silent and empty stretch of the Foregate, the great street that set out purposefully for London. He had taken care to be back in his loft well before the east began to lighten, and here he was, seated on an abandoned barrel, kicking his heels and eating one of Cadfael's apples, and wishing something would happen. From the slit air-vents enough light entered the loft to make a close, dim, straw-tinted day.

If wishes are prayers, Edwin's was answered with almost crude alacrity. He was used to hearing horses passing in the Foregate, and the occasional voices of people on foot, so he thought nothing of the leisurely hoof-beats and monosyllabic voices that approached from the town. But suddenly the great double doors below were hurled open, their solid weight crashing back to the wall, and the hoof-beats, by the sound of them of horses being walked on leading reins, clashed inward from the cobbles of the apron and thudded dully on the beaten earth floor within.

Edwin sat up, braced and still, listening with pricked ears. One horse...two...more of them, lighter in weight and step, small, neat hooves—mules, perhaps? And at least two grooms with them, probably three or four. He froze, afraid to stir, wary of even the crunching of his apple. Now if they were only meaning to stall these beasts during the day, all might yet be well, and all he had to do was keep quiet and sit out the time in hiding.

There was a heavy trapdoor in the cleared space of flooring, so that at need grooms could gain access to the loft without having to go outside, or carry the other key with them. Edwin slid from his barrel and went to stretch himself cautiously on the floor, and apply an ear to the crack.

A young voice chirruped soothingly to a restive horse, and Edwin heard a hand patting neck and shoulder. 'Easy there, now, my beauty! A very fine fellow you are, too. The old man knew his horse-flesh, I'll say that for him. He's spoiled for want of work. It's shame to see him wasted.'

'Get him into a stall,' ordered a gruff voice shortly, 'and come and lend a hand with these mules.'

There was a steady to-ing and fro-ing about settling the beasts. Edwin got up quietly, and put on his Benedictine habit over his own clothes, for if by ill-luck he was seen around this building, it would be the best cover he could have. Though it seemed that everything would probably pass off safely. He went back to his listening station just in time to hear a third voice say: 'Fill up the hay-racks. If there's not fodder enough down here, there's plenty above.'

They were going to invade his refuge, after all! There

was already a foot grating on the rungs of the ladder below. Edwin scrambled up in haste, no longer troubling to be silent, and rolled his heavy barrel on its rim to settle solidly over the trapdoor, for the bolts must be on the underside. The sound of someone wrestling them back from stiff sockets covered the noise of the barrel landing, and Edwin perched on top of his barricade, and wished himself three times as heavy. But it is very difficult to thrust a weight upwards over one's head, and it seemed that even his slight bulk was enough. The trap heaved a little under him, but nothing worse.

'It's fast,' called a vexed voice from below. 'Some fool's bolted it on top.'

'There are bolts on top. Use your brawn, man, you're no such weed as all that.'

'Then they've dumped something heavy over the trap. I tell you it won't budge.' And he rattled it again irritably to demonstrate.

'Oh, come down, and let a man try his arm,' said he of the gruff voice disgustedly. There was an alarming scrambling of heavier feet on the rungs, and the ladder creaked. Edwin held his breath and willed himself to grow heavier by virtue of every braced muscle. The trap shook, but lifted not an inch, and the struggling groom below panted and swore.

'What did I tell you, Will?' crowed his fellow, with satisfaction.

'We'll have to go round to the other door. Lucky I brought both keys. Wat, come and help me shift whatever's blocking the trap, and fork some hay down.'

Had he but known it, he needed no key, for the door was unlocked. The voice receded rapidly down the ladder, and footsteps stamped out at the stable-door. Two of them gone from below, but only a matter of moments before he would be discovered; not even time to burrow deep into the hay, even if that had been a safe stratagem when they came with forks. If they were only three in all, why not attempt the one instead of the two? Edwin as hastily rolled his barrel back to jam it against the door, and then flung himself upon the trap, hoisting mightily. It rose so readily that he was almost spilled backwards, but he recovered, and lowered himself hastily through. No time to waste in closing the trap again, all his attention was centred on the perils below.

They were four, not three! Two of them were still here among the horses, and though one of them had his back squarely turned, and was forking hay into a manger at the far end of the long stable, the other, a lean, wiry fellow with shaggy grey hair, was only a few feet from the foot of the ladder, and just striding out from one of the stalls.

It was too late to think of any change of plan, and Edwin never hesitated. He scrambled clear of the trap, and launched himself in a flying leap upon the groom. The man had just caught the sudden movement and raised his head sharply to stare at its source, when Edwin descended upon him in a cloud of overlarge black skirts, and brought him to the ground, momentarily winded. Whatever advantage the habit might have been to the boy was certainly lost after that assault. The other youth, turning at his companion's startled yell, was baffled only briefly at the sight of what appeared to be a Benedictine brother, bounding up from the floor with gown gathered in one hand, and the other reaching for the pikel his victim had dropped. No monk the groom had ever yet seen behaved in this fashion. He took heart and began an indignant rush which halted just as abruptly when the pikel was flourished capably in the direction of his middle. But by then the felled man was also clambering to his feet, and between the fugitive and the wide open doorway.

There was only one way to go, and Edwin went that way, pikel in hand, backing into the stall nearest him. Only then did he take note, with what attention he had to spare from his adversaries, of the horse beside him, the one which had been so restive, according to the young groom, spoiling for want of work and shamefully wasted. A tall, high-spirited chestnut beast with a paler

123

mane and tail, and a white blaze, stamping in excitement of the confusion, but reaching a nuzzling lip to Edwin's hair, and whinnying in his ear. He had turned from his manger to face the fray, and the way was open before him. Edwin cast an arm over his neck with a shout of recognition and joy.

'Rufus...oh, Rufus!'

He dropped his pikel, knotted a fist in the flowing mane, and leaped and scrambled astride the lofty back. What did it matter that he had neither saddle nor bridle, when he had ridden this mount bareback more times than he could remember, in the days before he fell utterly out of favour with the owner? He dug in his heels and pressed with his knees, and urged an all too willing accomplice into headlong flight.

If the grooms had been ready to tackle Edwin, once they realised his vocation was counterfeit, they were less eager to stand in the way of Rufus. He shot out of his stall like a cross-bow bolt, and they leaped apart before him in such haste that the older one fell backwards over a truss of hay, and measured his length on the floor a second time. Edwin lay low on the rippling shoulders, his fists in the light mane, whispering incoherent gratitude and encouragement into the laidback ears. They clattered out on to the triangle of the horse-fair, and by instinct Edwin used knee and heel to turn the horse away from the town and out along the Foregate.

The two who had mounted by the rear staircase, and had difficulty in getting the door open, not to mention finding it inexplicably unlocked in the first place, heard the stampede and rushed to stare out along the road.

'God save us!' gasped Wat, round-eyed. 'It's one of the brothers! What can he be at in such a hurry?'

At that moment the light wind filled Edwin's cowl and blew it back on to his shoulders, uncovering the bright tangle of hair and the boyish face. Will let out a wild yell, and began to scurry down the stairs. 'You see that? That's no tonsure, and no brother, either!

That's the lad the sheriff's hunting. Who else would be hiding in our barn?'

But Edwin was already away, nor was there a horse left in the stable of equal quality, to pursue him. The young groom had spoken the truth, Rufus was baulked and frustrated for want of exercise, and now, let loose, he was ready to gallop to his heart's content. There was now only one obstacle to freedom. Too late Edwin remembered Cadfael's warning not, in any circumstances to take the London road, for there was certainly a patrol out at St Giles, where the town suburbs ended, to check on all passing traffic in search of him. He recalled it only when he saw in the distance before him a party of four riders spread well across the road and approaching at a relaxed amble. The guard had just been relieved, and here was the off-duty party making its way back to the castle.

He could not possibly burst a way through that serried line, and the black gown would not deceive them for a moment, on a rider proceeding at this desperate speed. Edwin did the only thing possible. With pleading voice and urgent knees he checked and wheeled his displeased mount, and set off back the way he had come, at the same headlong gallop. And well behind him he heard a gleeful shout that told him he was now pursued by a posse of determined men-at-arms, fully persuaded they were on the heels of a miscreant, even if they were not yet certain of his identity.

Brother Mark, hurrying along the horse-fair after High Mass, primed with his part to enter the loft unobserved, so that no one should be able afterwards to swear that only one went in where two came out, arrived close to the barn just in time to hear the commotion of a hue and cry, and see Edwin on his elated war-horse come hurtling back along the Foregate, cowl and skirts streaming, head stooped low to the flying mane. He had never before set eyes on Edwin Gurney, but there was no doubt as to who this careering desperado must be; nor, alas, any doubt that Mark's own errand came much too late. The quarry was flushed from cover, though not yet taken. But there was nothing, nothing at all, Brother Mark could do to help him.

The head groom Will, a stout-hearted man, had hastily hauled out the best of the remaining horses in his care, and prepared to pursue the fugitive, but he had no more than heaved himself into the saddle when he beheld the chestnut thundering back again in the opposite direction. He spurred forward to try and intercept it, though the prospect was daunting; but his mount's courage failed of matching his, and it baulked and swerved aside before Rufus's stretched neck, laid-back ears and rolling eye. One of the undergrooms hurled a pikel towards the pounding hooves, but if truth be told rather half-heartedly, and Rufus merely made a startled side-wise bound, without checking speed, and was past and away towards the town.

Will might well have followed, though with small hope of keeping that yellow, billowing tail in sight; but by then the clamour of the pursuers was approaching along the Foregate, and he was only too glad to surrender the task to them. It was, after all, their business to apprehend malefactors, and whatever else this pseudo-monk had done, he had certainly stolen a horse belonging to the Widow Bonel, and in the abbey's care. Obviously the theft should be reported at once. He rode into the path of the galloping guards, waving a delaying hand, and all three of his colleagues closed in to give their versions of what had happened.

There was a substantial audience by then. Passers-by had happily declined to pass by such a promising mêlée, and people had darted out from nearby houses to discover what all the hard riding meant. During the pause to exchange information, several of the children had drawn close to listen and stare, and that in itself somewhat slowed the resumption of the chase. Mothers retrieved children, and managed to keep the way blocked a full minute more. But there seemed no reasonable explanation for the fact that at the last moment, when they were virtually launched, the horse under the captain of the guard suddenly shrieked indignantly, reared, and almost spilled his rider, who was not expecting any such disturbance, and had to spend some minutes mastering the affronted horse, before he could muster his men and gallop away after the fugitive.

Brother Mark, craning and peering with the rest of the curious, watched the guards stream away towards the town, secure that the chestnut horse had had time to get clean out of sight. The rest was up to Edwin Gurney. Mark folded his hands in his wide sleeves, drew his cowl well forward to shadow a modest face, and turned back towards the gatehouse of the abbey, with very mixed news. On the way he discarded the second pebble he had picked up by the barn. On his uncle's manor he had been set to work for his meagre keep at four years old, following the plough with a small sack full of stones, to scare off the birds that took the seed. It had taken him two years to discover that he sympathised with the hungry birds, and did not really want to harm them; but by then he was already a dead shot, and he had not lost his skills.

'And you followed as far as the bridge?' Cadfael questioned anxiously. 'And the bridge-keepers had not so much as seen him? And the sheriff's men had lost him?'

'Clean vanished,' Brother Mark reported with pleasure. 'He never crossed into the town, at least, not that way. If you ask me, he can't have turned from the road by any of the alleys short of the bridge, he wouldn't be sure he was out of sight. I think he must have dived down along the Gaye, the shoreward side where the orchard trees give some cover. But what he would do after that I can't guess. But they haven't taken him, that's certain. They'll be hounding his kin within the town, but they'll find nothing there.' He beamed earnestly into Cadfael's troubled face, and urged: 'You know you'll prove he has nothing to answer for. Why do you worry?'

It was more than enough worry to have someone

depending so absolutely on the victory of truth, and the credit with heaven of Brother Cadfael, but it seemed that this morning's events had cast no shadow upon young Mark, and that was matter for gratitude.

'Come to dinner,' said Cadfael thankfully, 'and then take your ease, for with such a faith as yours you can. I do believe when you come to cast a pebble with intent, it must hit the mark. Whoever named you foresaw your future. And since it arises, what is your own mark? A bishopric?'

'Pope or cardinal,' said Brother Mark happily. 'Nothing less.'

'Oh, no,' said Brother Cadfael seriously. 'Beyond bishop, and a pastoral cure, I think you would be wasted.'

All that day the sheriff's men hunted Edwin Gurney through the town, where they reckoned he must have sought help, somehow evading notice in crossing the bridge. Finding no trace there, they sent out patrols to cover all the major roads out of the peninsula. In a close loop of the Severn, Shrewsbury had only two bridges, one towards the abbey and London, by which he was thought to have entered, one towards Wales, with a fan of roads branching out westwards.

They were convinced that the fugitive would make for Wales, that being his quickest way out of their jurisdiction, though his future there might well be hazardous. So it came as a surprise when a party patrolling the abbey side of the river, where they had little expectation of picking up the trail, was accosted by an excited young person of about eleven, who ran to them through the fields to demand breathlessly if it was true the man they were looking for was in monk's gown, and riding a bright-brown horse with a primrose mane and tail. Yes, she had seen him, and only a short time since, breaking cautiously out of that copse and trotting away eastwards, as if he wanted to cross the next loop of the river and move round to join the highroad to London, some way past St Giles. Since he had first set out in that direction, and found the way blocked at the rim of the town, her report made sense. Evidently he had managed to find cover and lie up for a while, in the hope that the hunt would take the opposite direction, and now he felt secure in moving again. The girl said he might be making for the ford at Uffington.

They thanked her heartily, sent back one man to report the trail hot again and bring reinforcements after, and set off briskly for the ford. And Alys, having watched them out of sight, made her way back as briskly to the highroad and the bridge. No one was on the watch for eleven-year-old girls going in and out.

Beyond the ford at Uffington the hunters got their first glimpse of the quarry, jogging along almost sedately on the narrow road towards Upton. From the moment he turned and saw them, he flashed away at speed; the colour and the gait of the horse were unmistakable, and the pursuers could not but wonder why the rider had retained his purloined habit, which was now more liability than asset, for everyone in the countryside must be looking out for it.

It was then mid-afternoon, and the light beginning to dim. The chase went on for hours. The boy seemed to know every byway and every covert, and managed to lose them several times, and lead them into some unexpected and perilous places, often leaving the roads for marshy meadows where one stout man-at-arms was thrown into odorous bog, or broken places where it was soon impossible to see the easiest passage, and one horse picked up a stone and went lame. Through Atcham, Cound and Cressage he held them off, and from time to time lost them, until Rufus tired and stumbled in the woods beyond Acton, and they were on him and round him, grasping at gown and cowl and pinioning him fast. They pulled him down and tied his hands, and for the chase he had led them they gave him some rough handling, which he bore philosophically and in silence. All he asked was that the miles they had to go back to Shrewsbury should be taken at an easy pace, for the horse's sake.

At some stage he had rigged a serviceable bridle from the rope girdle of his habit. They borrowed that back to secure him behind the lightest weight among them, for fear he should leap clear even with bound hands, and make off into the darkening woods on foot. Thus they brought their prisoner back the lengthy journey to Shrewsbury, and turned in at the abbey gatehouse late in the evening. The stolen horse might as well be returned at once where he belonged; and since that was, at present, the only crime that stood manifestly proven against the culprit, his proper place, until further examination had been made of his deeds, was in the abbey prison. There he could safely be left to kick his heels until the law was ready to proceed against him on graver charges of acts committed outside the pale, and therefore within the sheriff's jurisdiction.

Prior Robert, courteously informed that the wanted youth was brought in captive, and must remain in abbey keeping at least overnight, was torn between satisfaction at the prospect of getting rid of the criminal implications of Master Bonel's death, in order to be able to deal more skilfully with the legal ones, and the vexation of having temporarily to accommodate the criminal within his own domain. Still, an arrest for the murder must follow in the morning, the inconvenience was not so great.

'You have this youth in the gatehouse now?' he asked the man-at-arms who had brought the news to his lodging.

'We have, Father. Two of your abbey sergeants are with him there, and if you please to give orders that they hold him in charge until tomorrow, the sheriff will certainly take him off your hands on the graver count. Would it please you come and examine him for yourself on the matter of the horse? If you see fit, there could be charges of assault against your grooms, a serious matter even without the theft.'

Prior Robert was not immune to human curiosity,

and was not adverse to taking a look at this youthful demon who had poisoned his own stepfather and led the sheriff's men a dance over half the shire. 'I will come,' he said. 'The church must not turn its back upon the sinner, but only deplore the sin.'

In the porter's room at the gatehouse the boy sat stolidly on a bench opposite the welcome fire, hunched defensively against the world, but looking far from cowed, for all his bruises and wariness. The abbey sergeants and the sheriff's patrol circled him with brooding eyes and hectoring questions, which he answered only when he chose to do so, and then briefly. Several of them were soiled and mud-stained from the hunt, one or two had scratches and bruises of their own to show. The boy's bright eyes flickered from one to another, and it even seemed that his lips twitched with the effort to suppress a smile when he contemplated the one who had gone head over heels in the meadows near Cound. They had stripped his borrowed habit from him and restored it to the porter's care; the boy showed now slender and light-haired, smooth and fair of skin, with ingenuous-seeming hazel eyes. Prior Robert was somewhat taken aback by his youth and comeliness; truly the devil can assume fair shapes!

'So young and marred!' he said aloud. The boy was not meant to hear that, it was uttered in the doorway as Robert entered, but at fourteen the hearing is keen. 'So, boy,' said the prior, drawing near, 'you are the troubler of our peace. You have much upon your conscience, and I fear it is even late to pray that you may have time to amend. I shall so pray. You know, for you are old enough to know, that murder is mortal sin.'

The boy looked him in the eye, and said with emphatic composure: 'I am not a murderer.'

'Oh, child, is it now of any avail to deny what is known? You might as well say that you did not steal a horse from our barn this morning, when four of our servants and many other people saw the act committed.'

'I did not *steal* Rufus,' the boy retorted promptly and

131

firmly. 'He is mine. He was my stepfather's property, and I am my stepfather's heir, for his agreement with the abbey has never been ratified, and the will that made me his heir is sound as gold. What belongs to me how could I steal? From whom?'

'Wretched child,' protested the prior, bristling at such bold defiance, and even more at a dawning suspicion that this imp, in spite of his dire situation, was daring to enjoy himself, 'think what you say! You should rather be repenting while you have time. Have you not yet realised that the murderer cannot live to inherit from his victim?'

'I have said, and say again, I am not a murderer. I deny, on my soul, on the altar, on whatever you wish, that ever I did my stepfather harm. Therefore Rufus *is* mine. Or when the will is proven, and my overlord gives his consent as he promised, Rufus and Mallilie and all *will* be mine. I have committed no crime, and nothing you can do or say can make me admit to any. And nothing you can do,' he added, his eyes suddenly flashing, 'can ever make me guilty of any.'

'You waste your goodwill, Father Prior,' growled the sheriff's sergeant, 'he's an obdurate young wretch meant for the gallows, and his come-uppance will be short.' But under Robert's august eye he refrained from clouting the impudent brat round the ears, as otherwise he might well have done. 'Think no more of him, but let your servants clap him into safe hold in your cell here, and put him out of your mind as worth no more pains. The law will take care of him.'

'See that he has food,' said Robert, not altogether without compassion, and remembering that this child had been in the saddle and in hiding all the day, 'and let his bed be hard, but dry and warm enough. And should he relent and ask...Boy, listen to me, and give a thought to your soul's welfare. Will you have one of the brothers come and reason and pray with you before you sleep?'

The boy looked up with a sudden sparkle in his eye that might have been penitent hope, but looked more like mischief, and said with deceptive meekness: 'Yes, and gratefully, if you could be so kind as to send for Brother Cadfael.' It was time, after all, to take thought for his own situation, he had surely done enough now.

He expected the name to raise a frown, and so it did, but Robert had offered a grace, and could not now withdraw it or set conditions upon it. With dignity he turned to the porter, who hovered at the door. 'Ask Brother Cadfael to come here to us at once. You may tell him it is to give counsel and guidance to a prisoner.'

The porter departed. It was almost the hour for retirement, and most of the brothers would certainly be in the warming-room, but Cadfael was not there, nor was Brother Mark. The porter found them in the workshop in the garden, not even compounding mysteries, either, but sitting somewhat glumly, talking in low and anxious tones. The news of the capture had not yet gone round; by day it would have been known everywhere within minutes. It was common knowledge, of course, how the sheriff's men had spent their day, but it was not yet common knowledge with what an achievement they had crowned it.

'Brother Cadfael, you're wanted at the gatehouse,' announced the porter, leaning in at the doorway. And as Cadfael looked up at him in surprise: 'There's a young fellow there asks for you as his spiritual adviser, though if you want my view, he's very much in command of his own spirit, and has let Prior Robert know it, too. A company of the sheriff's men rode in towards the end of Compline with a prisoner. Yes, they've taken young Gurney at last.'

So that was how it had ended, after all Mark's efforts and prayers, after all his own ineffective reasonings and seekings and faith. Cadfael got up in grieving haste. 'I'll come to him. With all my heart I'll come. Now we have the whole battle on our hands, and little time left. The poor lad! But why have they not taken him straight into the town?' Though of that one small mercy he was glad, seeing he himself was confined within the abbey walls, and only this odd chance provided him with a brief meeting.

'Why, the only thing they can charge him with, and nobody can question, is stealing the horse he rode off on this morning, and that was from our premises and our care, the abbey court has rights in it. In the morn they'll fetch him away on the count of murder.'

Brother Mark fell in at their heels and followed to the gatehouse, altogether cast down and out of comfort, unable to find a hopeful word to say. He felt in his heart that that was sin, the sin of despair; not despair for himself, but despair of truth and justice and right, and the future of wretched mankind. Nobody had bidden him attend, but he went, all the same, a soul committed to a cause about which, in fact, he knew very little, except the youth of the protagonist, and the absolute nature of Cadfael's faith in him, and that was enough.

Cadfael entered the porter's room with a heavy heart but not in despair; it was a luxury he could not afford. All eyes turned upon him, understandably, since he entered upon a heavy silence. Robert had abandoned his kindly meant but patronising exhortations, and the men of law had given up the attempt to get any admissions out of their captive, and were content to see him safely under lock and key, and get to their beds in the castle. A ring of large, well-equipped men on guard round a willowy lad in country homespun, bareheaded and cloakless on a frosty night, who sat braced and neat and alert on a bench by the wall, pleasantly flushed now from the fire, and looking, incredibly, almost complacent. His eyes met Brother Cadfael's eyes, and danced; clear, dark-fringed, greenish eyes. His hair was light brown, like seasoned oak. He was lightly built but tall for his years. He was tired, sleepy, bruised and dirty, and behind the wary eyes and solemn face he was undoubtedly laughing.

Brother Cadfael looked long, and understood much, enough at that moment to have no great worries about what as yet he did not understand. He looked round the attentive circle, looked last and longest at Prior Robert.

'Father Prior, I am grateful that you sent for me, and I welcome the duty laid on me, to do what may be done for the prisoner. But I must tell you that these gentlemen are in some error. I cast no doubt on what they may have to report of how this boy was taken, but I do advise them to make enquiry how and where he spent this morning's hours, when he is said to have escaped from the abbey barn on the horse belonging to Mistress Bonel. Gentlemen,' he informed the sheriff's bewildered patrol very gravely, 'this is not Edwin Gurney you have captured, but his nephew, Edwy Bellecote.'

Chapter 7

The abbey prison was two little cells attached to the
rear of the gatehouse, very clean, furnished with bench-
beds no worse than the novices endured, and very
rarely occupied. The summer period of Saint Peter's
fair was the chief populator of the cells, since it could
be relied upon to provide two happy drunken servants
or lay brothers nightly, who slept off their excesses and
accepted their modest fines and penances without ran-
cour, thinking the game well worth the candle. From
time to time some more serious disturbance might cast
up an inmate, some ill-balanced brother who nursed a
cloistered hate long enough to attempt violence, or a
lay servant who stole, or a novice who offended too
grossly against the imposed code. The abbey court was
not a busy one.

In one of the two cells Brother Cadfael and Edwy sat
side by side, warmly and companionably. There was a
grille in the door, but it was most improbable that anyone was paying attention to anything that could be
heard through it. The brother who held the keys was
sleepy, and in any case indifferent to the cause that
had brought him a prisoner. The difficulty would probably be to batter loudly enough to wake him when
Cadfael wanted to leave.

'It wasn't so hard,' said Edwy, sitting back with a
grateful sigh after demolishing the bowl of porridge a
tolerant cook had provided him, 'there's a cousin of
father's lives along the riverside, just beyond your property of the Gaye, he has an orchard there, and a shed
for the donkey and cart, big enough to hide Rufus. His

boy brought word into the town to us, and I took father's horse and came out to meet Edwin there. Nobody was looking for a bony old piebald like our Japhet, I never got a second glance as I crossed the bridge, and I didn't hurry. Alys came with me pillion, and kept watch in case they got close. Then we changed clothes and horses, and Edwin made off towards—'

'Don't tell me!' said Cadfael quickly.

'No, you can truly say you don't know. Plainly not the way I went. They were slow sighting me,' said Edwy scornfully, 'even with Alys helping them. But once they had me in view it was a matter of how long I could keep them busy, to give him time to get well away. I could have taken them still further, but Rufus was tiring, so I let them have me. I had to, in the end, it kept them happy several more hours, and they sent one man ahead to call off the hunt. Edwin's had a clear run. Now what do you think they'll do with me?'

'If you hadn't already been in abbey charge, and the prior by, at that,' said Cadfael frankly, 'they'd have had the hide off you for leading them such a dance and making such fools of them. I wouldn't say Prior Robert himself wouldn't have liked to do as much, but dignity forbids, and authority forbids letting the secular arm skin you on his behalf. Though I fancy,' he said with sympathy, viewing the blue bruises that were beginning to show on Edwy's jaw and cheekbone, 'they've already paid you part of your dues.'

The boy shrugged disdainfully. 'I can't complain. And it wasn't all one way. You should have seen the sergeant flop belly-down into the bog...and heard him when he got up. It was good sport, and we got Edwin away. And I've never had such a horse under me before, it was well worth it. But now what's to happen? They can't accuse *me* of murder, or of stealing Rufus, or even the gown, because I was never near the barn this morning, and there are plenty of witnesses to where I was, about the shop and the yard.'

'I doubt if you've broken any law,' agreed Cadfael, 'but you have made the law look very foolish, and no man in authority and office enjoys that. They could well keep you in close hold in the castle for a while, for helping a wanted man to escape. They may even threaten you in the hope of fetching Edwin back to get you out of trouble.'

Edwy shook his head vigorously. 'He need take no notice of that, he knows in the end there's nothing criminal they can lay against me. And I can sit out threats better than he. He loses his temper. He's getting better, but he has far to go yet.' Was he as buoyant about his prospects as he made out? Cadfael could not be quite sure, but certainly this elder of the pair had turned his four months seniority into a solid advantage, perhaps by reason of feeling responsible for his improbable uncle from the cradle. 'I can keep my mouth shut and wait,' said Edwy serenely.

'Well, since Prior Robert has so firmly demanded that the sheriff come in person tomorrow to remove you,' sighed Cadfael, 'I will at least make sure of being present, and try what can be got for you. The prior has given me a spiritual charge, and I'll stand fast on it. And now you'd better get your rest. I am supposed to be here to exhort you to an amended life, but to tell the truth, boy, I find your life no more in need of amendment than mine, and I think it would be presumption in me to meddle. But if you'll join your voice to mine in the night prayers, I think God may be listening.'

'Willingly,' said Edwy blithely, and plumped to his knees like a cheerful child, with reverently folded hands and closed eyes. In the middle of the prayers before sleeping his lips fluttered in a brief smile; perhaps he was remembering the extremely secular language of the sergeant rising dripping from the bog.

Cadfael was up before Prime, alert in case the prisoner's escort should come early. Prior Robert had been extremely angry at last night's comedy, but grasped readily at the plain fact that it gave him full justification for demanding that the sheriff should at once relieve him of an offender who had turned out to be no concern of his at all. This was not the boy who had taken away a Benedictine habit and a horse in Benedictine care, he was merely the mischievous brat who had worn the one and ridden the other to the ludicrous discomfiture of several gullible law officers. They could have him, and welcome; but the prior considered that it was due to his dignity—in this mood fully abbatial—that the senior officer then in charge, sheriff or deputy, should come in person to make amends for the inconvenience to which the abbey had been subjected, and remove the troublesome element. Robert wanted a public demonstration that henceforth all responsibility lay with the secular arm, and none within his sacred walls.

Brother Mark hovered close at Cadfael's elbow as the escort rode in, about half past eight in the morning, before the second Mass. Four mounted men-at-arms, and a spruce, dark, lightly built young nobleman on a tall, gaunt and self-willed horse, dappled from cream to almost black. Mark heard Brother Cadfael heave a great, grateful sigh at the sight of him, and felt his own heart rise hopefully at the omen.

'The sheriff must have gone south to keep the feast with the king,' said Cadfael with immense satisfaction. 'God is looking our way at last. That is not Gilbert Prestcote, but his deputy, Hugh Beringar of Maesbury.'

'Now,' said Beringar briskly, a quarter of an hour later, 'I have placated the prior, promised him deliverance from the presence of this desperate bravo, sent him off to Mass and chapter in tolerable content, and retrieved you, my friend, from having to accompany him, on the grounds that you have questions to answer.' He closed the door of the room in the gatehouse from which all his men-at-arms had been dismissed to wait his pleasure, and came and sat down opposite Cadfael at the table. 'And so you have, though not, quite as he supposes. So now, before we go and pick this small crab out of his shell, tell me everything you know about this curious business. I know you must know more of it than any other man, however confidently my sergeant sets

139

out his case. Such a break in the monastic monotony could never occur, and you not get wind of it and be there in the thick of it. Tell me everything.'

And now that it was Beringar in the seat of authority, while Prestcote attended dutifully at his sovereign lord's festal table, Cadfael saw no reason for reserve, at least so far as his own part was concerned. And all, or virtually all, was what he told.

'He came to you, and you hid him,' mused Beringar.

'I did. So I would again, in the same circumstances.'

'Cadfael, you must know as well as I the strength of the case against this boy. Who else has anything to gain? Yet I know you, and where you have doubts, I shall certainly not be without them.'

'I have no doubts,' said Cadfael firmly. 'The boy is innocent even of the thought of murder. And poison is so far out of his scope, he never would or could conceive the idea. I tested them both, when they came, and they neither of them even knew how the man had died, they believed me when I said he had been cut down in his blood. I stuck the means of murder under the child's nose, and he never paled. All it meant to him was a mild memory of sniffing the same sharp smell while Brother Rhys was having his shoulders rubbed in the infirmary.'

'I take your word for all that,' said Beringar, 'and it is good evidence, but it is not in itself proof. How if we should both of us underestimate the cunning of the young, simply because they *are* young?'

'True,' agreed Cadfael with a wry grin, 'you are none so old yourself, and of your cunning, as I know, the limit has not yet been found. But trust me, these two are not of the same make as you. I have known them, you have not; agreed? I have my duty to do, according to such lights as I see. So have you your duty to do, according to your office and commission. I don't quarrel with that. But at this moment, Hugh, I don't know and have no means of guessing where Edwin Gurney is, or I might well urge him to give himself up to you and rely on your integrity. You will not need me to tell you

140

that this loyal nephew of his, who has taken some sharp knocks for him, does know where he is, or at least knows where he set out to go. You may ask him, but of course he won't tell you. Neither for your style of questioning nor Prestcote's.'

Hugh drummed his fingers on the table, and pondered in silence for a moment. 'Cadfael, I must tell you I shall pursue the hunt for the boy to the limit, and not spare any tricks in the doing, so look to your own movements.'

'That's fair dealing,' said Cadfael simply. 'You and I have been rivals in trickery before, and ended as allies. But as for my movements, you'll find them monstrously dull. Did Prior Robert not tell you? I'm confined within the abbey walls, I may not go beyond.'

Hugh's agile black brows shot up to meet his hair. 'Good God, for what cloistered crime?' His eyes danced. 'What have you been about, to incur such a ban?'

'I spent too long in talk with the widow, and a stretched ear gathered that we had known each other very well, years ago, when we were young.' That was one thing he had not thought necessary to tell, but there was no reason to withhold it from Hugh. 'You asked me, once, how it came I had never married, and I told you I once had some idea of the kind, before I went to the Holy Land.'

'I do remember! You even mentioned a name. By now, you said, she must have children and grandchildren... Is it really so, Cadfael? This lady is your Richildis?'

'This lady,' said Cadfael with emphasis, 'is indeed Richildis, but mine she is *not*. Two husbands ago I had a passing claim on her, and that's all.'

'I must see her! The charmer who caught your eye must be worth cultivating. If you were any other man I should say this greatly weakens the force of your championship of her son, but knowing you, I think any scamp of his age in trouble would have you by the nose. I will see her, however, she may need advice or help,

141

for it seems there's a legal tangle there that will take some unravelling.'

'There's another thing you can do, that may help to prove to you what I can only urge. I told you the boys says he threw into the river an inlaid wooden box, quite small.' Cadfael described it minutely. 'If that could come to light, it would greatly strengthen his story, which I, for one, believe. I cannot go out and contact the fishermen and watermen of Severn, and ask them to keep watch for such a small thing in the places they'll know of, where things afloat do wash up. But you can, Hugh. You can have it announced in Shrewsbury and downstream. It's worth the attempt.'

'That I'll certainly do,' said Beringar readily. 'There's a man whose grim business it is, when some poor soul drowns in Severn, to know exactly where the body will come ashore. Whether small things follow the same eddies is more than I know, but *he*'ll know. I'll have him take this hunt in charge. And now, if we've said all, we'd better go and see this twin imp of yours. Lucky for him you knew him, they'd hardly have believed it if he'd told them himself that he was the wrong boy. Are they really so like?'

'No, no more than a general family look about them if you know them, or see them side by side. But apart, a man might be in doubt, unless he did know them well. And your men were after the rider of that horse, and sure who it must be. Come and see!'

He was still in doubt, as they went together to the cell where Edwy waited, by this time in some trepidation, exactly what Beringar meant to do with his prisoner, though he had no fear that any harm would come to the boy. Whatever Hugh might think about Edwin's guilt or innocence, he was not the man to lean too heavily upon Edwy's staunch solidarity with his kinsman.

'Come forth, Edwy, into the daylight,' said Beringar, holding the cell door wide, 'and let me look at you. I want to be in no doubt which of you I have on my hands, the next time you change places.' And when Edwy obediently rose and stepped warily out into the court, after one nervous side-glance to make sure Brother Cadfael was there, the deputy sheriff took him by the chin and raised his face gently enough, and studied it attentively. The bruises were purple this morning, but the hazel eyes were bright. 'I'll know you again,' said Hugh confidently. 'Now, young sir! You have cost us a great deal of time and trouble, but I don't propose to waste even more by taking it out of your skin. I'll ask you but once: Where is Edwin Gurney?'

The phrasing of the question and the cut of the dark face left in doubt what was to happen if he got no answer; in spite of the mild tone, the potentialities were infinite. Edwy moistened dry lips, and said in the most conciliatory and respectful tone Cadfael had heard from him: 'Sir, Edwin is my kin and my friend, and if I had been willing to tell where he is, I should not have gone to such pains to help him get there. I think you must see that I can't and won't betray him.'

Beringar looked at Brother Cadfael, and kept his face grave but for the sparkle in his eye. 'Well, Edwy, I expected no other, to tell the truth. Nobody does ill to keep faith. But I want you where I may lay hand on you whenever I need to, and be sure you are not stravaiging off on another wild rescue.'

Edwy foresaw a cell in Shrewsbury castle, and stiffened a stoical face to meet the worst.

'Give me your parole not to leave your father's house and shop,' said Beringar, 'until I give you your freedom, and you may go home. Why should we feed you at public expense over the Christmas feast, when I fancy your word, once given, will be your bond? What do you say?'

'Oh, I do give you my word!' gasped Edwy, startled and radiant with relief. 'I won't leave the yard until you give me leave. And I thank you!'

'Good! And I take your word, as you may take mine. My task, Edwy, is not to convict your uncle, or any man, of murder at all costs, it is to discover truly who did commit murder, and that I mean to do. Now come,

I'll take you home myself, a word with your parents may not come amiss.'

They were gone before High Mass at ten, Beringar with Edwy pillion behind him, the raw-boned dapple being capable of carrying double his master's light weight, the men-at-arms of the escort two by two behind. Only in the middle of Mass, when his mind should have been on higher things, did Cadfael recall vexedly two more concessions he might have gained if he had thought of them in time. Martin Bellecote, for certain, was now without a horse, and the abbey was willing to part with Rufus, while Richildis would surely be glad to have him settled with her son-in-law, and no longer be beholden to the abbey for his keep. It would probably have tickled Beringar's humour to restore the carpenter a horse, on the pretext of relieving the abbey of an incubus. But the other thing was more important. He had meant to go searching the shores of the pond for the poison vial the previous day, and instead had found himself confined within the walls. Why had he not remembered to ask Beringar to follow up that tenuous but important line of inquiry, while he was asking him to have the watermen watch for the pear-wood reliquary? Now it was too late, and he could not follow Beringar into the town to remedy the omission. Vexed with himself, he even snapped at Brother Mark, when that devoted young man questioned him about the outcome of the morning's events. Undeterred, Mark followed him, after dinner, to his sanctuary in the garden.

'I am an old fool,' said Cadfael, emerging from his depression, 'and have lost a fine chance of getting my work done for me, in places where I can no longer go myself. But that's no fault of yours, and I'm sorry I took it out on you.'

'If it's something you want done outside the walls,' said Mark reasonably, 'why should I be of less use today than I was yesterday?'

'True, but I've involved you enough already. And if I had had good sense I could have got the law to do it,

144

which would have been far better. Though this is not at all dangerous or blameworthy,' he reminded himself, taking heart, 'it is only to search once again for a bottle...'

'Last time,' said Mark thoughtfully, 'we were looking for something we hoped would *not* be a bottle. Pity we did not find it.'

'True, but this time it *should* be a bottle, if the omen of Beringar's coming instead of Prestcote means anything. And I'll tell you where.' And so he did, pointing the significance of a window open to the south, even in light frost, on a bright day.

'I'm gone,' said Brother Mark. 'And you may sleep the noon away with a good conscience. My eyes are younger than yours.'

'Mind, take a napkin, and if you find it, wrap it loosely, and touch only as you must. I need to see how the oil has run and dried.'

It was when the afternoon light was dimming that Brother Mark came back. There was half an hour yet before Vespers, but from this time on any search for a small thing in a narrow slope of grass would have been a blind and hopeless quest. Winter days begin so late and end so early, like the dwindling span of life past three score.

Cadfael had taken Brother Mark at his word, and dozed the afternoon away. There was nowhere he could go, nothing he could do here, no work needing his efforts. But suddenly he started out of a doze, and there was Brother Mark, a meagre but erect and austere figure, standing over him with a benign smile on the ageless, priestly face Cadfael had seen in him ever since his scared, resentful, childish entry within these walls. The voice, soft, significant, delighted, rolled the years back; he was still eighteen, and a young eighteen at that.

'Wake up! I have something for you!'

Like a child coming on a father's birthday: 'Look! I made it for you myself!'

The carefully folded white napkin was lowered gently into Cadfael's lap. Brother Mark delicately turned back the folds, and exposed the contents with a gesture of such shy triumph that the analogy was complete. There it lay to be seen, a small, slightly mis-shapen vial of greenish glass, coloured somewhat differently all down one side, where yellowish brown coated the green, from a residue of liquid that still moved very sluggishly within.

'Light me that lamp!' said Cadfael, gathering the napkin in both hands to raise the prize nearer his eyes. Brother Mark laboured industriously with flint and tinder, and struck a spark into the wick of the little oil-lamp in its clay saucer, but the conflict of light, within and without, hardly bettered the view. There was a stopper made of a small plug of wood wrapped in a twist of wool cloth. Cadfael sniffed eagerly at the cloth on the side that was coloured brown. The odour was there, faint but unmistakable, his nose knew it well. Frost had dulled but still retained it. There was a long trail of thin, crusted oil, long dried, down the outside of the vial.

'Is it right? Have I brought you what you wanted?' Brother Mark hovered, pleased and anxious.

'Lad, you have indeed! This little thing carried death in it, and, see, it can be hidden within a man's hand. It lay thus, on its side, as you found it? Where the residue has gathered and dried the length of the vial within? And without, too.... It was stoppered and thrust out of sight in haste, surely about someone's person, and if he has not the mark of it somewhere about him still, this long ooze of oil from the leaking neck is a great deceiver. Now sit down here and tell me where and how you found it, for much depends on that. And can you find the exact spot again, without fail?'

'I can, for I marked it.' Flushed with pleasure at having pleased, Brother Mark sat down, leaning eagerly against Cadfael's sleeve. 'You know the houses there have a strip of garden going down almost to the water, there is only a narrow footpath along the edge

146

of the pond below. I did not quite like to invent a reason for entering the gardens, and besides, they are narrow and steep. It would not be difficult to throw something of any weight from the house right to the edge of the water, and beyond—even for a woman, or a man in a hurry. So I went first along the path, the whole stretch of it that falls within reach from the kitchen window, the one you said was open that day. But it was not there I found it.'

'It was not?'

'No, but beyond. There's a fringe of ice round the edge of the pond now, but the current from the mill-race keeps all the middle clear. I found the bottle on my way back, after I'd searched all the grass and bushes there, and thought to look on the other side of the path, along the rim of the water. And it was there, on its side half under the ice, held fast. I've driven a hazel twig into the ground opposite the place, and the hole I prised it from will say unless we have a thaw. I think the bottle was thrown clear of whatever ice there may have been then, but not far enough out to be taken away by the mill current, and because the stopper was in it, it floated, and drifted back to be caught in the next frost. But, Cadfael, it couldn't have been thrown from the kitchen window, it was too far along the path.'

'You're sure of that? Then where? Is it the distance that seems too great?'

'No, but the direction. It's much too far to the right, and there's a bank of bushes between. The ground lies wrong for it. If a man threw it from the kitchen window it would not go where I found it, it could not. But from the window of the other room it very well could. Do you remember, Cadfael, was that window unshuttered, too? The room where they were dining?'

Cadfael thought back to the scene within the house, when Richildis met him and ushered him desperately through to the bedchamber, past the disordered table laid with three trenchers. 'It was, it was!—the shutter was set open, for the midday sun came in there.' From that room Edwin had rushed in indignant offence, and

147

out through the kitchen, where he was thought to have committed his crime and rid himself of the evidence later. But not for a moment had he been alone in that inner room; only in his precipitate flight had he been out of sight of all the household.

'You see, Mark, what this means? From what you say, this vial was either thrown from the window of the inner room, or else someone walked along that path and threw it into the pond. And neither of those things could Edwin have done. He might, as they suppose, have halted for a moment in the kitchen, but he certainly did not go along the path by the pond before making for the bridge, or Aelfric would have overtaken him. No, he would have been ahead of him, or met him at the gate! Nor did he have the opportunity, at any time afterwards, to dispose of the vial there. He hid with his bitter mood until Edwy found him, and from then on they were both in hiding until they came to me. This small thing, Mark, is proof that Edwin is as clear of guilt as you or I.'

'But it does not prove who the guilty man is,' said Mark.

'It does not. But if the bottle was indeed thrown from the window of that inner room, then it was done long after the death, for I doubt if anyone was alone in there for a moment until after the sergeant had come and gone. And if the one responsible carried this somewhere on him all that time, as ill-stoppered as it is now, then the marks of it will be on him. He might try to scrub the stain away, but it will not be easily removed. And who can afford to discard cotte or gown? No, the signs will be there to be found.'

'But what if it was someone else, not of the household, who did the deed, and flung the vial from the pathway? Once you did wonder, about the cook and the scullions...'

'I won't say it's impossible. But is it likely? From the path a man could make very sure the vial went into the mid-current and the deep of the pool, and even if it did not sink—though he would have had time in that case to ensure that it did!—it would be carried away back to the brook and the river. But you see it fell short, and lay for us to find.'

'What must we do now?' asked Brother Mark, roused and ready.

'We must go to Vespers, my son, or we shall be late. And tomorrow we must get you, and this witness with you, to Hugh Beringar in Shrewsbury.'

The lay contingent at Vespers was always thin, but never quite absent. That evening Martin Bellecote had come down out of the town to give a word of hearty thanks first to God, and then to Cadfael, for his son's safe return. After the service ended he waited in the cloister for the brothers to emerge, and came to meet Cadfael at the south door.

'Brother, it's to you we owe it that the lad's home again, if it is with a flea in his ear, and not lying in some den in the castle for his pains.'

'Not to me, for I could not free him. It was Hugh Beringar who saw fit to send him home. And take my word, in all that may happen you can rely on Beringar for a decent, fair-minded man who'll not tolerate injustice. In any encounter with him, tell him the truth.'

Bellecote smiled, but wryly. 'Truth, but not all the truth, even to him—though he showed generous indeed to my boy, I grant you. But until the other one's as safe as Edwy, I keep my own counsel on where he is. But to you, brother...'

'No,' said Cadfael quickly, 'not to me, either though soon, I hope, there may be no reason left for hiding him. But that time's not yet. Is all well, then, with your own family? And Edwy none the worse?'

'Never a whit the worse. Without a bruise or two he'd have valued his adventure less. It was all his own devising. But it's caused him to draw in his horns for a while. I never knew him so biddable before, and that's no bad thing. He's working with more zeal than he commonly shows. Not that we're overburdened with work, this close to the feast, but wanting Edwin, and now Meurig's gone to keep Christmas with his kin, I've enough on hand to keep my scamp busy.'

'So Meurig goes to his own people, does he?'

'Regularly for Christmas and Easter. He has cousins and an uncle or so up in the borders. He'll be back before the year ends. He sets store by his own folk, does Meurig.'

Yes, so he had said on the day Cadfael first encountered him. 'My kinship is my mother's kinship, I go with my own. My father was not a Welshman.' Naturally he would want to go home for the feast.

'May we all be at peace for the Lord's nativity!' said Cadfael, with heartier optimism since the discovery of the small witness now lying on a shelf in his workshop.

'Amen to that, brother! And I and my household thank you for your stout aid, and if ever you need ours, you have but to say.'

Martin Bellecote went back to his shop with duty done, and Brother Cadfael and Brother Mark went to supper with duty still to be done.

'I'll go early into the town,' said Brother Mark, earnestly whispering in Cadfael's ear in a corner of the chapter-house, during some very lame readings in the Latin by Brother Francis, after the meal. 'I'll absent myself from Prime, what does it matter if I incur penance?'

'You will not,' Brother Cadfael whispered back firmly. 'You'll wait until after dinner, when you are freed to your own work, as this will truly be legitimate work for you, the best you could be about. I will not have you flout any part of the rule.'

'As *you* would not dream of doing, of course!' breathed Mark, and his plain, diffident face brightened beautifully into a grin he might have borrowed from Edwin or Edwy.

'For no reason but matter of life and death. And owning my fault! And you are not me, and should not be copying my sins. It will be all the same, after dinner or before,' he said reassuringly. 'You'll ask for Hugh Beringar—no one else, mind, I would not be sure of any other as I am of him. Take him and show him where you found the vial, and I think Edwin's family will soon be able to call him home again.'

Their planning was largely vain. The next morning's chapter undid such arrangements as they had made, and changed everything.

Brother Richard the sub-prior rose, before the minor matters of business were dealt with, to say that he had an item of some urgency, for which he begged the prior's attention.

'Brother Cellarer has received a messenger from our sheepfold near Rhydycroesau, by Oswestry. Lay Brother Barnabas is fallen ill with a bad chest, and is in fever, and Brother Simon is left to take care of all the flock there alone. But more than this, he is doubtful of his skill to tend the sick brother successfully, and asks, if it's possible, that someone of more knowledge should come to help him for a while.'

'I have always thought,' said Prior Robert, frowning, 'that we should have more than two men there. We run two hundred sheep on those hills, and it is a remote place. But how did Brother Simon manage to send word, since he is the only able man left there?'

'Why, he took advantage of the fortunate circumstances that our steward is now in charge at the manor of Mallilie. It seems it is only a few miles from Rhydycroesau. Brother Simon rode there and asked that word be sent, and a groom was despatched at once. No time has been lost, if we can send a helper today.'

The mention of Mallilie had caused the prior to prick up his ears. It had also made Cadfael start out of his own preoccupations, since this so clearly had a bearing on the very problems he was pondering. So Mallilie was but a few short miles from the abbey sheepfolds near Oswestry! He had never stopped to consider that the exact location of the manor might have any significance, and this abrupt enlightenment started a number of mental hares out of their forms in bewildering flight.

151

'Clearly we must do so,' said Robert, and almost visibly reminded himself that the errand could with propriety be laid upon the abbey's most skilled herbalist and apothecary, which would effectively remove him not only from all contact with the Widow Bonel, but also from his meddlesome insistence on probing the unfortunate events which had made her a widow. The prior turned his silver, stately head and looked directly at Brother Cadfael, something he normally preferred not to do. The same considerations had dawned upon Cadfael, with the same pleasing effect. If I had devised this myself, he was thinking, it could not have been more apposite. Now young Mark can leave the errand to me, and remain here blameless.

'Brother Cadfael, it would seem this is a duty for you, who are accomplished in medicines. Can you at once put together all such preparations as may be needed for our sick brother?'

'I can and will, Father,' said Cadfael, so heartily that for a moment Prior Robert recoiled into doubt of his own wisdom and penetration. Why should the man be so happy at the prospect of a long winter ride, and hard work being both doctor and shepherd at the end of it? When he had been so assiduously poking his nose into the affairs of the Bonel household here? But the distance remained a guarantee; from Rhydycroesau he would be in no position to meddle further.

'I trust it may not be for very long. We shall say prayers for Brother Barnabas, that he may rally and thrive. You can again send word by the grooms at Mallilie, should there be need. And is your novice Mark well grounded, enough for minor ailments in your absence? In cases of serious illness we may call on the physician.'

'Brother Mark is devoted and able,' said Cadfael, with almost paternal pride, 'and can be trusted absolutely, for if he feels himself in need of better counsel he will say so with modesty. And he has a good supply of all those remedies that may most be needed at this season. We have taken pains to provide against an ill winter.'

'That's very well. Then in view of the need, you may leave chapter and make ready. Take a good mule from the stables, and have food with you for the way, and make sure you're well provided for such an illness as Brother Barnabas seems to have contracted. If there is any case in the infirmary you feel you should visit before leaving, do so. Brother Mark shall be sent to you, you may have advice for him before you go.'

Brother Cadfael went out from the chapter-house and left them to their routine affairs. God is still looking our way, he thought, bustling blithely into his workshop and raking the shelves for all that he needed. Medicines for throat, chest, head, an unguent for rubbing into the chest, goose-grease and strong herbs. The rest was warmth and care and proper food. They had hens at Rhydycroesau, and their own good milch-cow, fed through the winter. And last, a thing he need take only into Shrewsbury, the little green glass vial, still wrapped in its napkin.

Brother Mark came with a rush and out of breath, sent from his Latin studies under Brother Paul. 'They say you're going away, and I'm to be custodian here. Oh, Cadfael, how shall I manage without you? And what of Hugh Beringar, and this proof we have for him?'

'Leave that to me now,' said Cadfael. 'To go to Rhydycroesau one must go through the town, I'll bear it to the castle myself. You pay attention only to what you've learned from me, for I know how well it's been learned, and I shall be here with you in spirit every moment. Imagine that you ask me, and you'll find the answer.' He had a jar of unguent in one hand, he reached the other with absent affection and patted the young, smooth tonsure ringed by rough, thick, spiky straw-coloured hair. 'It's only for a short while, we'll have Brother Barnabas on his feet in no time. And listen, child dear, the manor of Mallilie, I find, is but a short way from where I shall be, and it seems to me that the answer to what we need to know may be there, and not here.'

'Do you think so?' said Brother Mark hopefully, forgetting his own anxieties.

'I do, and I have a thought—no more than the gleam of an idea, that they loosed in me at chapter... Now make yourself useful! Go and bespeak me a good mule at the stables, and see all these things into the saddlebags for me. I have an errand to the infirmary before I leave.'

Brother Rhys was in his privileged place by the fire, hunched in his chair in a contented half-doze, but awake enough to open one eye pretty sharply at every movement and word around him. He was in the mood to welcome a visitor, and brightened into something approaching animation when Cadfael told him that he was bound for the north-west of the county, to the sheepfolds of Rhydycroesau.

'Your own countryside, brother! Shall I carry your greetings to the borderland? You'll still have kinsfolk there, surely, three generations of them.'

'I have so!' Brother Rhys bared toothless gums in a dreamy smile. 'If you should happen to meet with my cousin Cynfrith ap Rhys, or his brother Owain, give them my blessings. Ay, there's a mort of my people in those parts. Ask after my niece Angharad, my sister Marared's girl—my youngest sister, that is, the one who married Ifor ap Morgan. I doubt Ifor's dead before this, but if you should hear of him living, say I remember, and give him my good word. The girl ought to come and visit me, now her lad's working here in the town. I remember her as a little lass no higher than a daisy, and that pretty...'

'Angharad was the girl who went as maidservant in the house of Bonel of Mallilie?' said Cadfael, gently prompting.

'She did, a pity it was! But they've been there many years now, the Saxons. You get used to foreigner families, in time. They never got further, though. Mallilie's nothing but a thorn stuck in the side of Cynllaith. Stuck far in—nigh broken off, as some day it may be yet! It touches Saxon land barely at all, only by a claw...'

'Is that truth!' said Cadfael. 'Then properly speaking Mallilie, for all it was held by an Englishman, and has been three generations now, is rightly within Wales?'

'As Welsh as Snowdon,' said Brother Rhys, harking back to catch once again a spark of his old patriotic fire. 'And all the neighbours Welsh, and most of the tenants. I was born just to the west of it, nearby the church of Llansilin, which is the centre of the commote of Cynllaith. Welsh land from the beginning of the world!'

Welsh land! That could not be changed, merely because a Bonel in William Rufus's reign had pushed his way in and got a hold on some acres of it, and maintained his grasp under the patronage of the earl of Chester ever since. Why did I never think, wondered Cadfael, to enquire earlier where this troublous manor lay? 'And Cynllaith has properly appointed Welsh judges? Competent to deal according to the code of Hywel Dda, not of Norman England?'

'Surely it has! A sound commote court as there is in Wales! The Bonels in their time have pleaded boundary cases, and suchlike, by whichever law best suited their own purposes, Welsh or English, what matter, provided it brought them gain? But the people like their Welsh code best, and the witness of neighbours, the proper way to settle a dispute. The just way!' said Brother Rhys righteously, and wagged his old head at Cadfael. 'What's all this of law, brother? Are you thinking of bringing suit yourself?' And he fell into a moist, pink-gummed giggling at the thought.

'Not I,' said Cadfael, rising, 'but I fancy one that I know of may be thinking of it.'

He went out very thoughtfully, and in the great court the low winter sun came out suddenly and flashed in his eyes, dazzling him for the second time. Paradoxically, in this momentary blindness he could see his way clearly at last.

Chapter 8

He would have liked to turn aside from the Wyle to
have a word with Martin Bellecote and see for himself
that the family were not being hounded, but he did not
do it, partly because he had a more urgent errand on
his mind, partly because he did not want to call attention to the house or the household. Hugh Beringar was
one man, of independent mind and a strong attachment
to justice, but the officers of the sheriffry of Shropshire
were a very different matter, looking for their lead
rather to Gilbert Prestcote, understandably enough,
since Prestcote was King Stephen's official represen-
tative in these parts; and Prestcote's justice would be
sharper, shorter-sighted, content with a brisk and tidy
ending. Prestcote might be away in Westminster, Beringar might be nominally in charge, but the sergeants
and their men would still be proceeding on their usual
summary course, making for the most obvious quarry.
If there was a watch set on Bellecote's shop, Cadfael
had no intention of giving it any provocation. If there
was not, so much the better, Hugh's orders had prevailed.

So Cadfael paced demurely up the Wyle and past the
Bellecote yard without a glance, and on through the
town. His way to the north-west lay over the bridge
that led towards Wales, but he passed that, too, and
climbed the hill to the High Cross; from that point the
road descended slightly, to mount again into the castle
gatehouse.

King Stephen's garrison was in full possession since
the summer siege, and the watch, though vigilant, was

assured and easy. Cadfael lighted down at the approach, and led his mule up the causeway and into the shadow of the gate. The guard waited for him placidly.

'Goodmorrow, brother! What's your will?'

'A word with Hugh Beringar of Maesbury,' said Cadfael. 'Tell him Brother Cadfael, and I think he'll spare me a short while of his time.'

'You're out of luck, brother, for the present while. Hugh Beringar is not here, and likely won't be till the light fails, for he's off on some search down the river with Madog of the Dead-boat.' That was news that heartened Cadfael as suddenly as the news of Hugh's absence had disheartened and dismayed him. He might have done better, after all, to leave the vial with Brother Mark, who could have paid a second visit after the first one had missed its mark. Of all but Beringar here, Cadfael had his doubts, but now he was caught in a situation he should have foreseen. Hugh had lost no time in setting the hunt in motion after Edwin's reliquary, and better still, was pursuing it himself instead of leaving it to underlings. But long delay here to wait for him was impossible; Brother Barnabas lay ill, and Cadfael had undertaken to go and care for him, and the sooner he reached him the better. He pondered whether to entrust his precious evidence to another, or keep it until he could deliver it to Beringar in person. Edwin, after all, was somewhere at liberty yet, no immediate ill could befall him.

'If it's the matter of the poisoning you're here about,' said the guard helpfully, 'speak a word to the sergeant who's left in charge here. I hear there's been strange goings-on down at the abbey. You'll be glad when you're left in quiet again, and the rascal taken. Step in, brother, and I'll tether your mule and send to let William Warden know you're here.'

Well, no harm, at any rate, in taking a look at the law's surrogate and judging accordingly. Cadfael waited in a stony anteroom within the gatehouse, and let the object of his visit lie hidden in his scrip until he made up his mind. But the first glimpse of the sergeant as he entered rendered it virtually certain that the vial would remain in hiding. The same officer who had first answered the prior's summons to Bonel's house, bearded, brawny, hawk-beaked, self-assured and impatient of caution once his nose had found an obvious trail. He knew Cadfael again just as promptly; large white teeth flashed in a scornful grin in the bushy beard.

'You again, brother? And still finding a dozen reasons why young Gurney must be blameless, when all that's wanting is a witness who stood by and watched him do the deed? Come to throw some more dust in our eyes, I suppose, while the guilty make off into Wales?'

'I came,' said Brother Cadfael, not strictly truthfully, 'to enquire whether anything had yet come to light, concerning what I reported to Hugh Beringar yesterday.'

'Nothing has and nothing will. So it was you who set him off on this fool's errand down the river! I might have guessed it! A glib young rogue tells you a tall tale like that, and you swallow it, and infect your betters into the bargain! Wasteful nonsense! To spare men to row up and down Severn in the cold, after a reliquary that never was! You have much to answer for, brother.'

'No doubt I have,' agreed Cadfael equably. 'So have we all, even you. But to exert himself for truth and justice is Beringar's duty, and so it is yours and mine, and I do it as best I may, and forbear from snatching at what offers first and easiest, and shutting my eyes to everything else in order to be rid of the labour, and at ease again. Well, it seems I've troubled you for nothing. But let Hugh Beringar know that I was here asking for him.'

He eyed the sergeant closely at that, and doubted whether even that message would be delivered. No, grave evidence that pointed the wrong way could not be left with this man, who was so sure of his rightness he might bend even circumstances and facts to match his opinions. No help for it, the vial would have to go on to Rhydycroèsau and wait its time, when Brother Barnabas was restored, and back among his sheep.

'You mean well, brother,' said William generously, 'but you are far out of your cloister in matters like these. Best leave them to those who have experience.'

Cadfael took his leave without further protest, mounted his mule, and rode back through the town to the foot of the hill, where the street turning off to the right led him to the westward bridge. At least nothing was lost, and Beringar was following up the lead he had given. It was time now to keep his mind on the journey before him, and put aside the affairs of Richildis and her son until he had done his best for Brother Barnabas.

The road from Shrewsbury to Oswestry was one of the main highroads of the region, and fairly well maintained. The old people, the Romans, had laid it long ago when they ruled in Britain, and the same road ran south-eastward right to the city of London, where King Stephen was now preparing to keep Christmas among his lords, and Cardinal-bishop Alberic of Ostia was busy holding his legatine council for the reform of the church, to the probable discomfiture of Abbot Heribert. But here, riding in the opposite direction, the road ran straight and wide, only a little overgrown with grass here and there, and encroached upon by the wild verges, through fat farming country and woods to the town of Oswestry, a distance of no more than eighteen miles. Cadfael took it at a brisk but steady pace, to keep the mule content. Beyond the town it was but four miles to the sheepfolds. In the distance, as he rode due west in the dimming light, the hills of Wales rose blue and noble, the great rolling ridge of Berwyn melting into a faintly misted sky.

He came to the small, bare grange in a fold of the hills before dark. A low, solid wooden hut housed the brothers, and beyond lay the much larger byres and stables, where the sheep could be brought in from ice and snow, and beyond again, climbing the gentle slopes, the long, complex grey-stone walls of the field enclosures, where they grazed in this relatively mild beginning of winter, and were fed roots and grain if ever stubble and grass failed them. The hardiest were still out at liberty in the hills. Brother Simon's dog began to bark, pricking his ears to the neat hooves that hardly made a sound in the thin turf of the ride.

Cadfael lighted down at the door, and Simon came eagerly out to welcome him, a thin, wiry, dishevelled brother, some forty years old but still distrait as a child when anything went wrong with other than sheep. Sheep he knew as mothers know their babes, but Brother Barnabas's illness had utterly undone him. He clasped Cadfael's hands in his, and shook them and himself in his gratitude at no longer being alone with his patient.

'He has it hard, Cadfael, you hear the leaves of his heart rustling as he breathes, like a man's feet in the woods in autumn. I cannot break it with a sweat, I've tried...'

'We'll try again,' said Cadfael comfortably, and went into the dark, timber-scented hut before him. Within it was blessedly warm and dry; wood is the best of armours against weather, where there's small fear of fire, as in this solitude there was none. A bare minimum of furnishing, yet enough; and within, in the inner room, Brother Barnabas lay in his bed neither asleep nor awake, only uneasily in between, rustling at every breath as Simon had said, his forehead hot and dry, his eyes half-open and vacant. A big, massive man, all muscle and bone, with reserves of fight in him that needed only a little guidance.

'You go look to whatever you should be doing,' said Cadfael, unbuckling his scrip and opening it on the foot of the bed, 'and leave him to me.'

'Is there anything you will need?' asked Simon anxiously.

'A pan of water on the fire, out there, and a cloth, and a beaker ready, and that's all. If I want for more, I'll find it.'

Blessedly, he was taken at his word; Brother Simon had a childlike faith in all who practised peculiar mysteries. Cadfael worked upon Brother Barnabas without haste all the evening, by a single candle that Simon brought as the light died. A hot stone wrapped in Welsh flannel for the sick man's feet, a long and vigorous rub for chest and throat and ribs, down to the waist, with an ointment of goose-grease impregnated with mustard and other heat-giving herbs, and chest and throat then swathed in a strip of the same flannel, cool cloths on the dry forehead, and a hot draught of wine mulled with spices and borage and other febrifuge herbs. The potion went down patiently and steadily, with eased breathing and relaxing sinews. The patient slept fitfully and uneasily; but in the middle of the night the sweat broke like a storm of rain, drenching the bed. The two attentive nurses lifted the patient, when the worst was past, drew the blanket from under him and laid a fresh one, rolled him close in another, and covered him warmly again.

'Go and sleep,' said Cadfael, content, 'for he does very well. By dawn he'll be wake and hungry.'

In that he was out by some hours, for Brother Barnabas, once fallen into a deep and troubled sleep, slept until almost noon the following day, when he awoke clear-eyed and with quiet breathing, but weak as a new lamb.

'Never trouble for that,' said Cadfael cheerfully. 'Even if you were on your feet, we should hardly let you out of here for a couple of days, or longer. You have time in plenty, enjoy being idle. Two of us are enough to look after your flock for you.'

Brother Barnabas, again at ease in his body, was content to take him at his word, and luxuriate in his convalescence. He ate, at first doubtfully, for savour had left him in his fever, then, rediscovering the pleasures of taste, his appetite sharpened into fierce hunger.

'The best sign we could have,' said Cadfael. 'A man who eats heartily and with enjoyment is on his way back to health.' And they left the patient to sleep again as thoroughly as he had eaten, and went out to the sheep, and the chickens and the cow, and all the rest of the denizens of the fold.

'An easy year so far,' said Brother Simon, viewing his leggy, tough hill-sheep with satisfaction. Sheep as Welsh as Brother Cadfael gazed towards the south-west, where the long ridge of Berwyn rose in the distance; long, haughty, inscrutable faces, and sharp ears, and knowing yellow eyes that could outstare a saint. 'Plenty of good grazing still, what with the grass growing so late; and the good pickings they had in the stubble after harvest. And we have beet-tops, they make good fodder, too. There'll be better fleeces than most years, when next they're shorn, unless the winter turns cruel later on.'

From the crest of the hill above the walled folds Brother Cadfael gazed towards the south-west, where the long ridge dipped towards lower land, between the hills. 'This manor of Mallilie will be somewhere in the sheltered land there, as I judge.'

'It is. Three miles round by the easy track, the manor-house drawn back between the slopes, and the lands open to the south-east. Good land for these parts. And main glad I was to know we had a steward there, when I needed a messenger. Have you an errand there, brother?'

'There's something I must see to, when Brother Barnabas is safely on the way to health again, and I can be spared.' He turned and looked back towards the east. 'Even here we must be a good mile or more the Welsh side of the old boundary dyke. I never was here before, not being a sheep man. I'm from Gwynedd myself, from the far side of Conwy. But even these hills look like home to me.'

Gervase Bonel's manor must lie somewhat further advanced into Welsh land even than these high pastures. The Benedictines had very little hold in Wales, Welshmen preferred their own ancient Celtic Christianity, the solitary hermitage of the self-exiled saint and the homely little college of Celtic monks rather than the shrewd and vigorous foundations that looked

162

to Rome. In the south, secular Norman adventurers had penetrated more deeply, but here Mallilie must, indeed, as Brother Rhys had said, be lodged like a single thorn deep in the flesh of Wales.

'It does not take long to ride to Mallilie,' said Brother Simon, anxiously helpful. 'Our horse here is elderly, but strong, and gets little enough work as a rule. I could very well manage now, if you want to go tomorrow.'

'First let's see,' said Cadfael, 'how Brother Barnabas progresses by tomorrow.'

Brother Barnabas progressed very well once he had the fever out of him. Before nightfall he was sick of lying in his bed, and insisted on rising and trying his enfeebled legs about the room. His own natural strength and stout heart were all he needed now to set him up again, though he swallowed tolerantly whatever medicines Cadfael pressed upon him, and consented to have his chest and throat anointed once again with the salve.

'No need to trouble yourself for me now,' he said. 'I shall be hale as a hound pup in no time. And if I can't take to the hills again for a day or two—though I very well could, if you would but let me!—I can see to the house here, and the hens and the cow, for that matter.'

The next morning he rose to join them for Prime, and would not return to his bed, though when they both harried him he agreed to sit snugly by the fire, and exert himself no further than in baking bread and preparing dinner.

'Then I will go,' said Cadfael, 'if you can manage alone for the day, Simon. If I leave now I shall have the best of the daylight, and be back with you in time for the evening work.'

Brother Simon went out with him to where the track branched, and gave him directions. After the hamlet of Croesau Bach he would come to a cross roads, and turn right, and from that point he would see how the hills were cleft ahead of him, and making straight for that cleft he would come to Mallilie, beyond which the track continued westward to Llansilin, the central seat of the commote of Cynllaith.

The morning was faintly misty, but with the sun bright through the mist, and the turf wet and sparkling with the hint of rime already melting. He had chosen to ride the horse from the grange rather than his mule, since the mule had had lengthy exercise on the way north, and was entitled to a rest. The horse was an ungainly bay, of homely appearance but amiable disposition and stout heart, willing and ready for work. It was pleasant to be riding here alone in a fine winter morning on cushioned turf, between hills that took him back to his youth, with no routine duties and no need for talk, beyond the occasional greeting for a woman splitting kindling in her yard, or a man moving sheep to a new pasture, and even that was a special pleasure because he found himself instinctively calling his good-day in Welsh. The holdings here were scattered and few until he came through Croesau into lower and richer ground, where the patterns of ordered tillage told him he was already entering Mallilie land. A brook sprang into life on his right hand, and accompanied him towards the cleft where the hill-slopes on either side drew close together. Within a mile it was a little river, providing level meadows on either bank, and the dark selions of ploughed land beyond. Trees clothed the upper slopes, the valley faced south-east into the morning sun; a good place, its tenant holdings sheltered and well found. Well into the defile, drawn back into a fold of the slope on his right, and half-circled with arms of woodland, he came to the manor-house.

A timber stockade surrounded it, massive and high, but the house stood on rising ground, and showed tall above it. Built of local stone, granite grey, with a great long roof of slates, gleaming like fish-scales in the sun as the frost on them turned to dew. When he had crossed the river by a plank-bridge and ridden in at the open gate of the stockade, the whole length of the house lay before him, a tall stone stair leading up to the main door of the living floor at the left-hand end. At ground

164

level three separate doors, wide enough to take in country carts, led into what was evidently a vaulted undercroft, with storage room enough for a siege. Judging by the windows in the gable end, there was yet another small room above the kitchen. The windows of hall and solar were stone-mullioned and generous. Round the inner side of the stockade there were ample outhouses, stables, mews and stores. Norman lordlings, promised heirs, Benedictine abbeys might well covet such a property. Richildis had indeed married out of her kind.

The servants here would be Bonel's servants, continuing their functions under a new rule. A groom came to take Cadfael's bridle, feeling no need to question one who arrived in a Benedictine habit. There were few people moving about the court, but those few assured in their passage; and impressive though the house was, it could never have needed a very numerous body to run it. All local people, surely, and that meant Welsh people, like the serving-maid who had warmed her lord's bed and borne him a disregarded son. It happened! Bonel might even have been an attractive man then, and given her pleasure, as well as a child; and at least he had kept her thereafter, and the child with her, though as mere indulged dependents, not members of his family, not his kin. A man who did not take more than he felt to be legally his, but would not forgo any item of what fell within that net. A man who let an unclaimed villein holding go to a hungry younger son from a free family, on terms of customary service, and then, with the law firmly behind him, claimed that questionable tenant as villein by reason of the dues rendered between them, and his progeny as unfree by the same code.

In this disputed borderland of soil and law, Cadfael found his heart and mind utterly Welsh, but could not deny that the Englishman had just as passionately held by his own law, and been sure that he was justified. He had not been an evil man, only a child of his time and place, and his death had been murder.

Properly speaking, Cadfael had no business at this

house but to observe, as now he had observed. But he went in, nevertheless, up the outdoor stair and into the passage screened off from the hall. A boy emerging from the kitchen louted to him and passed, accepting him as one of the breed, who would know his way here. The hall was lofty and strongly beamed. Cadfael passed through it to the solar. This must be where Bonel had intended to install the panelling commissioned from Martin Bellecote, the transaction which had first caused him to set eyes and heart on Richildis Gurney, who had once been Richildis Vaughan, daughter of an honest, unpretentious tradesman.

Martin had done good work, and fitted it into place here with skill and love. The solar was narrower than the hall, there being a garderobe off it, and a tiny chapel. It glowed and was scented with the polished and sparely carved oak panelling, the suave silvery grain glinting in the light from the wide window. Edwin had a good brother and a good master. He need not repine if he missed the illusory heritage.

'Your pardon, brother!' said a respectful voice at Cadfael's back. 'No one told me there was a messenger here from Shrewsbury.'

Cadfael turned, startled, to take a look at the abbey's steward here; a layman, a lawman, young enough to be deferential to his employers, mature enough to be in command of his own province.

'It's I who should ask your pardon,' said Cadfael, 'for walking in upon you without ceremony. Truth to tell, I have no errand here, but being in the neighbourhood I was curious to see our new manor.'

'If it is indeed ours,' said the steward ruefully, and looked about him with a shrewd eye, assessing what the abbey might well be losing. 'It seems to be in doubt at the moment, though that makes no difference to my commission here, to maintain it in good order, however the lot falls in the end. The place has been run well and profitably. But if you are not sent to join us here, brother, where is your domicile? As long as we hold the manor, we can well offer you lodging, if it please you to stay.'

'That I can't,' said Cadfael. 'I was sent from Shrewsbury to take care of an ailing brother, a shepherd at the folds by Rhydycroesau, and until he's restored I must take on his duties there.'

'Your patient is mending, I trust?'

'So well that I thought I might use a few hours to come and see what manner of property may be slipping through our fingers here. But have you any immediate reason for feeling that our tenure may be threatened? More than the obvious difficulty of the charter not being sealed in time?'

The steward frowned, chewing a dubious lip. 'The situation is strange enough, for if both the secular heir and the abbey lose their claim, the future of Mallilie is a very open question. The earl of Chester is the overlord, and may bestow it as he pleases, and in troublous times like these I doubt if he'll want to leave it in monastic hands. We could appeal to him, true, but not until Shrewsbury has an abbot again, with full powers. All we can do in the meantime is manage this land until there's a legal decision. Will you take your dinner here with me, brother? Or at least a cup of wine?'

Cadfael declined the offer of a midday meal; it was yet early, and he had a use for the remaining hours of daylight. But he accepted the wine with pleasure. They sat down together in the panelled solar, and the dark Welsh kitchen-boy brought them a flagon and two horns.

'You've had no trouble with the Welsh to west of you?' asked Cadfael.

'None. They've been used to the Bonels as neighbours for fifty years now, and no bad blood on either side. Though I've had little contact except with our own Welsh tenants. You know yourself, brother, both sides of the border here there are both Welsh and English living cheek by jowl, and most of those one side have kin on the other.'

'One of our oldest brothers,' said Cadfael, 'came from

this very region, from a village between here and Llansilin. He was talking of his old kinship when he knew I was coming to Rhydycroesau. I'd be glad to carry his greetings, if I can find his people. Two cousins he mentioned, Cynfrith and Owain ap Rhys. You haven't encountered either? And a brother by marriage, one Ifor ap Morgan...though it must be many years since he had any contact with any of them, and for ought I know this Ifor ap Morgan may be dead long ago. He must be round about Rhys's own age, and few of us last so long.'

The steward shook his head doubtfully. 'Cynfrith ap Rhys I've heard spoken of, he has a holding half a mile or so west of here. Ifor ap Morgan...no, I know nothing of him. But I tell you what, if he's living the boy will know, he's from Llansilin himself. Question him when you leave, and do it in Welsh, for all he knows English well enough. You'll get more out of him in Welsh...and all the more readily,' he added with a wry grin, 'if I'm not with you. They're none of them ill-disposed, but they keep their own counsel, and it's wonderful how they fail to understand English when it suits them to shut the alien out.'

'I'll try it,' said Cadfael, 'and my thanks for the good advice.'

'Then you'll forgive me if I don't accompany you to the gate and give you God-speed. You'll do better alone.'

Cadfael took the hint and his leave, there in the solar, and went out through the hall and by the screened way into the kitchen. They boy was there, backing red-faced from the oven with a tray of new loaves. He looked round warily as he set down his burden on the clay top to cool gradually. It was neither fear nor distrust, but the wariness of a wild creature alert and responsive to every living thing, curious and ready to be friendly, sceptical and ready to vanish.

'God save you, son!' said Cadfael in Welsh. 'If your bread's all out now, do a Christian deed, come out to the gate with me, and show a stranger the way to the holding of Cynfrith ap Rhys or his brother Owain.'

The boy gazed, eyes brightening into interest at

being addressed placidly in his own tongue. 'You are from Shrewsbury abbey, sir? A monk?'

'I am.'

'But Welsh?'

'As Welsh as you, lad, but not from these parts. The vale of Conwy is my native place, near by Trefriw.'

'What's your will with Cynfrith ap Rhys?' asked the boy directly.

Now I know I'm in Wales, thought Cadfael. An English servant, if he ventured to challenge your proceedings at all, would do it roundabout and obsequiously, for fear of getting his ears clipped, but your Welsh lad speaks his mind to princes.

'In our abbey,' he said obligingly, 'there's an old brother who used to be known in these parts as Rhys ap Griffith, and he's cousin to these other sons of Rhys. When I left Shrewsbury I said I'd take his greetings to his kin, and so I will if I can find them. And while we're about it there's one more name he gave me, and you may at least be able to tell me if the man's alive or dead, for he must be old. Rhys had a sister Marared, who married one Ifor ap Morgan, and they had a daughter Angharad, though I'm told she's dead years ago. But if Ifor is still living I'll speak the good word to him, also.'

Under this rain of Welsh names the boy thawed into smiles. 'Sir, Ifor ap Morgan is still alive. He lives a fair way beyond, nearly to Llansilin. I'll come out with you and show you the way.'

He skipped down the stone staircase lightly, ahead of Cadfael, and trotted before him to the gate. Cadfael followed, leading his horse, and looked where the boy pointed, westward between the hills.

'To the house of Cynfrith ap Rhys it is but half a mile, and it lies close by the track, on your right hand, with the wattle fence round the yard. You'll see his white goats in the little paddock. For Ifor ap Morgan you must go further. Keep to the same track again until you're through the hills, and looking down into the valley, then take the path to the right, that fords our

169

river before it joins the Cynllaith. Half a mile on, look to your right again, just within the trees, and you'll see a little wooden house, and that's where Ifor lives. He's very old now, but he lives alone still.'

Cadfael thanked him and mounted.

'And for the other brother, Owain,' said the boy cheerfully, willing enough now to tell all he knew that might be helpful, 'if you're in these parts two more days you may catch him in Llansilin the day after tomorrow, when the commote court meets, for he has a dispute that was put off from the last sitting, along with some others. The judges have been viewing the impleaded lands, and the day after tomorrow they're to give judgment. They never like to let bad blood continue at the Christmas feast. Owain's holding is well beyond the town, but you'll find him at Llansilin church, sure enough. One of his neighbours moved his boundary stone, or so he claims.'

He had said more than he realised, but he was serenely innocent of the impression he had made on Brother Cadfael. One question, perhaps the most vital of all, had been answered without ever having to be asked.

Cynfrith ap Rhys—the kinship seemed to be so full of Rhyses that in some cases it was necessary to list three generations back in order to distinguish them—was easily found, and very willing to pass the time of day even with a Benedictine monk, seeing that the monk spoke Welsh. He invited Cadfael in heartily, and the invitation was accepted with pleasure. The house was one room and a cupboard of a kitchen, a solitary man's domain, and there was no sign of any other creature here but Cynfrith and his goats and hens. A solid, thick-set, prominent-boned Welshman was Cynfrith, with wiry black hair now greying round the edges and balding on the crown, and quick, twinkling eyes set in the webs of good-humoured creases common to outdoor men. Twenty years at least younger than his cousin in the infirmary at Shrewsbury. He offered bread and goat's-milk cheese, and wrinkled, sweet apples.

'The good old soul, so he's still living! Many a time I've wondered. He's my mother's cousin in the first degree, not mine, but time was I knew him well. He'll be nearing fourscore now, I suppose. And still comfortable in his cloister? I'll send him a small flask of the right liquor, brother, if you'll be so kind as to carry it. I distil it myself, it will stand him in good stead through the winter, a drop in season is good for the heart, and does the memory no harm, either. Well, well, and to think he still remembers us all! My brother? Oh, be sure I'll pass on the word to Owain when I see him. He has a good wife, and grown sons, tell the old man, the elder, Elis, is to marry in the spring. The day after tomorrow I shall be seeing my brother, he has a judgment coming up at the commote court at Llansilin.'

'So they told me at Mallilie,' said Cadfael. 'I wish him good speed with it.'

'Ah, well, he claims Hywel Fychan, who lives next him, shifted one of his boundary stones, and I daresay he did, but I wouldn't say but what Owain has done the like by Hywel in his time. It's an old sport with us...But I needn't tell you, you being of the people yourself. They'll make it up as the court rules, they always do until the next time, and no hard feelings. They'll drink together this Christmas.'

'So should we all,' said Cadfael, somewhat sententiously.

He took his leave as soon but as graciously as he well might, truthfully claiming another errand and the shortness of the daylight, and rode on his way by the little river, both heartened and chastened by contact with open and fearless goodwill. The little flask of powerful home-distilled spirit swung in his scrip; he was glad he had left the other, the poisoned one, behind at the sheepfold.

He came through the defile, and saw the valley of the Cynllaith open before him, and the track to the right weaving a neat line through rising grass to ford the little tributary. Half a mile beyond, woodland clothed the slope of the ridge, and in the full leaf of summer it might have been difficult to detect the low wooden house within the trees; but now, with all the leaves fallen, it stood clear behind the bare branches like a contented domestic hen in a coop. There was clear grass almost to its fence, and on one side continuing behind it, the veil of trees drawn halfway round like a curtain. Cadfael turned in towards it, and circled with the skirt of grass, seeing no door in the side that faced the track. A horse on a long tether came ambling round the gable end, placidly grazing; a horse as tall and rakish and unbeautiful as the one he rode, though probably some years older. At sight of it he pulled up short, and sat at gaze for a moment, before lighting down into the coarse grass.

There must, of course, be many horses that would answer to the description given: a bony old piebald. This one was certainly that, very strikingly black and white in improbable patterns. But they could not all, surely, be called by the same name?

Cadfael dropped his bridle and went softly forward towards the serenely feeding beast, which paid him no attention whatever after a single glance. He chirruped to it, and called quietly: 'Japhet!'

The piebald pricked long ears and lifted a gaunt, amiable head, stretching out a questing muzzle and dilated nostrils towards the familiar sound, and having made up his mind he was not mistaken, advanced confidently and briskly to the hand Cadfael extended. He ran caressing fingers up the tall forehead, and along the stretched, inquisitive neck. 'Japhet, Japhet, my friend, what are you doing here?'

The rustle of feet in the dry grass, while all four feet of this mild creature were still, caused Cadfael to look up sharply towards the corner of the house. A venerable old man stood looking at him steadily and silently; a tall old man, white-haired and white-bearded, but still with brows black and thick as gorse-bushes, and eyes as starkly blue as a winter sky beneath them. His dress was the common homespun of the countryman, but his carriage and height turned it into purple.

'As I think,' said Cadfael, turning towards him with one hand still on Japhet's leaning neck, 'you must be Ifor ap Morgan. My name is Cadfael, sometime Cadfael ap Meilyr ap Dafydd of Trefriw. I have an errand to you from Rhys ap Griffith, your wife's brother, who is now Brother Rhys of the abbey of Shrewsbury.'

The voice that emerged from the long, austere, dry lips was deep and sonorous, a surprising music. 'Are you sure your errand is not to a guest of mine, brother?'

'It was not,' said Cadfael, 'it was to you. Now it is to both. And the first thing I would say is, keep this beast out of sight, for if I can know him again from a mere description, so can others.'

The old man gave him a lengthy, piercing blue stare. 'Come into the house,' he said, and turned on his heel and led the way. But Cadfael took time to lead Japhet well behind the house and shorten his tether to keep him there, before he followed.

In the dimness within, smoky and wood-scented, the old man stood with a hand protectively on Edwin's shoulder; and Edwin, with the impressionable generosity of youth, had somehow gathered to himself a virgin semblance of the old man's dignity and grace, and stood like him, erect and quiet within his untried body as was Ifor ap Morgan in his old and experienced one, copied the carriage of his head and the high serenity of his regard.

'The boy tells me,' said Ifor, 'that you are a friend. His friends are welcome.'

'Brother Cadfael has been good to me,' said Edwin, 'and to my nephew, Edwy, also, as Meurig told us. I have been well blessed in my friends. But how did you find me?'

'By not looking for you,' said Cadfael. 'Indeed, I've been at some pains *not* to know where you had taken yourself, and certainly I never rode this way to find you. I came with a harmless errand to Ifor ap Morgan here, from that same old brother you visited with Meurig in our infirmary. Your wife's brother, friend, Rhys ap Griffith, is still living, and for his age hale, too, in our convent, and when he heard that I was bound into these parts he charged me to bring his kinsmen his greetings and prayers. He has not forgotten his kin, though it's long since he came among you, and I doubt he'll come no more. I have been with Cynfrith ap Rhys, and sent the same word by him to his brother Owain, and if there are any others of his generation left, or who would remember him, be kind enough to give them word, when chance offers, that he remembers his blood and his own soil yet, and all those whose roots are in it.'

'So he would,' said Ifor, melting suddenly into a warm smile. 'He was always a loyal kinsman, and fond of my child and all the other young in our clan, having none of his own. He lost his wife early, or he'd have been here among us yet. Sit down a while, brother, and tell me how he does, and if you'll take my blessings back to him, I'll be grateful.'

'Meurig will have told you much of what I can tell,' and Cadfael, settling beside him on a bench at the rough table, 'when he brought you Edwin to shelter. Is he not here with you?'

'My grandson is away making the round of all his kin and neighbours,' said the old man, 'for he comes home rarely now. He'll be here again in a few days, I daresay. He did tell me he'd been to see the old man, along with the boy here, but he stayed only an hour or so before making off about his visiting. There'll be time to talk when he comes back.'

It was in Cadfael's mind that he ought to cut short his own stay, for though it had never entered his mind that the officers of the law might find it worth while to keep a watch on him when he left Shrewsbury, the too easy discovery of Edwin in this house had shaken his assurance. It was true that he had neither expected nor wished to trace the boy as yet, but even Hugh Beringar, let alone his underlings, might well have considered the contrary as a possibility, and set a discreet hound on his trail. But he could not flatly deliver his message and go, while the old man clearly took pleasure in polishing up old memories. He was rambling away happily about the time when his wife was with him, and his daughter a fair and lively child. Now all that remained to him was a single grandson, and his own dignity and integrity.

Exile and refuge in this remote place and this impressive company had had a strong effect on Edwin. He withdrew into the shadows to leave his elders undisturbed, making no plea, asking no question yet concerning his own troubled affairs. Quietly he went and brought beakers and a pitcher of mead, and served them unobtrusively and neatly, all dignity and humility, and again absented himself, until Ifor turned to reach a long arm and draw him to the table.

'Young man, you must have things to ask of Brother Cadfael, and things to tell him.'

The boy had not lost his tongue, after all, once invited he could talk as volubly and vehemently as ever. First he asked after Edwy, with an anxiety he would never have revealed to the object of it, and was greatly eased to hear how that adventure had ended better than it had threatened. 'And Hugh Beringar was so fair and generous? And he listened to you, and is looking for my box? Now if he could but find it...! I was not happy leaving Edwy to play that part for me, but he would have it so. And then I took Japhet a roundabout way to a place we used to play sometimes, a copse by the river, and Meurig met me there, and gave me a token to carry to his grandfather here, and told me how to find the place. And the next day he came, too, as he said he would.'

'And what,' asked Cadfael gently, 'had you planned to do, if truth never did come out? If you could not go back? Though God forbid it should end so, and God granting, I'll see that it does not.'

The boy's face was solemn but clear; he had thought much, here in his haven, and spent so much time contemplating the noble face of his patron that a kind of shining likeness had arisen between them. 'I'm strong, I can work, I could earn my keep in Wales, if need be, even if it must be as an outlander. Other men have had to leave their homes because of unjust accusations, and have made their way in the world, and so could I. But I'd rather go back. I don't want to leave my mother, now that she's alone, and her affairs in such disorder. And I don't want to be remembered as the man who poisoned his stepfather and ran away, when I know I never did him harm or wished him any.'

'That shall not happen,' said Cadfael firmly. 'You lie close in cover a few days more, and put your trust in God, and I believe we shall get to the truth, and you can go home openly and proudly.'

'Do you believe that? Or is it just to hearten me?'

'I believe it. Your heart is not in want of bolstering up with false cheer. And I would not lie to you, even for good cause.' Yet there were lies, or at least unspoken truths, hanging heavy on his mind in this house, and he had better make his farewells and go, the passing of time and daylight giving him a sound excuse. 'I must get back to Rhydycroesau,' he said, making to rise from the table, 'for I've left Brother Simon to do all the work alone, and Brother Barnabas still shaky on his legs yet. Did I tell you I was sent there to get a sick man well again, and to supply his place while he was mending?'

'You'll come again if there's news?' said Edwin, and if his voice was resolutely steady, his eyes were anxious.

'I'll come again *when* there's news.'

'You'll be in Rhydycroesau some days yet?' asked Ifor ap Morgan. 'Then we shall see you again at more leisure, I trust.'

He was leading the way to the door to speed his guest, his hand again possessive on Edwin's shoulder, when he halted suddenly, stiffening, and with the other hand, outstretched with spread fingers, halted them, too, and enjoined silence. Age had not dulled those ancient ears; he was the first to catch the muted sound of voices. Not muted by distance, close and deliberately quiet. The dry grass rustled. In the edge of the trees one of the tethered horses whinnied enquiringly, giving notice of other horses approaching.

'Not Welsh!' said Ifor in a soundless whisper. 'English! Edwin, go into the other room.'

The boy obeyed instantly and silently; but in a moment he was back, shadowy in the doorway. 'They're there—two, outside the window. In leather, armed...'

The voices had drawn nearer, outside the house-door, their whispers grew louder, satisfied, abandoning stealth.

'That's the pied beast...no mistaking it!'

'What did I tell you? I said if we found the one we'd find the other.'

Someone laughed, low and contentedly. Then abruptly a fist thudded at the door, and the same voice called aloud, peremptorily: 'Open to the law!' The formality was followed up immediately by a strong thrust, hurling the door inwards to the wall, and the doorway was filled by the burly figure of the bearded sergeant from Shrewsbury, with two men-at-arms at his back. Brother Cadfael and William Warden confronted each other at a distance of a couple of feet; mutual recognition made the one bristle and the other grin.

'Well met, Brother Cadfael! And sorry I am I have no writ for you, but my business is with the young man behind you. I'm addressed to Edwin Gurney. And you, I think, my lad, are he?'

Edwin came forward a step from the inner doorway, pale as his shirt and huge-eyed, but with a chin jutting valiantly, and a stare like a levelled lance. He had learned a great deal in his few days here. 'That is my name,' he said.

'Then I arrest you on suspicion of the murder of Gervase Bonel by poison, and I'm here to take you back in custody to answer the charge in Shrewsbury.'

Chapter 9

Ifor ap Morgan drew himself up in a single long breath, seeming to grow half a head in the process, and stood forth to face his unexpected visitor.

'Fellow,' he said in his deep voice, in itself a weapon, 'I am the master of this house, and you have not, as yet, addressed yourself to me. There are visitors I invite, there are some I welcome, unexpected. You I do not know and have not invited, and you I do not welcome. Have the courtesy to make yourself known to me, if you have business with me or with others under my roof. Otherwise, leave this house.'

It could not be said that the sergeant was abashed, since he was protected by his office from any personal humiliation; but he did make a shrewd appraisal of this venerable person, and abate what would otherwise have been a boldly abrasive manner. 'I understand that you are Ifor ap Morgan. I am William Warden, a sergeant serving under Gilbert Prestcote, the sheriff of Shropshire, and I am in pursuit of Edwin Gurney on suspicion of murder. My commission is to bring him by whatever means to Shrewsbury, where the charge stands, and that I shall do, as I am bound. You also, as an elder of this region, are bound by law.'

'But not by English law,' said Ifor simply.

'By law! Knowing murder for murder, by whatever law. Murder by poison, grandsire!'

Brother Cadfael glanced once at Edwin, who stood motionless and pale, one hand advanced to take the old man pleadingly and comfortingly by the arm, but too much in awe and love of him to complete the gesture.

178

Cadfael did it for him, laying a hand gently on the lean old wrist. For whatever was done and said now, they would take the boy with them. If there were three of them there, and two guarding the rear of the house, who was to stop them? And this was a self-assured, arrogant man, who might take petty revenges for past impudent reverses, but who would also have full regard for his own skin when dealing with a deputy sheriff of Beringar's measure, who might unaccountably have strict scruples about the handling of prisoners. Better not alienate Warden unnecessarily, when a little sweet reasonableness might do more to protect Edwin.

'Sergeant, you know me, and know I do not believe this boy has any guilt to answer for. But I know you, too, and know you have your duty to do. You must obey your orders, and we cannot stand in your way. Tell me, was it Hugh Beringar sent you here to look for me? For I'm sure I was not followed from Shrewsbury. What brought you to this house?'

The sergeant was by no means averse to detailing his own cleverness. 'No, we never thought to have you followed, brother, after you left us, for we thought you were bound back to your abbey. But when Hugh Beringar came back empty-handed from his follies down the river, and heard you'd been asking for him, he went down to the abbey after you, only to find you were gone north to Rhydycroesau. I bethought me then how close Bonel's manor was, and took it upon me to bring a party up here to enquire what you were up to. The steward at the manor never questioned it when an officer from Shrewsbury came asking for Brother Cadfael. Why should he? Or his servants, either? They told us you'd been asking directions to a couple of houses this side the hills, and here at the second we've overtaken you. Where the one casts up, I said, the other won't be far.'

So no one had wittingly informed on the fugitive; that would be some compensatory good news for Ifor ap Morgan, who would have felt himself shamed and dishonoured for ever if one of his kin had betrayed the

179

guest in his house. It was news of no less vital importance to Cadfael.

'Then Hugh Beringar did not send you on this quest? "*I took it upon me*," you said. What's he about, while you're doing his work for him?'

'He's off on some more tomfoolery down the river. Madog of the Dead-boat sent up to him early this morning to come down to Atcham, and off he went as hopeful as ever, though nothing will come of it. So I took the chance of following my own notions, and a fine surprise he'll get by this evening, when he comes back with nothing to show for his day, and finds I've brought him his prisoner.'

That was reassuring, since he was clearly looking forward to the presentation of his prize, and pleased with his own success, therefore the less likely to find satisfaction in rough-handling the boy.

'Edwin,' said Cadfael, 'will you be guided now by me?'

'I will,' said Edwin steadily.

'Then go with them peaceably, and make no trouble. You know you have done no wrong, therefore you cannot be proven guilty, and on that you must take your stand. When you are delivered into the hand of Hugh Beringar, answer freely whatever he may ask of you, and tell him all the truth. I promise you, you will not be long in prison.' And God stand by me, he thought, and help me make that good! 'If the boy gives you his pledge to go with you of his own will, sergeant, and attempt no escape, you surely need not bind him. It's a long ride, and you'll be pressing before the dark comes.'

'He may have the use of his hands, and welcome,' said Warden indifferently, 'seeing the two men I have outside are archers, and masters of their craft. If he tried to evade us he would not get many yards.'

'I shall not try,' said Edwin firmly. 'I give you my word. I'm ready!' He went to Ifor ap Morgan, and bent the knee to him reverently. 'Grandfather, thank you

180

for all your goodness. I know I'm not truly of your kinship—I wish I were!—but will you give me your kiss?'

The old man took him by the shoulders, and stooped to kiss his cheek. 'Go with God! And come again free!'

Edwin took up his saddle and bridle from the corner where they were stowed, and marched out with his head up and his chin jutting, his attendants closing in on either side. In a few minutes the two left behind, gazing through the open door, saw the little cortège form and move off, the sergeant ahead, the boy between two men-at-arms riding close, the archers behind. The day was already chilling, though the light had not yet dimmed. They would not reach Shrewsbury until after dark; a drear journey, and a stony cell in Shrewsbury castle at the end of it. But please God, not for long. Two or three days, if all went well. But well for whom?

'What am I to tell my grandson Meurig,' said the old man sadly, 'when he returns, and finds I have let his guest be taken?'

Cadfael closed the door upon the last glimpse of Edwin's brown head and slight figure; well grown as he was, he looked very small and young between his brawny guards.

'Tell Meurig,' he said after heavy thought, 'that he need have no fears for Edwin, for in the end truth will out, and the truth will deliver him.'

He had one day of inactivity left to live through now, and since there was nothing he could do of use to Edwin's cause in that time, it behoved him at least to try to turn the waiting time into a day of grace by some other means. Brother Barnabas, heartily convalescent, could at least be persuaded to forbear from the heavier work and keep the warmth of the house for a little longer. Brother Simon could take his own day of rest, all the more since on the morrow Cadfael would again be absent. Moreover, they could observe together all the main offices of the day, as if they had been home in the abbey of St Peter. The patient recital of the proper forms must surely in itself be regarded as prayer.

There was time for thought all that day, while he scattered grain for the hens, milked the cow, groomed the old bay horse, and moved the sheep to a fresh hill-pasture. Edwin was lodged in his prison by now, though only, Cadfael hoped, after a long and calming interview with Hugh Beringar. Had Martin Bellecote yet heard that he was taken? Did Edwy know that his decoy ride had been all for nothing? And Richildis...Had Beringar seen it as his duty to visit her and tell her of her son's capture? It would be done as courteously and kindly as possible, but there was no way of allaying the pain and dread she would feel.

But Cadfael was even more exercised in mind for the old man Ifor ap Morgan, left alone now after his brief experience of being trusted and revered by a creature fresh and young, like a vision of his own youth returning. The unruly vigour which had made Edwin rebel and wage war against Gervase Bonel had all been charmed and tamed into willing duty and service by Ifor ap Morgan. We are all both the victims and the heirs of our fellow-men.

'Tomorrow,' said Cadfael at supper, round the brazier hissing with resiny logs and giving forth a blue, weaving smoke as aromatic as his workshop at Shrewsbury, 'I must set out very early.' The commote court would sit as soon as there was daylight, and hope to adjourn in time for all present to reach their homes before night. 'I'll try to be back to fold the sheep in the evening. You have not asked me where I go this time.'

'No, brother,' agreed Simon mildly. 'We've seen that you have much on your mind, and would not trouble you yet with questions. When you wish it, you will tell us what we need to know.'

But it was a long story, of which they, here in this solitude and with their own tranquil world undisturbed, knew not even the beginnings. Better say nothing.

* * *

He rose before dawn and saddled his horse, taking the same track he had ridden two days previously as far as the ford, where he had turned aside to cross the tributary and make his way to Ifor's house. This time he did not turn aside, but rode on into the valley of the Cynllaith, and crossed by a wooden bridge. From there it was little more than a mile into Llansilin, and the sun was up, veiled but bright. The village was wide awake, and full of people, converging on the timber church. Every house in the neighbourhood must have given shelter overnight to friends and kin from other parts of the commote, for the normal population of this hamlet could be no more than a tenth part of those met here on this day. Cadfael turned his horse into the paddock by the churchyard, where there was a stone water-trough and peaceful grazing, and joined the leisurely procession of men entering the church. Out in the roadway he was conspicuous in his black Benedictine habit, the species being so rare here, but within, he could be well hidden in a retired corner. He had no wish to be noticed too soon.

He was glad that Ifor ap Morgan did not appear among the elders who came to see justice done, the duty of neighbours who knew the land and the people involved. Better by far the testimony of these familiar and respected men than the legal arguments of professional lawmen, though these, too, would be here in plenty. Nor did he see Cynfrith ap Rhys until after the bench of three judges had taken their places, and the first adjourned case was called. Then, when the plaintiff was asked to stand forth with his guarantors on one side, Cadfael recognised Cynfrith among his brother's backers. Owain was the younger of the two, but very like his brother. Hywel Fychan, the defendant, was a wiry, dark man of belligerent aspect, with his own little cluster of witnesses at his back.

The presiding judge gave the verdict of the bench. They had viewed the two disputed holdings on the spot, and taken measurements to match with old charters. Their judgment was that Hywel Fychan had indeed moved the corner boundary stone in such a way as to filch some yards of his neighbour's land, but they had also found that Owain ap Rhys, more discreetly, and admittedly after he had discovered the defendant's fraud, had countered by shifting a whole length of fencing between them by a cautious yard, adequately repaying himself for his loss. They therefore decreed that both marks should be restored to their former positions, and amerced both parties by a negligible fine. Predictably, Owain and Hywel clasped hands amicably enough in acceptance of the verdict; and probably they would be drinking away together, later in the day, the excess of their expected fines over those imposed. The game would be resumed next year. Cadfael was familiar with the national sport.

There were two more boundary disputes which had been awaiting a judgment arrived at on the disputed land, the one settled amicably, the other accepted with some bitterness by the losing party, but none the less accepted. There was a widow who claimed a patch of land against her husband's kin, and won her claim by the testimony of no less than seven neighbours. The morning wore away, and Cadfael, constantly looking over his shoulder towards the door, began to wonder if he had been utterly mistaken in his reading of the probabilities. How if he had interpreted all the signs wrongly? Then he had all to do again, and Edwin was in genuine peril, and his only resort was Hugh Beringar, whose rule would end when Gilbert Prestcote returned from the king's Christmas.

The grateful widow was withdrawing with her witnesses, flushed and happy, when the door of the church opened wide. The light of day flowed across the crowded assembly, and so remained for some minutes, as a numerous group entered the nave. Cadfael looked round, as half those met there were also doing, and saw Meurig advance into the open aisle, and there take his stand, with seven grave elders at his back.

He was wearing, Cadfael noted, the same cotte and hose in which he had always seen him, no doubt his best, worn to the commote court as they were worn to visit the abbey at Shrewsbury. His only other garment would be those he wore at work. And the linen scrip hanging by its leather thongs from his belt was the same Cadfael had seen on him at the infirmary, where he had laboured, certainly out of kindliness and with nothing to gain, to coax the aches and pains out of an old man's rusty joints. Such scrips cost money, and are durable for many years. Doubtful if he even owned another such.

An ordinary enough figure, this square, sturdy, black-avised young fellow, anybody's son or brother; but not ordinary now. He stood in the middle of the open aisle, feet spread, arms down at his sides but braced, as if either hand had a weapon within reach, though he surely had not so much as a hunting-knife on him, here in a place doubly sacred as church and court. He was shaven and bathed clean, and the subdued light within the nave found and plucked into relief every bony line of his powerful face, the outline of a skull drawn white and taut, shadowy dark flesh clothing it sparely. His eyes were like burning lamps sunk into cavernous hollows; he looked both piteously young and age-old, and hungry to starving.

'With the court's leave,' he said, and his voice was high and clear, 'I have a plea that will not wait.'

'We were about to declare this sitting at an end,' said the presiding judge mildly. 'But we are here to serve. Declare yourself and your business.'

'My name is Meurig, son of Angharad, daughter of Ifor ap Morgan, who is known to all men here. By this same Angharad I am the son of Gervase Bonel, who held the manor of Mallilie while he lived. I am here to advance my claim to that manor, by reason of my birth, as the son, and the only child, of Gervase Bonel. I am here to introduce testimony that that same land is Welsh land, and subject to Welsh law, and that I am that man's son, and the only child he ever engendered. And by Welsh law I lay claim to Mallilie, for by Welsh law a son is a son, whether born in or out of wedlock,

provided only that his father has acknowledged him.'
He drew breath, and the pale, drawn lines of his face
sharpened yet further with tension. 'Will the court hear
me?'

The shudder and murmur that rippled through the
church caused even the dark timber walls to quiver.
The three on the bench stirred and peered, but kept
their more than human balance and calm. The president said with the same restraint: 'We must and will
hear whoever comes with an urgent plea, however prof-
fered, with or without legal advice, but the cause may
involve adjournment for proper procedure. On that consideration, you may speak.'

'Then first, as to the land of Mallilie, here with me
are four respected men, known to all here, who hold
land bordering the manor, and their boundaries between them encircle nine-tenths of the manor lands.
Only the remaining tenth touches English soil. And all
is on the Welsh side of the dyke, as all men know. I
ask my witnesses to speak for me.'

The oldest said simply: 'The manor of Mallilie is
within the land of Wales, and causes within it and
concerning it have been tried by Welsh law within my
lifetime, on two occasions, even though the manor was
in English hands. True it is that some cases have also
been heard in English court and by English law, but
Gervase Bonel himself twice preferred to plead in this
court and by Welsh law. I hold that Welsh law has
never lost its right in any part of that land, for whatever
its ownership, it is part of the commote of Cynllaith.'

'And we hold the same opinion,' said the second of
the elders.

'That is the view of you all?' asked the judge.

'It is.'

'Is there any present here who wishes to refute that
opinion?'

There were several, on the contrary, who spoke up
in confirmation of it, one indeed who recalled that he
had been the party in dispute with Bonel on the last
occasion, over a matter of cattle straying, and had had

his case heard in this court, by a bench on which one of the present judges had sat with two others. As doubtless the judge in question recalled without need of reminders.

'The bench is in agreement with the witness of neighbours,' said the president, having consulted his colleagues with hardly more than a glance and a nod. 'There is no question that the land involved is within Wales, and any plaintiff advancing a claim on it is entitled to Welsh law if he desires it. Proceed!'

'As to the second matter of substance,' said Meurig, moistening lips dry with tension, 'I declare that I am the son of Gervase Bonel, his only son, his only child. And I ask these who have known me from birth to testify to my parentage, and any here who may also know the truth to speak up in support of me.'

This time there were many in the body of the church who rose in turn to confirm the declaration of the elders: Meurig, son of Angharad, daughter of Ifor ap Morgan, had been born on the manor of Mallilie, where his mother was a maidservant, and it had been known to everyone before his birth that she was with child by her lord. It had never been any secret, and Bonel had housed and fed the boy.

'There is a difficulty here,' said the presiding judge. 'It is not enough that the common opinion should be that a certain man is father, for common opinion could be mistaken. Even the acceptance of the duty of providing for a child is not in itself proof of acknowledgement. It must be shown that the father has himself acknowledged the child as his. That is the validation the kinship requires for the admittance of a young man into full rights, and that is the validation necessary before property can be inherited.'

'It is no difficulty,' said Meurig proudly, and drew out from the bosom of his cotte a rolled parchment. 'If the court will examine this, they will see that in this indenture, when I took up a trade, Gervase Bonel himself called me his son, and set his seal to it.' He came forward and handed up the parchment to the judges' clerk, who unrolled and studied it.

'It is as he says. This is an agreement between Martin Bellecote, master-carpenter, of Shrewsbury, and Gervase Bonel, for the young man Meurig to be taken and taught the whole craft of the carpenter and carver. A payment was made with him, and a small allowance made to him for his keep. The seal is in order, the young man is described as "my son". There is no doubt in the matter. He was acknowledged.'

Meurig drew breath deep, and stood waiting. The bench conferred in low and earnest tones.

'We are agreed,' said the president, 'that the proof is irrefutable, that you are what you purport to be, and have the right to make claim upon the land. But it's known that there was an agreement, never completed, to hand over the manor to the abbey of Shrewsbury, and on that ground, before the man's unfortunate death, the abbey placed a steward in the house to administer the estate. A claim by a son, in these circumstances, must be overwhelmingly strong, but in view of the complications it should be advanced through the channels of law. There is an English overlord to be taken into account, as well as such claims as the abbey may advance, by virtue of Bonel's having shown his intent even in an uncompleted agreement. You will have to bring formal suit for possession, and we would advise that you brief a man of law at once.'

'With respect,' said Meurig, paler and brighter than ever, and with hands cupped and curled at his sides, as if he had already filled them with the desired and coveted soil, 'there is a provision in Welsh law by which I may take possession even now, before the case is tried. Only the son may do so, but I am the son of this man who is dead. I claim the right of *dadanhudd*, the right to uncover my father's hearth. Give me the sanction of this court, and I will go, with these elders who uphold my claim, and enter the house which is mine by right.'

Brother Cadfael was so caught into the intensity of this consuming passion that he almost let the just moment slip by him. All his Welsh blood rose in helpless sympathy with so strong a hunger and love for the land, which Meurig's blood would have granted him, but by Norman-English law his birth had denied him. There was almost a nobility about him in this hour, and the bleak force of his longing carried with him judges, witnesses, even Cadfael.

'It is the court's judgment that your claim is justified,' said the president gravely, 'and your right to enter the house cannot be denied you. For form's sake we must put it to this assembly, since no notice has been given beforehand. If there is any here who has anything to raise an objection, let him stand forward now, and speak.'

'Yes,' said Cadfael, wrenching himself out of his daze with a great effort. 'Here is one who has somewhat to say before this sanction is granted. There is an impediment.'

Every head turned to peer and crane and stare. The judges ranged the ranks looking for the source of the voice, for Cadfael was no taller than the majority of his fellow-countrymen, and even his tonsure could be matched by many here conferred by time rather than a cloistered order. Meurig's head had turned with a wild start, his face suddenly fixed and bloodless, his eyes blank. The voice had pierced him like a knife, but he did not recognise it, and for the moment was too blind to be able to mark even the undulation of movement as Cadfael pushed his way clear of the crowd to be seen.

'You are of the Benedictine order?' said the presiding judge, bewildered, as the sturdy, habited figure emerged and stood in the aisle. 'A monk of Shrewsbury? Are you here to speak on behalf of your abbey?'

'No,' said Brother Cadfael. He stood no more than two yards from Meurig now, and the mist of shock and unbelief had cleared from the black, brilliant eyes; they recognised him all too well. 'No, I am here to speak on behalf of Gervase Bonel.'

By the brief, contorted struggle of Meurig's throat, he made an attempt to speak, but could not.

'I do not understand you, brother,' said the judge patiently. 'Explain yourself. You spoke of an impediment.'

'I am a Welshman,' said Cadfael. 'I endorse and approve the law of Wales, that says a son is a son, in or out of marriage, and has the same rights though English law may call him a bastard. Yes, a son born out of wedlock may inherit—but not a son who has murdered his father, as this man has.'

He expected uproar, and instead there was such a silence as he had seldom known. The three judges sat rigid and staring, as though turned to stone, and every breath in the church seemed to be held in suspense. By the time they all stirred out of their daze, and turned almost stealthily, almost fearfully, to look at Meurig, he had regained his colour and his hardihood, though at a price. Forehead and high cheekbones had a wet sheen of sweat, and the muscles of his neck were drawn like bow-strings, but he had himself in hand again, he could look his accuser in the face, refrain from hurling himself upon him, even turn from him with dignity and calm to look at the judges, in eloquent protest against a charge he disdained to deny except by silent contempt. And probably, Cadfael reflected ruefully, there are some here who will take for granted that I am an agent sent by my order to prevent, or at least delay, the surrender of Mallilie to its rightful owner. By any means, however base, even by accusing a decent man of murder.

'This is a most grave charge,' said the presiding judge, formidably frowning. 'If you are in earnest, you must now stand to it, and make good what you have said, or withdraw.'

'That I will do. My name is Cadfael, a brother of Shrewsbury, and the herbalist who made the oil with which Gervase Bonel was poisoned. My honour is involved. The means of comfort and healing must not be used to kill. I was called to attend the dying man, and

I am here now to demand justice for him. Allow me, if you will, to tell you how this death befell.'

He told the story very baldly, the narrow circle of those present, of whom one, the stepson, seemed then to be the only one with anything to gain from the death.

'Meurig, as it seemed to us, had nothing to gain, but you and I have now seen how much, indeed, was at stake for him. The agreement with my abbey had not been completed, and by Welsh law, which we had not understood could be invoked in the matter, he is the heir. Let me tell you his story as I see it. Ever since he grew a man he has been well aware that by Welsh law his position as heir was unassailable, and he was well content to wait for his father's death, like any other son, before claiming his inheritance. Even the will Gervase Bonel made, after his second marriage, making his stepson his heir, did not trouble Meurig, for how could such a claim stand against his right as a true son of the man's blood? But it was a different case when his father granted his manor to the abbey of Shrewsbury in return for housing, food and comfort for life, after the usual fashion of such retirements. I do believe that if that agreement had been completed and sealed at once, all would have been over, and this man would have grown reconciled to his loss and never become a murderer. But because my abbot was summoned away to London, with good reason to think that another may be appointed in his place, he would not complete the charter, and that respite caused Meurig to hope again, and to look about him desperately for the means to prevent it ever being completed. For, see, if the abbey ever established its legal right by final ratification, his position at law would have been hopeless. How could he fight Shrewsbury abbey? They have influence enough to ensure that any suit should be tried in an English court and by English law, and by English law, I acknowledge it with regret and shame, such children as Meurig are deprived, and cannot inherit. I say it was mere chance, and that resulting from an act of kindness, that showed him where to find the means to kill, and tempted him to use it. And great pity it is, for he was never meant to be a murderer. But here he stands in his guilt, and must not and cannot enter into possession of the fruit of his crime.'

The presiding judge sat back with a heavy and troubled sigh, and looked at Meurig, who had heard all this with a motionless face and a still body. 'You have heard and understood what is charged against you. Do you wish now to answer?'

'I have nothing to answer,' said Meurig, wise in his desperation. 'This is nothing but words. There is no substance. Yes, I was there in the house, as he has told you, with my father's wife, the boy her son, and the two servants. But that is all. Yes, by chance I have been in the infirmary, and did know of this oil he speaks of. But where is there any thread to link me with the act? I could as well put forward the same story against any of those in that household that day, and with as little proof, but I will not. The sheriff's officers have held from the beginning that my father's stepson did this thing. I don't say that is true. I say only that there is no proof to entangle me rather than any other.'

'Yes,' said Cadfael, 'there is such proof. There is one small matter that makes this crime all the more grievous, for it is the only proof that it was not all impulsive, done in an angry instant and regretted after. For whoever took away a portion of my monk's-hood oil from our infirmary must have brought with him a bottle in which to put it. And that bottle he had to conceal afterwards, as long as he was observed, but dispose of as soon as he privately might. And the place will show that it could not have been put there by the boy Edwin Gurney, Bonel's stepson. By any other of the household, yes, but not by him. His movements are known. He ran straight from the house to the bridge and the town, as there are witnesses to declare.'

'We have still nothing but words, and deceptive words, too,' said Meurig, gaining a little confidence. 'For this bottle has *not* been found, or we should have
192

known it from the sheriff's men. This is a whole-cloth tale compounded for this court alone.'

For of course he did not know; not even Edwin knew, not even Hugh Beringar, only Cadfael and Brother Mark. Thank God for Brother Mark, who had done the finding and marked the place, and was in no suspicion of being anyone's corrupted agent.

Cadfael reached into his pouch, and brought forth the vial of flawed green glass, unwrapping it carefully from the napkin in which it was rolled. 'Yes, it has been found. Here it is!' And he held it out sharply at the full stretch of his arm into Meurig's appalled face.

The instant of sick disintegration passed valiantly, but Cadfael had witnessed it, and now there was no shadow of doubt left, none. And it was a piercing grief to him, for he had liked this young man.

'This,' said Cadfael, whirling to face the bench, 'was found, not by me, but by an innocent novice who knew little of the case, and has nothing to gain by lying. And it was found—the place is recorded—in the ice of the mill-pond, under the window of the inner room of that house. In that room the boy Edwin Gurney was never for one moment alone, and could not have thrown this out from that window. Inspect it, if you will. But carefully, for the marks of the oil are there in a dried stream down one outer side of the vial, and the dregs are still easily identifiable within.'

Meurig watched the small, dreadful thing being passed among the three in its napkin, and said with arduous calm: 'Even granted this—for we have not the finder here to speak for himself!—there were four of us there who could well have gone in and out of that inner room the rest of the day. Indeed, I was the only one to leave, for I went back to my master's shop in the town. They remained there, living in the house.'

Nevertheless, it had become a trial. Even with his admirable and terrible gallantry, he could not entirely prevent the entry of a note of defence. And he knew it, and was afraid, not for himself, for the object of his absorbing love, the land on which he had been born.

Brother Cadfael was torn in a measure he had hardly expected. It was time to end it, with one fatal cast that might produce success or failure, for he could not bear this partition of his mind much longer, and Edwin was in a prison cell, something even Meurig did not yet know, something that might have reassured him if he had been aware of it, but no less might have moved and dismayed him. Never once, in that long afternoon of questioning, had Meurig sought to turn suspicion upon Edwin, even when the sergeant pointed the way.

'Draw out the stopper,' said Cadfael to the three judges, almost strident now in his urgency. 'Note the odour, it is still strong enough to be recognised again. You must take my word for it that it was the means of death. And you see how it has run down the vial. It was stoppered in haste after the act, for all was then done in haste. Yet some creature carried this vial on his person for a considerable while after, until the sheriff's officers had come and gone. In this condition, oiled without as well as within. It would leave a greasy stain not easy to remove, and a strong smell—yes, I see you detect the smell.' He swung upon Meurig, pointing to the coarse linen scrip that hung at his belt. 'This, as I recall, you wore that day. Let the judges themselves examine, with the vial in their hands, and see whether it lay within there an hour, two hours or more, and left its mark and its odour. Come, Meurig, unbuckle and give up your scrip.'

Meurig indeed dropped a hand to the buckles, as though stunned into obedience. And after this while, Cadfael knew, there might be nothing to find, even though he no longer had any doubts that the vial had indeed lain within there all that prolonged and agonising afternoon of Bonel's death. It needed only a little hardihood and a face of brass, and the single fragile witness against Meurig might burst like a bubble, and leave nothing but the scattered dew of suspicion, like the moisture a bubble leaves on the hand. But he could not be sure! He could not be sure! And to examine the scrip and find nothing would not be to exonerate him completely, but to examine it and find the seam stained with oil, and still with the penetrating scent clinging, would be to condemn him utterly. The fingers that had almost withdrawn the first thong suddenly closed into a clenched fist denying access.

'No!' he said hoarsely. 'Why should I submit to this indignity? He is the abbey's man sent to besmirch my claim.'

'It is a reasonable requirement,' said the presiding judge austerely. 'There is no question of your surrendering it to anyone but this court. There can be no suspicion that we have anything to gain by discrediting you. The bench requires you to hand it over to the clerk.'

The clerk, accustomed to having the court's orders respected without demur, advanced trustingly, extending a hand. Meurig dared not take the risk. Suddenly he whirled and sprang for the open door, scattering the old men who had come to back his claim. In a moment he was out into the wintry light of the morning, running like a deer. Behind him uproar broke out, and half of those in the church poured out after the fugitive, though their pursuit was half-hearted after the first instinctive rush. They saw Meurig vault the stone wall of the churchyard and head for the fringes of woodland that clothed the hillside behind. In a moment he was lost to view among the trees.

In the half-deserted church a heavy silence fell. The old men looked at one another helplessly, and made no move to join the hunt. The three judges conferred in low and anxious tones. Cadfael stood drooping in a weariness that seemed temporarily to have deprived him of energy or thought, until at last he drew breath long and deeply, and looked up.

'It is not a confession, nor has there been a formal charge, or any suit as yet brought against him. But it is evidence for a boy who is now in prison at Shrewsbury on suspicion of this crime. Let me say what can and should be said for Meurig: he did not know Edwin Gurney had been taken, of that I am sure.'

'We have now no choice but to pursue him,' said the presiding judge, 'and it will be done. But certainly the record of this court must be sent, out of courtesy, to the sheriff at Shrewsbury, and at once. Will that content you?'

'It's all I ask. Send also, if you will, the vial, concerning which a novice by the name of Mark will testify, for it was he who found it. Send all to Hugh Beringar, the sheriff's deputy, who is in charge, and deliver the report only to him, of your kindness. I wish I might go, but I have still work to do here.'

'It will take some hours for our clerks to make the necessary copies and have them certified. But by tomorrow evening, at latest, the report shall be delivered. I think your prisoner will have nothing more to fear.'

Brother Cadfael uttered his thanks, and went out from the church into a village thronging with agitated, head-shaking neighbours. The tale of the morning's events was on the wing by now, surely already being carried over the hills throughout the commote of Cynllaith, but even rumour had not flown so fast as Meurig, for nothing was seen of him all that day. Cadfael led his horse from the paddock, and mounted and rode. The weariness that had fallen upon him when the need for effort ended so suddenly was subsiding slowly into a desperate sadness, and that again into a drear but grateful calm. He took the journey back very slowly, for he needed time to think, and above all, time for another to do some even more urgent thinking. He passed by the manor-house of Mallilie with only a rueful glance. The ending would not be there.

He was very well aware that it was not yet over.

'You are back in good time, brother,' said Simon, stoking the brazier with fresh fuel for the evening. 'Whatever your business, I trust God prospered it.'

'He did,' said Cadfael. 'And now it must be your turn to rest, and leave the remaining work to me. I've stabled and groomed and fed the horse, he's not overdone for I took things gently with him. After supper there'll be time for shutting the hen-house and seeing to the cow, and light enough still to bring down the ewes in lamb to the barn, for I think there may be harder frost in the night. Curious how the light lies in these hills a good half-hour longer than in the town.'

'Your Welsh eyes, brother, are only just regaining their proper vision. There are few nights here that a man could not travel safely even among the upland bogs, knowing the ground at all well. Only in the woods is it ever truly dark. I talked with a wandering brother from the north once, a rough red-haired man with a tongue I could barely understand, a Scot. He said in his far country there were nights when the sun barely set before it rose again on the other side, and you could see your way in an endless afterglow. But I do not know,' said Brother Simon wistfully, 'if he was romancing. I have never been further than Chester.'

Brother Cadfael forbore from citing his own travels, remembered now with the astonished contentment of a man at rest. To tell the truth, he had enjoyed the storms no less than he now enjoyed the calm, if this was indeed calm: but each had its own time and place.

'I've been glad of this stay with you,' he said, and that at least was true. 'It smells like Gwynedd here. And the folk hereabouts have me speaking Welsh to them, and that's gain, for I use it little enough in Shrewsbury.'

Brother Barnabas came with the supper, his own good bread, barley gruel, ewe's-milk cheese and dried apples. He breathed without labour, and strode round the house unwearied and energetic. 'You see I'm ready and able for work, brother, thanks to your skills. I could fold the ewes myself tonight.'

'You will not,' said Cadfael firmly, 'for I've taken that task for myself, having been truant all day. You be content to see us devouring this baking of yours, for that's one art I have not, and at least I have the grace to know it, and be thankful for the skills of other men.'

They ate early at Rhydycroesau, having normally laboured out of doors from early morning. There was still a muted half-light, the east a clear, deep blueness, the west a pallid glow, when Cadfael went out to climb to the nearer crest and bring down the ewes already heavy with lamb. They were few but precious, once in a while they even dropped twins, and with care both survived. Cadfael discerned a deep and tranquil satisfaction in the shepherd's life. The children of his solicitude were seldom killed, unless disease, injury or decrepitude threatened, or in time of desperation the flock could not all be fed through the winter. Their wool and milk were of more value than their meat, and their precious skins could be garnered only once, and better when for distress they had to be slaughtered. So they remained through their natural lives, growing into familiarity and affection, trusting and being understood, even acquiring names. Shepherds had a community of their own, peopled with gentle, obstinate, quiet companions, who did no murder or theft or banditry, broke no laws, made no complaints, fuelled no rebellions.

All the same, he thought, climbing the hill in long, easy strides, I could not be a shepherd for long. I should miss all the things I deplore, the range and grasp of man for good and evil. And instantly he was back with the struggles and victories and victims of the day.

On the crest of the ridge he stood to contemplate the coming night, aware that he must be seen from a good distance around. The sky above was immense and very lofty, a very deep blue, with a faint dappling of stars so new and fine that they were visible only when seen from the corner of the eye, and a direct stare immediately put them out. He looked down at the cluster of walled folds and the snug dark huddle of buildings, and could not be quite sure whether he had seen a mere quiver of movement at the corner of the barn. The ewes, accustomed to extra pampering, were gathering about him of their own will, ready to go down into the steamy, wool-scented warmth of the barn for the night. Their rounded sides and bellies swayed contentedly as they walked. By this light only an occasional gleam showed the disconcerting yellow stare of their eyes.

When at last he stirred, and began slowly to descend the hill, they followed daintily on their little, agile feet, crowding close, jostling one another, the mild, warm, greasy smell of their fleeces making a flowing cloud about them. He counted, called softly back to one or two stragglers, young ones in their first lamb, and irresponsible, though they came hurrying at his call. Now he had them all.

Apart from himself and his little flock, the night was empty and still, unless that was the momentary intrusion and instant withdrawal of some live thing he had caught between the buildings below. Blessedly, Brother Simon and Brother Barnabas had taken him at his word, and remained contentedly in the warmth of the house, by this time probably nodding over the brazier.

He brought his charges down to the large barn, half of which was cleared by now for their housing at night until they gave birth. The wide doors opened inwards, he thrust them open before him and ushered his flock within, where there was a rack filled for their use, and a trough of water. These needed no light to find their way. The interior of the barn was still peopled with vague, bulky shadows, but otherwise dark, and smelled of dried grass and clover and the fat scent of fleeces. The mountain sheep had not the long, curly wool of the lowlands, but they brought a very thick, short fleece that carried almost as much wool of a somewhat less valuable kind, and they converted handsomely the pasture their spoiled lowland cousins could not make use of. Their cheeses alone were worth their keep.

Cadfael chided the last and most unbiddable of his charges into the barn, and passed in after her, advancing into the dimness that left him temporarily blind. He felt the sudden presence behind him, and stood, every muscle stilled. The blade that was laid cold and sudden against the skin of his throat started no movement; he had had knives at his throat before, he was not such a fool as to provoke them into malice or fright, especially when he approached them forewarned.

An arm encircled him from behind, pinning both arms fast to his body, and he made no move to recoil or resist. 'And did you think when you destroyed me, brother,' panted a suffocating voice in his ear, 'that I would go into the dark alone?'

'I have been expecting you, Meurig,' said Brother Cadfael quietly. 'Close the door! You may safely, I shall not move. You and I have no need now of witnesses.'

Chapter 10

'No,' said the voice in his ear, low and savagely, 'no need of witnesses. My business is with you alone, monk, and brief enough.' But the arms withdrew from him, and in a moment the heavy doors closed with a hollow sound upon the glimpse of sky in which, from this walled darkness within, the stars showed doubly large and bright.

Cadfael stood motionless, and heard the soft brushing of cloth as Meurig leaned back against the closed door, arms spread, drawing deep breaths to savour the moment of arrival, and anticipate the last vengeful achievement. There was no other way out, and he knew his quarry had not moved by so much as a step.

'You have branded me murderer, why should I draw back now from murder? You have ruined me, shamed me, made me a reproach to my own kin, taken from me my birthright, my land, my good name, everything that made my existence worth calling a life, and I will have your life in recompense. I cannot live now, I cannot even die, until I have been your death, Brother Cadfael.'

Strange how the simple act of giving his victim a name changed everything, even this blind relationship, like the first gleam of light. Further light could only assist the change.

'Hanging behind the door, where you are,' said Cadfael practically, 'you'll find a lantern, and on another nail there a leather bag with flint and steel and tinder in it. We may as well see each other. Take care with the sparks, you've nothing against our sheep, and fire would bring people running. There's a shelf where the lantern will stand.'

'And you will make your bid to keep your forfeit life...I know!'

'I shall not move hand or foot,' said Cadfael patiently. 'Why do you suppose I have made so certain the last work tonight should fall to me? Did I not say I was expecting you? I have no weapon, and if I had I would not use it. I finished with arms many years ago.'

There was a long pause, during which, though he felt that more was expected of him, he added nothing more. Then he heard the creek of the lantern as Meurig's questing hand found it, the grating noise of the horn shutter being opened, the groping of fingers to find the shelf, and the sound of the lantern being set down there. Flint and steel tapped sharply several times, sparks flashed and vanished, and then a corner of charred cloth caught and held the tiny fire, and Meurig's face hung ghostlike over it, blowing until the wick caught in its turn, and sent up a lengthening flame. Dim yellow light brought into being the feeding-rack, the trough, the forest of shadows in the network of beams above, and the placid, incurious ewes; and Cadfael and Meurig stood looking intently at each other.

'Now,' said Cadfael, 'you can at least see to take what you came for.' And he sat down and settled himself solidly on a corner of the feeding-rack.

Meurig came towards him with long, deliberate strides through the straw-dust and chaff of the floor. His face was fixed and grey, his eyes sunken deep into his head and burning with frenzy and pain. So close that their knees touched, he advanced the knife slowly until the point pricked Cadfael's throat; along eight inches of steel they eyed each other steadily.

'Are you not afraid of death?' asked Meurig, barely above a whisper.

'I've brushed elbows with him before. We respect each other. In any case there's no evading him for ever, we all come to it, Meurig. Gervase Bonel...you...I. We have to die, every one of us, soon or late. But we do not *have* to kill. You and I both made a choice, you only a week or so ago, I when I lived by the sword. Here am I, as you willed it. Now take what you want of me.'

He did not take his eyes from Meurig's eyes, but he saw at the edge of vision the tightening of the strong brown fingers and the bracing of the muscles in the wrist to strike home. But there was no other movement. All Meurig's body seemed suddenly to writhe in an anguished attempt to thrust, and still he could not. He wrenched himself backward, and a muted animal moan came from his throat. He cast the knife out of his hand to whine and stick quivering in the beaten earth of the floor, and flung up both arms to clasp his head, as though all his strength of body and will could not contain or suppress the pain that filled him to overflowing. Then his knees gave under him, and he was crouched in a heap at Cadfael's feet, his face buried in his arms against the hay-rack. Round yellow eyes, above placidly chewing muzzles, looked on in detached surprise at the strangeness of men.

Broken sounds came from Meurig's buried mouth, muffled and sick with despair: 'Oh, God, that I could so face my death...for I owe it, I owe it, and dare not pay! If I were clean...if I were only clean again...' And in a great groan he said: 'Oh, Mallilie...'

'Yes,' said Cadfael softly. 'A very fair place. Yet there is a world outside it.'

'Not for me, not for me...I am forfeit. Give me up! Help me...help me to be fit to die...' He raised himself suddenly, and looked up at Cadfael, clutching with one hand at the skirts of his habit. 'Brother, those things you said of me...never meant to be a murderer, you said...'

'Have I not proved it?' said Cadfael. 'I live, and it was not fear that stayed your hand.'

'Mere chance that led me, you said, and that because of an act of simple kindness....Great pity it is, you said! Pity...Did you mean all those things, brother? Is there pity?'

'I meant them,' said Cadfael, 'every word. Pity, indeed, that ever you went so far aside from your own nature, and poisoned yourself as surely as you poisoned your father. Tell me, Meurig, in these last days you have not been back to your grandfather's house, or had any word from him?'

'No,' said Meurig, very low, and shuddered at the thought of the upright old man now utterly bereft.

'Then you do not know that Edwin was fetched away from there by the sheriff's men, and is now in prison in Shrewsbury.'

No, he had not known. He looked up aghast, seeing the implication, and shook with the fervour of his denial: 'No, that I swear I did not do. I was tempted....I could not prevent that they cast the blame on him, but I did not betray him...I sent him here, I would have seen that he got clear....I know it was not enough, but oh, this at least don't lay to my charge! God knows I liked the boy well.'

'I also know it,' said Cadfael, 'and know it was not you who sent them to take him. No one wittingly betrayed him. None the less, he was taken. Tomorrow will see him free again. Take that for one thing set right, where many are past righting.'

Meurig laid his clasped hands, white-knuckled with tension, on Cadfael's knees, and lifted a tormented face into the soft light of the lantern. 'Brother, you have been conscience to other men in your time, for God's sake do as much by me, for I am sick, I am maimed, I am not my own. You said...great pity! Hear me all my evil!'

'Child,' said Cadfael, shaken, and laid his own hand over the stony fists that felt chill as ice, 'I am not a priest, I cannot give absolution, I cannot appoint penance...'

'Ah, but you can, you can, none but you, who found out the worst of me! Hear me my confession, and I shall be better prepared, and then deliver me to my penalty, and I will not complain.'

'Speak, then, if it gives you ease,' said Cadfael heavily, and kept his hand closed over Meurig's as the story spilled out in broken gouts of words, like blood from a wound: how he had gone to the infirmary with no ill thought, to pleasure an old man, and learned by pure chance of the properties of the oil he was using for its true purpose, and how it could be put to a very different use. Only then had the seed been planted in his mind. He had a few weeks, perhaps, of grace before Mallilie was lost to him for ever, and here was a means of preventing the loss.

'And it grew in me, the thought that it would not be a hard thing to do...and the second time I went there I took the vial with me, and filled it. But it was still only a mad dream...Yet I carried it with me, that last day, and I told myself it would be easy to put in his mead, or mull wine for him....I might never have done it, only willed it, though that is sin enough. But when I came to the house, they were all in the inner room together, and I heard Aldith saying how the prior had sent a dish from his own table, a dainty to please my father. It was there simmering on the hob, a spoon in it...The thing was done almost before I knew I meant to do it...And then I heard Aelfric and Aldith coming back from the table, and I had no time for more than to step quickly outside the door again, as if I had just opened it, and I was scraping my shoes clean to come in when they came into the kitchen....What could they think but that I had only just come? A score of times in the next hour, God knows how wildly, I wished it undone, but such things cannot be undone, and I am damned....What could I do but go forward, when there was no going back?'

What, indeed, short of what he was doing now, and this had been forced on him. Yet it was not to kill that he had flown like a homing bird to this meeting, whatever he himself had believed.

'So I went on. I fought for the fruit of my sin, for Mallilie, as best I could. I never truly hated my father, but Mallilie I truly loved, and it was mine, mine...if only I could have come by it cleanly! But there is justice, and I have lost, and I make no complaint. Now deliver me up, and let me pay for his death with mine, as is due. I will go with you willingly, if you will wish me peace.'

He laid his head on Cadfael's steadying hand with a great sigh, and fell silent; and after a long moment Cadfael laid his other hand on the thick dark hair, and held him so. Priest he might not be, and absolution he could not give, yet here he was in the awful situation of being both judge and confessor. Poison is the meanest of killings, the steel he could respect. And yet... Was not Meurig also a man gravely wronged? Nature had meant him to be amiable, kindly, unembittered, circumstances had so deformed him that he turned against his nature once, and fatally, and he was all too well aware of his mortal sickness. Surely one death was enough, what profit in a second? God knew other ways of balancing the scale.

'You asked your penance of me,' said Cadfael at last. 'Do you still ask it? And will you bear it and keep faith, no matter how terrible it may be?'

The heavy head stirred on his knee. 'I will,' said Meurig in a whisper, 'and be grateful.'

'You want no easy penalty?'

'I want all my due. How else can I find peace?'

'Very well, you have pledged yourself. Meurig, you came for my life, but when it came to the stroke, you could not take it. Now you lay your life in my hands, and I find that I cannot take it, either, that I should be wrong to take it. What benefit to the world would your blood be? But your hands, your strength, your will, that virtue you still have within you, these may yet be of the greatest profit. You want to pay in full. Pay, then! Yours is a lifelong penance, Meurig, I rule that you shall live out your life—and may it be long!— and pay back all your debts by having regard to those who inhabit this world with you. The tale of your good may yet outweigh a thousand times the tale of your evil. This is the penance I lay on you.'

Meurig stirred slowly, and raised a dazed and wondering face, neither relieved nor glad, only utterly bewildered. 'You mean it? This is what I must do?'

'This is what you must do. Live, amend, in your dealings with sinners remember your own frailty, and in your dealings with the innocent, respect and use your own strength in their service. Do as well as you can, and leave the rest to God, and how much more can saints do?'

'They will be hunting for me,' said Meurig, still doubting and marvelling. 'You will not hold that I've failed you if they take and hang me?'

'They will not take you. By tomorrow you will be well away from here. There is a horse in the stable next to the barn, the horse I rode today. Horses in these parts can very easily be stolen, it's an old Welsh game, as I know. But this one will not be stolen. I give it, and I will be answerable. There is a whole world to reach on horseback, where a true penitent can make his way step by step through a long life towards grace. Were I you, I should cross the hills as far west as you may before daylight, and then bear north into Gwynedd, where you are not known. But you know these hills better than I.'

'I know them well,' said Meurig, and now his face had lost its anguish in open and childlike wonder. 'And this is all? All you ask of me?'

'You will find it heavy enough,' said Brother Cadfael. 'But yes, there is one thing more. When you are well clear, make your confession to a priest, ask him to write it down and have it sent to the sheriff at Shrewsbury. What has passed today in Llansilin will release Edwin, but I would not have any doubt or shadow left upon him when you are gone.'

'Neither would I,' said Meurig. 'It shall be done.'

'Come, then, you have a long pilgrimage to go. Take up your knife again.' And he smiled. 'You will need it to cut your bread and hunt your meat.'

It was ending strangely. Meurig rose like one in a dream, both spent and renewed, as though some rainfall from heaven had washed him out of his agony and out of his wits, to revive, a man half-drowned and wholly transformed. Cadfael had to lead him by the hand, once they had put out the lantern. Outside, the night was very still and starlit, on the edge of frost. In the stable Cadfael himself saddled the horse.

'Rest him when you safely may. He's carried me today, but that was no great journey. I'd give you the mule, for he's fresh, but he'd be slower, and more questionable under a Welshman. There, mount and go. Go with God!'

Meurig shivered at that, but the pale, fixed brightness of his face did not change. With a foot already in the stirrup, he said with sudden inexpressibly grave and burdened humility: 'Give me your blessing! For I am bound by you while I live.'

He was gone, up the slope above the folds, by ways he knew better than did the man who had set him free to ride them, back into the world of the living. Cadfael looked after him for only a moment, before turning down towards the house. He thought as he went: Well, if I have loosed you on the world unchanged and perilous, if this cleansing wears off once you are safe, then on me be the guilt. But he found he could not feel greatly afraid; the more he reviewed the course he had taken, the more profound became his soul's tranquillity.

'You were a long time, brother,' said Simon, welcoming him with pleasure into the evening warmth within the house. 'We were wondering about you.'

'I was tempted to stay and meditate among the ewes,' said Brother Cadfael. 'They are so calming. And it is a beautiful night.'

Chapter 11

It was a good Christmas; he had never known one more firelit and serene. The simple outdoor labour was bliss after stress, he would not have exchanged it for the ceremonial and comparative luxury of the abbey. The news that came in from the town, before the first snow discouraged travel, made a kind of shrill overtone to the homely Christmas music they made between them, with three willing but unskilled voices and three contented and fulfilled hearts. Hugh Beringar sent word, not only that he had received the record of the Llansilin court, but also that Edwin's well-meant conciliatory gift had been cast up in the shallows near Atcham, in considerable disarray, but still recognisable. The boy was restored to his doting mother, and the Bonel household could breathe freely again, now that the culprit was known. The apologetic report that the horse belonging to the Rhydycroesau sheepfolds had gone missing, due to Brother Cadfael's reprehensible failure to bar the stable door securely, had been noted with appropriate displeasure by the chapter of the abbey, and repayment in some form awaited him on his return.

As for the fugitive Meurig, cried through Powys for murder, the hunt had never set eyes on him since, and the trail was growing cold. Even the report of his voluntary confession, sent by a priest from a hermitage in Penllyn, did not revive the scent, for the man was long gone, and no one knew where. Nor was Owain Gwynedd likely to welcome incursions on his territory in pursuit of criminals against whom he had no complaint, and who should never have been allowed to slip through authority's fingers in the first place.

In fact, all was very well. Cadfael was entirely happy among the sheep, turning a deaf ear to the outer world. He felt he had earned a while of retreat. His only regret was that the first deep snow prevented him from riding to visit Ifor ap Morgan, to whom he owed what consolation there was to be found for him. Frail though it might seem, Cadfael found it worth cherishing, and so would Ifor; and the very old are very durable.

They had no less than three Christmas morning lambs, a single and twins. They brought them all, with their dams, into the house and made much of them, for these innocents shared their stars with the Christchild. Brother Barnabas, wholly restored, nursed the infants in his great hands and capacious lap, and was as proud as if he had produced them of his own substance. They were very merry together, in a quiet celebration, before Brother Cadfael left them to return to Shrewsbury. His patient was by this time the most vigorous force within twenty miles round, and there was no more need for a physician here at Rhydycroesau.

The snow had abated in a temporary thaw, when Cadfael mounted his mule, three days after the feast, and set out southwards for Shrewsbury.

He made a long day of it because he did not take the direct road to Oswestry, but went round to pay his delayed visit on Ifor ap Morgan before cutting due east from Croesau Bach to strike the main road well south of the town. What he had to say to Ifor, and what Ifor replied to him, neither of them ever confided to a third. Certainly when Cadfael mounted again, it was in better heart that he set out, and in better heart that Ifor remained alone.

By reason of this detour it was already almost dusk when Cadfael's mule padded over the Welsh bridge into Shrewsbury, and through the hilly streets alive with people and business again after the holiday. No time now to turn aside from the Wyle for the pleasure of being let in by the shrewd little housewife Alys, and viewing the jubilation of the Bellecote family; that would have to keep for another day. No doubt Edwy was long since released from his pledge to keep to home, and off with his inseparable uncle on whatever work, play or mischief offered. The future of Mallilie still lay in the balance; it was to be hoped that the lawmen would not manage to take the heart out of it in their fees, before anyone got acknowledged possession.

And here round the curve of the Wyle the arc of the river showed before him, the waning day regaining half its light as he stepped on to the open span and passed through the gates on to the draw-bridge. Here Edwin checked in his indignant flight to hurl away his despised offering. And here beyond was the level road opening before him, and on his right the house where Richildis must still be living, and the mill-pond, a dull silver plane in the twilight; then the wall of the abbey enclosure, the west front and the parish door of the great church looming before him, and on his right hand the gatehouse.

He turned in and checked in astonishment at the bustle and noise that met him. The porter was out at his door, brushed and flushed and important as though for a bishop's visitation, and the great court was full of brothers and lay brothers and officials running to and fro busily, or gathered in excited groups, conversing in raised voices, and looking round eagerly at every creature who entered at the gate. Cadfael's coming caused one such stir, which subsided with unflattering promptness when he was recognised. Even the school-boys were out whispering and chirruping together under the wall of the gatehouse, and travellers crowded into the doorway of the guest-hall. Brother Jerome stood perched on the mounting-block by the hall, his attention divided between giving orders left and right, and watching every moment at the gate. In Cadfael's absence he seemed, if anything, to have grown more self-important and officious than ever.

Cadfael lighted down, prepared to stable his own

beast, but unsure whether the mules might still be housed in the barn on the horse-fair; and out of the weaving excitement around him Brother Mark came darting with a whoop of pleasure.

'Oh, Cadfael, what joy to see you! Such happenings! And I thought you would be missing everything, and all the while you were in the thick of it. We've heard about the court at Llansilin...Oh, you're so welcome home again!'

'So I see,' said Cadfael, 'if this reception is for me.'

'*Mine* is!' said Brother Mark fervently. 'But this...Of course, you won't have heard yet. We're all waiting for Abbot Heribert. One of the carters was out to St Giles a while ago, and he saw them, they've made a stop at the hospital there. He came to give the word. Brother Jerome is waiting to run and tell Prior Robert as soon as they come in at the gate. They'll be here any moment.'

'And no news until they come? Will it still be *Abbot* Heribert, I wonder?' said Cadfael ruefully.

'We don't know. But everybody's afraid...Brother Petrus is muttering awful things into his ovens, and vowing he'll quit the order. And Jerome is *unbearable*!'

He turned to glare, so far as his mild, plain face was capable of glaring, at the incubus of whom he spoke, and behold, Brother Jerome had vanished from his mounting-block, and was scurrying head-down for the abbot's lodging.

'Oh, they must be coming! Look—the prior!'

Robert sailed forth from his appropriated lodging, immaculately robed, majestically tall, visible above all the peering heads. His face was composed into otherworldly serenity, benevolence and piety, ready to welcome his old superior with hypocritical reverence, and assume his office with hypocritical humility; all of which he would do very beautifully, and with noble dignity.

And in at the gate ambled Heribert, a small, rotund, gentle elderly man of unimpressive appearance, who rode like a sack on his white mule, and had the grime and mud and weariness of the journey upon him. He wore, at sight, the print of demotion and retirement in his face and bearing, yet he looked pleasantly content, like a man who has just laid by a heavy burden, and straightened up to draw breath. Humble by nature, Heribert was uncrushable. His own clerk and grooms followed a respectful few yards behind; but at his elbow rode a tall, spare, sinewy Benedictine with weathered features and shrewd blue eyes, who kept pace with him in close attendance, and eyed him, Cadfael thought, with something of restrained affection. A new brother for the house, perhaps.

Prior Robert sailed through the jostling, whispering brothers like a fair ship through disorderly breakers, and extended both hands to Heribert as soon as his foot touched ground. 'Father, you are most heartily welcome home! There is no one here but rejoices to see you back among us, and I trust blessed and confirmed in office, our superior as before.'

To do him justice, thought Cadfael critically, it was not often he lied as blatantly as that, and certainly he did not realise even now that he was lying. And to be honest, what could he or any man say in this situation, however covetously he exulted in the promotion he foresaw for himself? You can hardly tell a man to his face that you've been waiting for him to go, and he should have done it long ago.

'Indeed, Robert, I'm happy to be back with you,' said Heribert, beaming. 'But no, I must inform all here that I am no longer their abbot, only their brother. It has been judged best that another should have charge, and I bow to that judgment, and am come home to serve loyally as a simple brother under you.'

'Oh, *no!*' whispered Brother Mark, dismayed. 'Oh, Cadfael, look, he grows taller!'

And indeed it seemed that Robert's silver head was suddenly even loftier, as if by the acquisition of a mitre. But equally suddenly there was another head as lofty as his; the stranger had dismounted at leisure, almost unremarked, and stood at Heribert's side. The ring of thick, straight dark hair round his tonsure was hardly touched with grey, yet he was probably at least as old as Robert, and his intelligent hatchet of a face was just as incisive, if less beautiful.

'Here I present to you all,' said Heribert almost fondly, 'Father Radulfus, appointed by the legatine council to have rule here in our abbey as from this day. Receive your new abbot and reverence him, as I, Brother Heribert of this house, have already learned to do.'

There was a profound hush, and then a great stir and sigh and smile that ran like a quiet wave all through the assembly in the great court. Brother Mark clutched Cadfael's arm and buried what might otherwise have been a howl of delight in his shoulder. Brother Jerome visibly collapsed, like a pricked bladder, and turned the identical wrinkled mud-colour. Somewhere at the rear there was a definite crow, like a game-cock celebrating a kill, though it was instantly suppressed, and no one could trace its origin. It may well have been Brother Petrus, preparing to rush back into his kitchen and whip all his pots and pans into devoted service for the newcomer who had disjointed Prior Robert's nose in the moment of its most superb elevation.

As for the prior himself, he had not the figure or the bearing to succumb to deflation like his clerk, nor the kind of complexion that could be said to blench. His reaction was variously reported afterwards. Brother Denis the hospitaller claimed that Robert had rocked back on his heels so alarmingly that it was a wonder he did not fall flat on his back. The porter alleged that he blinked violently, and remained glassy-eyed for minutes afterwards. The novices, after comparing notes, agreed that if looks could have killed, they would have had a sudden death in their midst, and the victim would not have been the new abbot, but the old, who by so ingenuously acknowledging his future subordination to Robert as prior had led him to believe in his expected promotion to the abbacy, only to shatter the illusion next moment. Brother Mark, very fairly, said that only a momentary marble stillness, and the subsequent violent agitation of the prior's Adam's-apple as he swallowed gall, had betrayed his emotions. Certainly he had been forced to a heroic effort at recovery, for Heribert had proceeded benignly:

'And to you, Father Abbot, I make known Brother Robert Pennant, who has been an exemplary support to me as prior, and I am sure will serve you with the same selfless devotion.'

'It was *beautiful!*' said Brother Mark later, in the garden workshop where he had submitted somewhat self-consciously to having his stewardship reviewed, and been relieved and happy at being commended. 'But I feel ashamed now. It was wicked of me to feel such pleasure in someone else's downfall.'

'Oh, come, now!' said Cadfael absently, busy unpacking his scrip and replacing the jars and bottles he had brought back with him. 'Don't reach for the halo too soon. You have plenty of time to enjoy yourself, even a little maliciously sometimes, before you settle down to being a saint. It *was* beautiful, and almost every soul there rejoiced in it. Let's have no hypocrisy.'

Brother Mark let go of his scruples, and had the grace to grin. 'But all the same, when Father Heribert could meet him with no malice at all, and such affection...'

'Brother Heribert! And you do yourself less than justice,' said Cadfael fondly. 'You're still endearingly green, it seems. Did you think all those well-chosen words were hit upon by accident? "A simple brother *under* you..." He could as well have said among you, since he was speaking to us all a moment before. And "with the same selfless devotion", indeed! Yes, the very same! And by the look of our new abbot, Robert will be waiting a long, long time before there's another vacancy there.'

Brother Mark dangled his legs from the bench by

the wall, and gaped in startled consternation. 'Do you mean he did it all *on purpose*?'

'He could have sent one of the grooms a day ahead, couldn't he, if he'd wished to give warning? He could at least have sent one on from St Giles to break the news gently. And privately! A long-suffering soul, but he took a small revenge today.' He was touched by Brother Mark's stricken face. 'Don't look so shocked! You'll never get to be a saint if you deny the bit of the devil in you. And think of the benefit he's conferred on Prior Robert's soul!'

'In showing the vanity of ambition?' hazarded Mark doubtfully.

'In teaching him not to count his chickens. There, now be off to the warming-room, and get me all the gossip, and I'll join you in a little while, after I've had a word or two with Hugh Beringar.'

'Well, it's over, and as cleanly as we could have hoped,' said Beringar, comfortable beside the brazier with a beaker of mulled wine from Cadfael's store in his hand. 'Documented and done with, and the cost might well have been higher. A very fine woman, by the way, your Richildis, it was a pleasure to hand her boy back to her. I've no doubt he'll be in here after you as soon as he hears you're back, as he soon will, for I'll call at the house on my way into the town.'

There had been few direct questions asked, and few but oblique answers. Their conversation was often as devious as their relationship was easy and secure, but they understood each other.

'I hear you lost a horse while you were up on the borders,' said Beringar.

'*Mea culpa!*' owned Cadfael. 'I left the stable unlocked.'

'About the same time as the Llansilin court lost a man,' observed Hugh.

'Well, you're surely not blaming me for that. I found him for them, and then they couldn't keep their hold on him.'

'I suppose they'll have the price of the horse out of you, one way or the other?'

'No doubt it will come up at chapter tomorrow. No matter,' said Brother Cadfael placidly, 'as long as no one here can dun me for the price of the man.'

'That can only be charged at another chapter. But it could come high.' But Hugh's sharp, dark face behind the quivering vapour from the brazier was smiling. "I've been saving a piece of news for you, Cadfael, my friend. Every few days a new wonder out of Wales! Only yesterday I got word from Chester that a rider who gave no name came into one of the granges of the monastery of Beddgelert, and left there his horse, asking that the brothers would give it stable-room until it could be returned to the Benedictine brothers at the sheepfolds of Rhydycroesau, whence it had been borrowed. They don't yet know of it at Rhydycroesau, for they had their first snow before us, up there in Arfon, and there was no chance of getting a messenger through overland, and I gather is none even yet. But the horse is there, and safe. Whoever the stranger was,' said Hugh innocently, 'he must have left it there no more than two days after our own vanished malefactor made his confession in Penllyn. The word came by way of Bangor, when they could reach it, and by sea to Chester with one of the coastal boats. So it seems you'll get a shorter penance than you bargained for.'

'Beddgelert, eh!' said Cadfael, pondering. 'And left there on foot, it seems. Where do you suppose he was bound, Hugh? Clynnog or Caergybi, and oversea to Ireland?'

'Why not into the cells of the *clas* as Beddgelert?' Hugh suggested, smiling into his wine. 'After all your buffeting around the world, you came into a like harbour.'

Cadfael stroked his cheeks thoughtfully. 'No, not that. Not yet! He would not think he had paid enough for that, yet.'

Hugh gave a brisk bark of laughter, set down his cup, and got to his feet, clapping Cadfael heartily on the shoulder. 'I'd better be off. Every time I come near you I find myself compounding a felony.'

'But it may end like that, some day,' said Cadfael seriously.

'In a felony?' Hugh looked back from the doorway, still smiling.

'In a vocation. More than one has gone from the one to the other, Hugh, and been profitable to the world in between.'

It was in the afternoon of the following day that Edwy and Edwin presented themselves at the door of the workshop, in their best, very well brushed and trimmed, and both looking slightly shocked into unusually discreet behaviour, at least at first. This subdued demeanour rendered them so alike that Cadfael had to look closely for the brown eyes and the hazel to be certain which of them was which. Their thanks were cheerfully and heartily expressed, their contentment had made total peace between them for the time being.

'This ceremonial finery,' said Cadfael, eyeing the pair of them with cautious benevolence, 'can hardly be for me.'

'The lord abbot sent for me,' explained Edwin, his eyes rounding in awe at the recollection. 'My mother made me put on my best. *He* only came with me out of curiosity, he wasn't invited.'

'And *he* fell over his feet in the doorway,' Edwy countered promptly, 'and blushed red as a cardinal's hat.'

'I did not!'

'You did! You're doing it now.' And indeed he was; the very suggestion produced the flooding crimson.

'So Abbot Radulfus sent for you,' said Cadfael. Clearing up unfinished business, he thought, and briskly, too. 'And what did you think of our new abbot?'

Neither of these two was going to own to being impressed. They exchanged a considering glance, and Edwy said: 'He was very fair. But I'm not sure I'd want to be a novice here.'

'He said,' reported Edwin, 'that it would be matter for discussion with my mother, and with the lawmen, but clearly the manor can't belong to the abbey, the agreement is void, and if the will is proven, and the earl of Chester confirms his assent as overlord, Mallilie will be mine, and until I'm of age the abbey will leave a steward there to manage it, and the lord abbot himself will be my guardian.'

'And what did you say to that?'

'I thanked him and said yes, very heartily. What else? Who knows better how to run a manor? I can learn all the art from them. And we are to return there, my mother and I, as soon as we wish, and that will be very soon, if we don't get more snows.' Edwin's eager brightness, though not dimmed, nevertheless grew very solemn. 'Brother Cadfael, it was a terrible thing — about Meurig. Hard to understand...'

Yes, for the young very hard, and almost impossible to forgive. But where there had been liking and trust there still remained a residue of unquenchable warmth, incompatible with the revulsion and horror he felt for a poisoner.

'I wouldn't have let him have Mallilie without a fight,' said Edwin, dourly intent on absolute honesty. 'But if he'd won, I don't think I'd have grudged it to him. And if I'd won...I don't know! *He* would never have shared it, would he? But I'm glad he got away! If that's wicked, I can't help it. I am glad!'

If it was wicked, he had company in his fault, but Cadfael said nothing of that.

'Brother Cadfael.... As soon as we're home again in Mallilie, I mean to go and visit Ifor ap Morgan. He did give me the kiss when I asked him. I can be a kind of grandson.'

Thank God I didn't make the mistake of suggesting it to him, thought Cadfael devoutly. There's nothing the young hate and resent so much as to be urged to a good act, when they've already made the virtuous resolve on their own account.

'That's very well thought of,' he said warmly. 'He'll

be glad of you. If you take Edwy with you to his house, better teach him how to tell you apart, his eyes may not be quite so sharp as mine.'

They both grinned at that. Edwy said: '*He* still owes me for the buffeting I got on his account, and the night I spent in prison here. I mean to have a foot in the door of Mallilie as often as I please on the strength of that.'

'I had *two* nights of it,' objected Edwin smartly, 'and in a much worse place.'

'*You*? Never a bruise on you, and in clover there with Hugh Beringar looking after you!'

And thereupon Edwin jabbed Edwy smartly in the middle with a stiff forefinger, and Edwy hooked a knee under Edwin's, and spilled him to the floor, both laughing. Cadfael looked on tolerantly for a while, and then grasped two separate handfuls of thick, curling hair, and plucked them apart. They rolled clear and came obligingly to their feet, grinning broadly, and looking much less immaculate than before.

'You are a pestilential pair, and I wish Ifor ap Morgan joy of you,' said Cadfael, but very complacently. 'You're the lord of a manor now, young Edwin, or will be when you're of age. Then you'd better be studying your responsibilities. Is that the kind of example uncle should set before nephew?'

Edwin stopped shaking and dusting himself into order with abrupt gravity, and stood erect, large-eyed. 'I have been thinking of my duties, truly. There's much I don't yet know, and have to learn, but I told the lord abbot...I don't like it, I never liked it, that my stepfather entered suit against Aelfric, and made him villein, when he thought himself born free, as his fathers had been before him. I asked him if I could free a man, or if I had to wait until I was of age, and got seisin myself. And he said certainly it could be done at will, and he would be sponsor for me. I am going to see Aelfric a free man. And I think...that is, he and Aldith...'

'*I* told him,' said Edwy, giving himself a brief shake, like a dog, and settling back at ease on the bench, 'that

220

Aldith likes Aelfric, and once he's free they will certainly marry, and Aelfric is lettered, and knows Mallilie, and will make a splendid steward, when the abbey hands over the manor.'

'*You told me*! I knew very well she liked him, only he wouldn't say how much he liked her. And what do you know about manors and stewards, you prentice carpenter?'

'More than you'll ever know about wood, and carving, and craftsmanship, you prentice baron!'

They were at it again, locked in a bear's hug, propped in the corner of the bench, Edwy with a grip on Edwin's russet thatch, Edwin with fingers braced into Edwy's ribs, tickling him into convulsions of laughter. Cadfael hoisted the pair of them in his arms, and heaved them towards the door.

'Out! Take your cantrips off these premises, where they hardly belong. There, go and find a bear-pit!' Even to himself he sounded foolishly proud and proprietary.

At the door they fell apart with bewildering ease and neatness, and both turned to beam at him. Edwin remembered to plead, in penitent haste: 'Brother Cadfael, will you please come and see my mother before we leave? She begs you!'

'I will,' said Cadfael, helpless to say otherwise, 'I will, surely!'

He watched them go, out towards the great court and the gatehouse, again wrangling amiably, arms round each other in ambiguous embrace and assault. Strange creatures at this age, capable of heroic loyalty and gallantry under pressure, earnest in pursuing serious ends, and reverting to the battle-play of pups from one litter when all was serene in their world.

Cadfael turned back into his workshop, and barred the door against all the rest of the world, even Brother Mark. It was very quiet in there, and very dim with the darkness of the timber walls and the faint blue smoke from the brazier. A home within a home to him now, and all he wanted. It was well over, as Hugh

221

Beringar had said, with no more waste than was inevitable. Edwin would have his manor, Aelfric would have his freedom, a secure future, good ground for loosening his tongue and declaring himself to Aldith; and no doubt, if he proved obstinate about it, she would find the means of prompting him. Brother Rhys would have a long gossip about his kin, and his little flask of the right spirit, and hazy memory would film over the gap left by a lost great-nephew. Ifor ap Morgan would have a grief of his own, never mentioned, but a hope of his own, too, and a substitute grandchild only a short ride away. And Meurig, somewhere at large in the world, had the long penance before him, and good need of other men's prayers. He would not want for Cadfael's.

He settled himself at ease on the bench where the boys had wrestled and laughed, and put up his feet comfortably. He wondered if he could legitimately plead that he was still confined within the enclave until Richildis left for Mallilie, and decided that that would be cowardly only after he had decided that in any case he had no intention of doing it.

She was, after all, a very attractive woman, even now, and her gratitude would be a very pleasant indulgence; there was even a decided lure in the thought of a conversation that must inevitably begin to have: 'Do you remember...?' as its constant refrain. Yes, he would go. It was not often he was able to enjoy an orgy of shared remembrances.

In a week or two, after all, the entire household would be removing to Mallilie, all those safe miles away. He was not likely to see much of Richildis after that. Brother Cadfael heaved a deep sigh that might have been of regret, but might equally well have been of relief.

Ah, well! Perhaps it was all for the best!